SHADOW OF SHADOWS

By the same author

The Other Side of Silence

Ted Allbeury
SHADOW OF SHADOWS

CHARLES SCRIBNER'S SONS
New York

Library of Congress Cataloging in Publication Data

Allbeury, Ted.
  Shadow of shadows.

  I. Title.
PR6051.L52S5   1982   823'.914   82-10338
ISBN 0-684-17628-9

With much love to my mother-in-law

Czeslawa Felinska

The Light of Lights looks always on the motive, not the
  deed,
The Shadow of Shadows on the deed alone.

W. B. Yeats: *The Countess Cathleen*

1

As Petrov came out of the ground at Highbury he stuffed the programme into his pocket and looked around for a taxi. The crowds were still pouring out, and the traffic was virtually at a standstill. He made his way down Avenell Road, pushing his way through the crowds. At Aubert Park he saw a taxi, waved and hurried across the road. He gave the driver the address and settled back in the seat, closing his eyes. Trying not to think.

He had thought the game would take his mind off his worries, but it had only made them worse. He wiped his hand over his face where the tears had dried on his cheeks. It was only an end-of-the-season friendly game. Arsenal v. Moscow Dynamo. But it had seemed like the old days when the blue shirts came out of the tunnel into the sunshine, kicking the ball about before the home team came on to the field. And after the kick-off he, like the rest of the crowd, had been absorbed by the football. When the band came on at half-time they'd played 'Moscow Nights' and 'Maybe It's Because I'm a Londoner' and the crowd had loved it. When the final whistle blew he was delighted that his team had won 2-1. Not that it mattered, it was only a friendly. But when he heard the announcement booming over the loudspeakers — Moscow Dynamo 2, Arsenal 1 — it had been like an electric shock. Moscow Dynamo wasn't his team. It *had* been, once. He had sat in the stand with Maria. A privileged spectator, because the Moscow Dynamo Club was sponsored by the KGB, and he, Anatoli Mikhailovich Petrov, was a KGB major. But whatever he was, he wasn't that now. He was a defector to the West. A collaborator with his old enemies. Telling them all they wanted to know. And scared as hell of both sides.

Only two days before, something had happened that had

7

been like a clap of thunder warning of an impending storm. He had gone over the pros and cons a hundred times, but his conclusion was always the same. Neither the people in Moscow nor the people in London would have any reason to let him live once he'd finished telling them what they wanted to know. Bringing them up to date. There were faint rays of hope. The British had sent him to the Harley Street clinic for cosmetic surgery. They'd straightened out his nose, pulled back his ears and taken the bags from under his eyes. And with the beard he had grown he certainly looked different. Younger, in fact. If they were going to kill him why should they have bothered? If it was just a gesture to allay his fears why had the surgery been so thorough? And if they killed him they knew that the word would eventually filter through, and there'd be no more KGB and GRU men defecting to the West. The intelligence grape-vine worked, and the British knew that as well as he did.

He opened his eyes and shivered, despite his heavy coat. He looked out of the taxi and wondered where he was. He knew the street-guides to London by heart but cities never looked the same on the ground. And then he saw the big statue and the roundabout. They were at Buckingham Palace and turning into Buckingham Palace Road. It wasn't far now. He closed his eyes again. Not to block out his thoughts, but because his head ached from thinking. He had nobody to confide in. Only Silvester and the interrogator knew who he was. And then the tears came again as he realized that that was no longer true. The man had shown no sign of recognition and it had only been a fleeting glance. And they had worked together a long time ago. In the days when he was a successful operator. The man in command. He wondered if even Maria would recognize him now. As the taxi passed Victoria Station he put his head in his hands, slowly shaking his head in despair, as he remembered that scene three years before at the house near Edenbridge.

2

Lawler had already packed the two leather cases and he sat on the bed checking the other bits and pieces. A ticket for a Lufthansa single flight to Düsseldorf, economy class; two hundred D-marks in fifty-mark notes; two paperbacks and a green-covered Republic of Ireland passport. As he leafed through the passport his face, looking slightly bug-eyed from the flash, stared back at him from the small photograph. And the name was there, beautifully handwritten, short and crisp — Patrick Keeler, born Skibbereen, Co. Cork. Skibbereen was one of SIS's little in-jokes, and Patrick Keeler wasn't his real name. Otherwise the passport was genuine, or *had* been when an IRA man originally squeezed it out of one of the clerks at Foreign Affairs in Dublin. After SIS had picked it up in Belfast it had been sent for a bit of face-lifting in the basement at Petty France, and now it was his. At least it was for the couple of months he would be in Cologne.

He slid the money and the passport into his jacket pocket and looked at his watch. It would be at least another fifteen minutes before the car came to take him to Gatwick. He picked up the two paperbacks. The very thin one was Elizabeth Smart's *By Grand Central Station I Sat Down and Wept*, which he had read so many times in the past year. The thick, heavy one was Gibbon's *Decline and Fall*, which he had never read. The Gibbon was a sort of first-aid kit, an insurance against being caught in some benighted place with nothing to read except some hotel's fire instructions, or a railway company's bye-laws. Apart from its latent reading pleasure it felt good and smelled nice when he opened it. That haunting, lovely smell of printer's ink on thin, smooth paper that is like balm to avid book-readers.

With the comfort of the Gibbon heavy in his hands he

9

looked around the room. Rooms, houses, gardens, places, no longer meant very much to him. Only people mattered, and this particular room was too recent an acquisition for him to have put down even the shallowest of roots. Apart from the books on the shelves there were few things in the flat that were his. The original Ansel Adams photograph of some rock formation in the Yosemite he had bought in New York. And beside the photograph, hung above the fire-place, was an oil-painting of a young girl in a long dress, her pale feet in a clear shallow brook as she sat on a daisy-strewn bank. Her long blonde hair emphasized the calm of her pre-Raphaelite face. He had bought it from a gallery in Bond Street. Alongside the hi-fi on the bottom bookshelf was a row of cassettes and a black and white photograph of a pretty blonde, set in an old-fashioned silver frame. And propped up against the cushions on the window seat was a doll, its silver blonde hair and baby clothes still pristine. He had bought it some months back when he thought Sarah was coming.

It was at that moment that the bell rang. He thought at first that it must be the driver at the street door then, as the ringing continued, he walked over to the phone and picked it up.

'Yes?'

'Lawler?'

'I'm afraid you've got the wrong number.' But he recognized Silvester's voice.

'It's me, Jimmy, Silvester. Has the driver arrived yet?'

'No.'

'When he does, send him back. I'm on my way to see you. I'll be round in about twenty minutes.'

'What's going on, Adam?'

'Nothing. A change of plan, that's all. I'll explain when I see you.'

'What about the flight?'

'Facilities are dealing with that. Don't worry. See you.'

Lawler stood with the receiver in his hand for a few moments before he laid it back on the cradle. Silvester was one of MI6's Old China Hands, and was not given to panic, but there had been a faint echo of alarm in his voice. Operation Oberon in Cologne had a high priority, and *he* was Operation Oberon. All of it.

He walked into the small, neat kitchen and opened one of the cupboards. Silvester would want a Scotch. He found the half-bottle of Dimple Haig, dusted it off, and put it on a tray with a glass and a jug of water. Then he put the kettle on and made himself a pot of tea.

While the tea was brewing he looked along the row of cassettes, wondering what might soothe Silvester's savage breast. He guessed that it would probably be Elgar or Delius. Silvester was very Brit, and TV documentaries about Britain's rolling landscape always had 'The Wand of Youth' for background music as the clouds sailed over the hilltops. And nature programmes always had 'The Walk to the Paradise Gardens'. But he wasn't in the mood for either of them and he put on Glière's Concerto for Harp.

He left the door to the small kitchen open so that he could hear the music. It reminded him of his father, although it was his mother who was the musician. Like Glière's music his father wore his heart on his sleeve; not that his mother didn't do that too, but her temperament was extrovert and flamboyant. His father was a quiet man; those who didn't know him well concluded that it was the wife who wore the trousers in the Lawler household. But they were quite wrong. The quietness was the calm of a strength that yielded willingly to his affection and love for the Irish girl whose liveliness had kept him going in the days of struggle and uncertainty about his talent.

James Lawler himself was thirty-seven and unmarried, although that was not for want of wishing it otherwise. Recruited to the Diplomatic Service in his final year at Cambridge, he had served for two years at the Moscow embassy as Third Secretary and his already fluent Russian had made his transfer to SIS almost inevitable. And, as so often happens, his early years in SIS were spent in places where his Russian was of little use – Brazil, Washington, Cairo and the Caribbean. Only in the last two years, in Europe, in operations against the KGB, had his Russian been usefully employed. But by now he had worked for all five of SIS's sections concerned with anti-KGB operations in Europe and the Americas.

As with his father, his appearance and demeanour were deceptive. A pale, lean, poet's face and what seemed an easy-going personality gave a faintly academic air to a man who had learned early on how to survive in back-streets from Rio to Belize. He had learned from experience that you were more likely to survive if you trusted no one, and believed no one. There was no litmus paper that distinguished friend from foe or truth from lies. Just experience and intuition. The poet's face and the amiable manner served him well.

He was still wondering what it was all about when the doorbell rang and he went down the steep, narrow stairs to let Silvester in. Operation Oberon was nothing to do with Silvester; it had been Dyer's baby right from the start. And there was no love lost between Silvester and Dyer.

Silvester, in white tie and tails, stood on the pavement, one foot on the bottom step and one hand on the cast-iron finial of the railings. He looked handsome in his Brit sort of way. Big features, a square jaw, and an old-fashioned moustache that gave a nice balance to his face. As he made his way up the narrow stairs his broad shoulders seemed to fill the whole space between the walls.

In the sitting-room Silvester stood in front of the empty fireplace, a white silk scarf with fringes draped round his neck, his big hands in his jacket pockets, the thumbs outside. He stood with his feet planted well apart like heroes stand in boys' adventure stories. It wasn't phoney in any way, despite the fact that so far as Lawler knew Silvester had never needed to be a hero. In five more years he'd get his knighthood, and a fine figure of a knight he would make.

'A whisky, Adam?'

'Excellent, Jimmy. With soda, please.'

'No soda, I'm afraid.'

'No matter. Ginger ale will do fine.'

'No ginger ale, Adam. Sorry. How about water?'

12

For a moment Silvester looked at Lawler's face as if he might be having his leg pulled. Then, reassured, he shrugged, and said, 'Well then. Water it shall be.'

Lawler poured the water into Silvester's glass and the older man stared at the mixture with pursed, judicial lips before he held up the glass.

'Cheers, my boy.'

There was a lot of genuine *noblesse oblige* about Silvester, and there were many who said that he would have preferred to serve out his time with his regiment rather than get mixed up in the cat's-cradle of MI6.

Silvester slid off his scarf and looked around for a place to sit, and chose the big club armchair. It was leather, a man's chair, unlike the tapestry settee.

Silvester looked at him over the top of his glass.

'Got a problem, James. My prize Russian's gone sour on me. You won't have got wind of him. But his name's Petrov. Anatoli Petrov.'

Lawler shook his head. 'No. I haven't heard of him. What's the problem?'

'Don't rightly know. Hints about wanting to go back. Mother Russia and all that sort of thing. Understandable, but it's definitely not on.'

'How old is he?'

'Forty-two, forty-three, something like that.'

'What sort of man?'

'You'd better read his file and make your own judgement.'

'Who's got it?'

'It's with my secretary. I've told her that you might be asking for it. It's highly classified so you'll have to read it in my office.'

'Does he say *why* he wants to go back?'

Silvester leaned forward and put his empty glass on the coffee table. He settled back in his chair and looked at Lawler for several seconds before he spoke.

'Oddly enough, he never says outright that he does want to go back. Just hints about it. Drags it into the conversation. What would we do if he wanted to go back. That sort of thing.'

'And what do you say when he talks about it?'

'I just try and smooth him down. I say that we should have to consider it if it ever arose. That sort of crap.'

'And what's his reaction to that?'

'Seems to cool him down for a bit, but sooner or later he comes back to it.'

'How do I come into it?'

Silvester's thick forefinger stroked his bushy moustache slowly as he looked back at Lawler.

'I want you to take him over. If he's genuinely homesick you'll have to help him settle down. Make him feel at home here. If it's not homesickness then find out what the hell he wants.'

'Why does he matter so much?'

Silvester shifted uneasily in his chair, reaching down for his fallen scarf, arranging it slowly and carefully on the arm of the chair. It slid back to the floor again as he turned to look at Lawler.

'He's probably the most important defector we've ever had. For the two years before he came over he was in Directorate "S", responsible for all illegals in English-speaking countries. We've been de-briefing him slowly and carefully for three months. Up to a couple of weeks ago he'd been entirely co-operative. Right now we're stuck.'

'Why did you pick on me?'

Lawler could see the relief in Silvester's eyes as he assumed that the question implied agreement.

'We thought you were a bit like him. A bit Russian. And your Russian's fluent.'

Silvester had the good grace to smile as he said it, but it obviously hadn't been meant as a joke.

'In what way am I like him?'

'Romantic. You know what I mean. The arts, that sort of thing. Emotional ups and downs.' Silvester waved his big hand limply, and let it fall on the arm of the chair.

'How long is this for?'

'As long as it takes.'

'Any restrictions?'

14

'Yes. Don't let the bugger do a flit.'

'Did anything happen that might have caused him to stop co-operating?'

'Nothing that I've been able to pin down. He was talking all we wanted, and then he started being evasive. Couldn't remember names, that sort of thing. I got the quack to check him over and he said there was nothing wrong that he could identify. It was the same interrogator all the time. We weren't pressuring him. We hadn't needed to.'

'What sort of private life does he have?'

'He's got a small place in Ebury Street, and a girl-friend. He's under observation of course but he can do pretty much what he wants. He gets a regular income.'

'Is the girl-friend one of ours?'

'No. She's the genuine article but I understand she plays him up. He wants to marry her but she won't have him.'

'Would you let him go back if he insists?'

Silvester slowly shook his head without speaking. And somehow it seemed more definite than if he had said it aloud.

'Is he in any danger?'

'I don't think so. He's had cosmetic surgery and he's got high-grade cover. We keep a good eye on him. Several good eyes.'

'Does he know about me?'

'I've told him that he needs a rest and that you'll be looking after him. And I told him that you're totally trusted and secure.'

'What about his de-briefing?'

'Forget it. It's not working anymore. It's a waste of time.'

'How many people know about him?'

'I do. The Chief does. Tony Reid's been interrogating him. And one of our people in Berlin brought him over. Nobody else knows who he is or what he's doing. The Soviets have kept quiet about him apart from the routine protests. We've denied all knowledge of him. And it's got to stay like that. The KGB have been nosing around but we're pretty sure that even they wouldn't recognize him

15

now. But we're taking no chances. Everything on paper is in my own safe.'

'Has what he's told you been useful?'

'Yes. But it stops short, by about two years. He's only up to '68 and we're desperate for the rest. He knows it. And he knows he can afford to play games. You don't discuss this with anyone but me. You understand?'

'Yes. What's his cover?'

'He speaks reasonable English and fluent German so we've given him documentation as a West German journalist. A free-lance.'

'What about Operation Oberon?'

'What the hell's that?'

'The operation I was on.'

'Oh, forget it,' Silvester said dismissively.

'Does Dyer know it's off?'

'He's been told that you've been transferred to me until further notice.'

'He doesn't know what I'll be doing?'

'Of course not.'

'And if he asks?'

'You say absolutely nothing. Just refer him to me.'

'How did he react when you told him that I was taken off Oberon?'

Silvester raised his eyebrows. He didn't like under-strappers enquiring into their elders and betters' little fights. 'I've no idea, James. But none of us is indispensable.'

Lawler wasn't sure whether the implied dispensability was directed at him or at Dyer. But he didn't dwell on it.

'When do you want me to start?'

Silvester threw two keys on to the coffee table. 'Tonight. He's in our block of flats at the far end of Ebury Street. There's one key for the main door, and one for his flat. Flat number 324. Both the porters are ours. Draw your cash from Cooper. Spend what you need, there'll be no accounting within reason. Keep me informed. Cooper can always get me if I'm not at the office. Contact me any time. Night or day.'

Lawler saw Silvester down to the door. At the bottom of

16

the stairs Silvester turned to look at him.

'How are things with Joanna?'

'Much the same.'

'Anything I could do?'

Lawler shook his head. 'No thanks. There's nothing anyone can do.'

Silvester sighed. 'You know that creep's in drugs?'

'I guessed he was. But I'd never be able to prove it.'

Silvester hesitated, and then said, 'If you ever *do* want to prove it, see me.'

And then with a wave of his arm he walked down the four stone steps looking each way for a taxi.

Lawler walked slowly back up the stairs and tried not to look at the face in the silver frame. The bedroom door was open and he walked in. It took about twenty minutes to unpack and put his things away. He slid the pistol down into the toe of one of the black shoes in his wardrobe.

He checked the other two bedrooms and walked back into the sitting-room. The flat seemed even more alien now that he was staying. The latest in the series of temporary places that he had used in the last seven months. He had been lucky to get it, even with Facilities' influence. But he had a year's lease with an option to renew, and in the spring of 1970 that was more than most tenants had. It was clean and reasonably furnished compared with the tatty pads that he had used for a month or two at a time, but its reasonableness didn't comfort his restless mind. He didn't want to have any time to think about his life and the shambles of his relationship with Joanna. He had been so stupid, so unforgivably stupid. Stupid to care for her in the first place. He should have let her continue her Gadarene rush alone. He closed his eyes to block out the vision of three-year-old Sarah. That had been more than stupidity. Irresponsible and unforgivable. A small and charming, pretty ghost, to haunt the edges of his mind for the rest of his days.

He brought his thoughts back to the present. Over the years he'd had some pretty odd things to do in his time with SIS, but acting as wet-nurse and psychiatrist for a homesick KGB defector was something new. He didn't really fancy it, it was a bit too open-ended for his liking. Too indefinite. It lacked . . . he tried to think of the word they so often used in crosswords . . . parameters. It lacked parameters.

He looked at his watch. It was seven o'clock, with an unplanned evening ahead of him. The driver hadn't appeared so he guessed that Facilities must have got to him before he left the garage. He'd have a look at Petrov's file before he met him.

At Century House the duty officer had checked with Silvester's girl and then taken him up to her office. The file was in the safe but it took twenty minutes to get clearance for the combination.

As he sat at the desk and opened the thin file he realized that only the basic facts concerning Petrov had been included. Maybe that was all they had. Anatoli Mikhailovich Petrov had been born on 17 October 1928 in Leningrad, and until the German artillery had smashed the area to rubble, he had lived with his parents in one of the back streets behind the Finlyansky Station. In 1940 his father, an engineer at the waterworks, had been called up to a pioneer regiment and had never been heard of since. Petrov's mother had been killed by an aerial land-mine towards the end of 1943. The fifteen-year-old boy had lived in the Leningrad ruins with other children for six months and had then been rounded up by a Red Army patrol and sent to an orphanage in Vologda. At the end of the war he had been sent to an orphanage in Kiev. After two years at Kiev University taking English and German he had shown such promise that he was transferred to Moscow University and registered as an officer candidate for the Red Army.

In 1949, aged twenty-one, he was sent to the KGB training school in Samarkand. Two years later he was posted to the Illegals Directorate of the First Chief Directorate. After almost three years' individual training in Moscow Petrov had been sent to Berlin to take charge of all KGB networks into West Berlin and West Germany.

In February 1958 he had been recalled to Moscow with the rank of major in the KGB. By 1970, as a full colonel, his responsibilities had been solely for operations in Britain.

18

He had married in 1958, with special permission, a pretty Polish girl from Krakow. Despite the careful security checks into her background there had been a problem. Not in their relationship. They loved one another dearly. But as an all too often open critic of the subservience of Russians to their bureaucracy she had been a constant embarrassment, and finally an actual danger to them both. Much as he loved her he had eventually had to submit to the pressures from his seniors. And once the hint had been made that unless he divorced her she would be sent to a labour camp, he had reluctantly agreed to a divorce, and the girl had been shipped back to Warsaw.

Despite his sacrifice his status and promotion possibilities had seemed to be irretrievably damaged. The girl's comments on Soviet life, and her Polish independence about the petty restrictions on even the privileged élite were neither forgiven nor forgotten just because she had been removed. It was suggested that he would be moved to either Sofia or East Berlin, but in the end he had been promoted and kept in Moscow in charge of all illegals in Britain.

He had made his first tentative approaches to SIS in West Berlin. It had taken six months of cautious negotiations before the arrangements were made for him to come over during a duty visit to Amsterdam.

There was no photograph and no physical description.

3

Lawler walked to Waterloo Station, waited until someone
else took the first taxi on the rank and then took the second.
It dropped him in Lower Belgrave Street, opposite Victoria
Station.

It had been cold all day, colder than mid-April should be.
But now the wind had dropped, and there was a faint touch
of spring in the night air. Ebury Street had been ravished
by architects at the Victoria Station end. The style was New
Brutal, but the developers and the architects seemed to
have surrendered about a third of the way up the street and
the pleasant old houses had survived. He walked to the far
end of the street to where the small block of flats stood
isolated on its small mat of dusty, green grass.

The porter who opened the big glass door was wearing a
brown frock-coat trimmed with gold braiding, and he
stopped Lawler just inside the foyer. He was almost bald,
with a shiny apple face, and all the signs of an ex-NCO.
Lawler showed him his ID card and the porter walked over
with him to the lift and pressed the button for the fifth floor.
For some reason Flat 324 was located on the fifth floor.

As the lift gates folded back at the fifth floor Lawler saw
the sign on the wall that pointed to the right for 320, 322 and
324. 324 was the last flat before the steel door marked
'Fire'.

The corridor was carpeted, but the walls and ceiling were
painted an institutional yellow with no relieving
decoration.

He stood facing the door of 324 for a moment and then
pressed the button beside the door. There was a faint smell
of disinfectant in the corridor.

Nobody came to the door and he rang again. He waited,
looking down at the bar of light at the bottom of the door.

He knocked on the door but still nobody came. Finally he took out the two keys. The first one fitted the lock and turned, opening the door without any hindrance.

To the right he could see a half-open door that led to a kitchen. He pushed the kitchen door fully open. The light was on, and there were crockery and utensils piled in the sink and the remains of a meal for one on the small table.

There was a good-sized living-room and two bedrooms. A double and a single. Somebody had been very subtle in furnishing the flat. The décor, the furniture, everything, was Moscow early 1950s. A chessboard, with the pieces set out, was on a small bamboo table by one of the armchairs.

A couple of dozen books were on the shelves on the far wall. A Russian–English dictionary, paperbacks in English of Tolstoy, Turgenev and Chekhov, John Barron's *KGB*, L. P. Hartley's *The Go-Between* and half a dozen Galsworthy novels.

There was a long, heavy, mahogany sideboard with an old-fashioned embroidered runner along its top, a bowl of fruit at the centre, and a new-looking music-centre alongside a row of records. They were mainly classical and jazz. About fifty of them. He switched on the radio. It was on the short-wave band and was tuned to Radio Moscow which was doing its version of the news in German. He switched it off and sat down on the big three-seater settee.

It was almost an hour before the door opened. The man who came in was tall and slim, and good-looking in a hawkish sort of way. Only for a second did his eyes flicker as he saw Lawler sitting there. He was wearing a raincoat and a brown trilby hat which he raised with old-fashioned courtesy as he walked over holding out his hand.

Unsmiling he said, 'Mr Lawler,' and shook hands, his dark brown eyes on Lawler's face. 'They gave you a key, I expect.'

'Yes. But I forgot to check out your cover name.'

Petrov smiled. 'Not very imaginative, I'm afraid. Peters. Anton Peters. But do sit down. Please,' and he waved Lawler back to the settee. As Petrov turned to hang up his hat and raincoat he said, with his back turned, 'Have you helped yourself to a drink?'

'No. And I haven't been through your drawers and cupboards either.'

Petrov swung round, his eyebrows raised, his forehead creased. Then with a half-smile he said, 'I was taught *"qui s'excuse, s'accuse"*.'

Lawler laughed. 'You sound like Khrushchev, Anatoli.'

The Russian relaxed and grinned. 'Are you staying here the night?'

'I wondered if you'd care to move into my place – it's not far away. There's plenty of room and it might be easier for both of us.'

'Where is it?'

'King's Road, Chelsea.'

'Very nice.' Petrov looked down at his shoes for a few moments, then lifting his head to look at Lawler he said, 'Am I under orders? Do I *have* to move?'

'Of course not. But we both live alone and I thought we might be company for one another.'

'You're not married?'

Lawler hesitated. 'No.'

'Girl-friend?'

'No.'

'Boy-friend?'

'No.'

Petrov suddenly looked tired, almost sad. His shoulders sagged and a muscle flickered below his left eye.

'Not a very lively couple, are we?'

Lawler smiled. 'We'll survive, Tolya. Pack your things for tonight and we'll go out for a drink.'

'I'll have to make a phone call first.'

'OK. Take your time.'

Petrov walked over to the phone and dialled. He waited, then hung up and dialled again. He waited for several minutes and finally hung up. He sighed, and without speaking walked into the bedroom.

As Lawler sat there alone he realized that he hadn't been very professional. He had given no thought as to how he would deal with Petrov, or what their relationship should

22

be. He should have ignored Silvester's pressure and left their first meeting until he had learned a lot more about Petrov's character and background. He should have talked to the interrogator. Instead of which he had just barged in without thought or preparation, and inside five minutes they sounded like a couple of elderly queers, bristling at one another over some suspected infidelity.

Then Petrov was standing there, canvas bag in one hand, the other hand supporting him against the door-frame.

'*Vy gavarete pa—Russki?*'

'*Da.*'

And that seemed to cheer up Petrov. He walked over for his raincoat and hat. Then he turned, looked round the room and said, 'I'm ready.'

They had a couple of drinks at the Markham Arms and then walked back to Lawler's flat. They were still talking at midnight and it wasn't until then that Lawler seized the nettle.

'Tell me about your problem, Tolya.'

'What problem?'

'Maybe problem is the wrong word. Silvester said that he thought you were worried about something.'

'What am I supposed to be worried about?'

'I don't really know, but I want to help you if I can.'

'What do you know about me?'

'Very little. Your name. Your job in Moscow. That you have a girl-friend. That's about it.'

'Who told you to call me Tolya?'

'Nobody.'

'So why do you use that name?'

'Your full name is Anatoli. Tolya is the diminutive. It's just more friendly.'

'Why don't you keep to my cover name, Anton?'

Lawler shrugged. 'I don't know. You don't look like an Anton to me. But I'll use whatever name you wish.'

Petrov looked at Lawler's face intently for several minutes, his eyes alert like an eagle's eyes, his mouth tight with tension. When he spoke his voice was very low as if he feared that he could be overheard.

'Tell me, are they going to try and do another Behar?'

'I don't understand.'

Petrov sighed. 'OK. Forget it. I think I'll go to bed.'

'How about a night-cap? A whisky, perhaps?'

'Have you got hot chocolate?'

Lawler smiled. 'Yes. We'll both have one. Get to bed and I'll bring it to you.'

When Lawler put the glass of chocolate on the table at the side of the bed Petrov was half-sitting, half-lying against the pillows, his eyes closed. Without opening his eyes he said, 'What kind of a man are you, Lawler?'

Lawler turned slowly at the door and looked at the figure in the bed. He walked back and sat on the bed at the far end.

'What do you want to know, Tolya?'

'Are you the one who has to kill me?'

'Nobody's going to kill you, Tolya. Why should they?'

The brown eyes looked at him as if they were trying to make a judgement. To weigh him up. Petrov sighed deeply and gripped the bed cover so tightly that his hand was trembling.

'I'm scared, my friend.'

'Of what?'

Petrov shook his head silently and Lawler said softly, 'Would you rather I found someone else to take care of you?'

'It makes no difference.' Petrov's voice was flat and dull.

Lawler reached out and covered Petrov's hand with his own. 'Don't worry, Tolya. Nothing unpleasant is going to happen. You are highly valued. You must know that.'

'We'll see, my friend. We'll see.'

Lawler stood up and walked slowly to the door.

'Goodnight, Tolya.'

'*Da zaftra.*'

'*Da.*'

4

Lawler was still asleep when the telephone extension on his bedside table rang the next morning. He looked at his watch as he reached for the phone. It was already 9.30. Silvester was on the line.

'How did you get on last night, Jimmy?'

'Hard to say.'

'Have you got somebody with you?'

'Yes.'

'Our friend?'

'Yes.'

'That's a good move. Was it difficult?'

'No.'

'OK. I'll get out of your hair. Keep in touch.'

'OK.'

Standing at the window in his dressing-gown, Lawler looked out on to the King's Road. It was a Saturday and the shoppers were out. He watched the doors swinging at Tesco's and his eyes moved on to Royal Avenue. A Chelsea Pensioner in his walking-out uniform was sitting on the bench and a man in jeans and a plaid shirt was sitting beside him, talking to him. Then he saw the younger man's eyes look up towards the window. He looked away quickly as he saw Lawler but his face had been visible long enough for Lawler to recognize him. His name was Bridges or Bridger, Lawler couldn't remember which; but what puzzled him was that whatever his name he was watching the flat, and he was Special Branch. Special Branch were MI5 not MI6. And the two intelligence services never shared services, and seldom co-operated except at the topmost levels. Even at the top the co-operation was limited and grudging.

He turned as Petrov came out of his bedroom.

25

'A good night, Tolya?'

'Very good. What do I call you to be friendly?'

'My first name is James. How about some breakfast?'

'I'd like some toast and coffee if you've got it.'

As they sat in the kitchen drinking a second cup of coffee, Lawler said, 'Where have you been outside London?'

'I've never been outside London.'

'Is there anywhere particular you'd like to go?'

'I don't know anywhere.'

'How about Stratford-on-Avon?'

'Why there? Is it specially beautiful?'

'It's where Shakespeare was born.'

Petrov looked pleased and interested. 'That would be fine. I'd like that.'

'We'll go to your place and you can pack some clothes.'

'OK.'

Lawler looked across at the Russian. 'D'you want to bring your girl-friend?'

'Silvester told you, yes?'

'He just said you had a girl-friend.'

'Nothing more than that?'

'He said you had a problem there, but he didn't say exactly what it was.'

'Could she come with us?'

'Of course.'

'She thinks I'm German. A foreign correspondent.'

'I know. That's no problem.'

'How long do we go for?'

'A couple of days. We can stay longer if you want to.'

'Is OK I telephone her?'

'Sure. Go ahead.'

Lawler pointed to the telephone in the sitting-room, and Petrov dialled a number.

Her name was Siobhan, and Petrov's voice as he talked to her was ingratiating, almost pleading, and it was obvious that he was having problems. He eventually put his hand over the mouthpiece and said, 'She is asking who you are and why you go with us.'

'We want tourists from Germany. I'm from the Foreign

Office to show you the English countryside so that you can write a travel piece.'

It took another five minutes of persuasion before she agreed. She would be ready and waiting in a couple of hours' time.

Petrov smiled. 'She says maybe I am a queer and you too. She often speaks of me like that.'

'I hope she's very pretty.'

Petrov's face clouded. 'Why do you hope that?'

'A girl who told me that I was a queer would have to be *very* pretty or I'd tell her to go to hell.'

Petrov nodded. 'She is very pretty. Maybe too pretty for me.'

'Are you fond of her?'

'Is "fond" more than to love, or less?'

'Less, but more than just liking.'

'I love her very much.'

'Do you sleep with her?'

Petrov nodded, and sat down again at the table. 'This is part of my problem with her. She gives me sex whenever I want. Plenty, plenty of sex. All the time if I want. I ask her to marry me. She says no every time I ask.'

'Why?'

'She says she is not interested, and anyway that I have no family. She says maybe I want to marry her to get British passport.'

Lawler smiled. 'I'll have to work on her for you. Let's get dressed or we shall keep her waiting.'

With a suitcase each in the boot of the car they made their way to Pimlico. Siobhan Nolan lived in two rooms in a house converted into flats, off Lupus Street. Lawler sat in the Rover while Petrov went to fetch her.

He saw her coming down the stone steps with the Russian and she was much more than pretty. She was beautiful. Slightly taller than Petrov and very shapely. Despite the full bosom and the long legs it was her face that he stared at as they walked towards the car. Big eyes, heavy-lidded, a wide mouth, a neat nose, and long, glossy black hair.

Then Petrov opened the rear door and introduced her.

When her suitcase was in the boot Petrov slid on to the back seat beside her. She was easy to talk to and, with that lovely Irish accent, even easier to listen to. It was hard to imagine her as being difficult. She laughed a lot, and seemed easy to please, and Lawler thought that most men would have settled happily for the lots of sex if she didn't want to get married. But he knew all too well how Petrov must feel. That need to belong. Someone to love and be loved by. Exclusively, and not shared. For the first few weeks it would be enough just to enjoy that lush young body, but slowly the need to be the only one would become an obsession. So why the talk of going back to Moscow?

They stopped on the M1 for petrol and coffee, and he checked the Yellow Pages for a hotel in Stratford, and phoned through to book three adjoining rooms.

It was a pleasant hotel near the Avon and Petrov was obviously impressed. The girl seemed barely to notice what it was like.

After they were settled in their rooms he walked them over the bridge into the town, and they 'did' Holy Trinity Church and Shakespeare's house on Henley Street. The hotel managed to get them seats at the theatre for *Henry V* for that evening, and even the girl seemed impressed.

After the performance they walked back along the river bank, through the gardens and over the bridge, Petrov slightly ahead, holding the girl's hand. There was a small breeze off the river but the evening air was mild. They looked like any other couple walking home after the theatre. Relaxed and happy and normal. Lawler wondered what the other people strolling along the river bank in the moonlight would think if they knew that the man with the girl was the most important KGB defector since the war. Unhappy with their country and contemplating return to the Soviet Union. A Russian who knew more about what was going on in their country than they did. Who knew which trades union leader was getting a stipend from Prague. Which MP picked up his instructions from Moscow

28

when he bought the seventh LP from the second row in a record shop in Kensington. And maybe which well-respected officer of the intelligence services had been playing footsie with Moscow for years because twenty million Russians had been killed by the Germans in World War II and the same Germans had smashed his home to rubble and his parents to pulp on an April night in Coventry in 1941. He would know the SIS codes that had been broken by Moscow but were still being operated; and which Cabinet ministers were against the stationing of US missiles in East Anglia. And whether Moscow was intending to let British Leyland survive.

It was midnight when they finally went up to their rooms, and with the door locked Lawler put a call through to London. The duty officer at Century House traced Cooper, and Silvester called him back twenty minutes later.

'How's it going?'

'Slowly, but he's very much on edge.'

'Any idea why?'

'He seems to have an idea we're planning to knock him off. He asked if I was the one who was going to do it.'

'For Christ's sake. Why should we want to do that? He's valuable property.'

'I know, but I guess he doesn't see it that way.'

'Try and find out more, Jimmy. No wonder the stupid bastard has clammed up if he thinks we're going to do him in. Anything else?'

'No. I don't think so. Nothing significant anyway. Oh yes. He said, "Are they going to try and do another Behar?"'

'What's that mean?'

'I've no idea.'

'You're sure that you heard him right?'

'Pretty sure.'

'Ask him then. Ask him what he means. Maybe it's a name, or it's a mispronunciation of some word he's seen written down.'

'I'll leave it for a day or two. He's just beginning to relax and I don't want to get him wound up again.'

29

'I'll leave it to you. You seem to be doing OK.'

'I'll keep in touch.'

''Night.'

'Ciao.'

He lay on the bed reading John O'Hara short stories trying not to think of Siobhan Nolan and her long legs and beautiful breasts.

The bedside light was still on when the phone woke him. The hotel operator sounded half asleep as he told him that there was a personal call for him from London. Lawler asked the time. It was ten past three, and the caller was Silvester.

'Is that you, James?'

'Yes.'

'Are you alone?'

'Of course I am. Did you think we were having a threesome?'

'Behar. The word Behar. Are you sure that was what he said?'

'Yes. But like you said, it may not be a name, of course. He said, "Are you doing a Behar?" He may have picked up some word somewhere and got hold of the wrong meaning.'

'I don't think so. I'm sure I know now what he means.'

'What does he mean?'

'He means George Blake.'

'Who's George—? Jesus. You mean the guy who got out of the Scrubs and back to Moscow?'

'Yes.'

'And what does Behar mean?'

'That was his real name. He only called himself Blake after he came to this country.'

'But that doesn't make sense,' Lawler said slowly.

'Why not?'

'Why does he associate Blake getting away, with being killed? He said it in the same sentence. Was I the one to kill him? Were we doing another Behar? But we didn't kill Blake, the bastard got away. And what does "doing a Blake" mean in Petrov's case? Maybe it's an odd way of saying will we let him go back. But it doesn't hang together.'

'All the same I think this is what's at the bottom of his problem. You'd better fish around those words as soon as you can.'

'I can't rush in like that, I'll have to take my time.'

'When are you coming back to London?'

'Tomorrow. Or the next day if he wants to stay a bit longer. He's enjoying himself down here.'

'We need this information, Jimmy.'

'Adam, I'll blow it if I don't go carefully. I've only had a couple of nights and a day.'

Silvester sighed. 'OK. I'll leave it to you.'

Lawler had slept until he heard the knock on the door. He looked at his watch. It was past ten and he called out, 'Come in.'

It was Siobhan Nolan in a white woollen dress, and she walked to the window and pulled back the curtains. The sun was bright and she was smiling as she walked over to the bed.

'Come on, my boy. Everybody's up.'

'Where's Tony?'

'Gone down to the river to feed the swans. He got some bread from the kitchens.'

She bounced down on to the bed, smiling as she looked at his face.

'Who were you dreaming of, honey?'

Lawler smiled. 'How many sisters have you got, Siobhan?'

'Two. D'you want one?'

'Only one?'

She laughed, and then said softly, 'What am I going to do with that guy?'

'What guy?'

'Tony.'

'What's wrong with Tony?'

'He wants me to marry him.'

'So?'

31

'I don't know a goddamn thing about him. He's got no relations. He says he's a journalist. But he's not. He's a phoney.'

'So why do you sleep with him?'

She shrugged. 'I like what he does.'

'Would you like him any more if you knew he wasn't a phoney?'

'Maybe.'

'What about the other guys?'

'He told you?'

'Not a word.'

'So how'd you know?'

'Every guy who sees you looks at your face, your boobs and your legs, and then mentally has you. You know this, but you don't react. It takes more than one man to give a girl that much self-assurance. You know that you've only got to lift an eyebrow and they'll come running. And you know that because when you want to, you *do* lift an eyebrow.'

She smiled. 'So what?'

'So Tony's in love with you. It's not just bed. He wants more than bed.'

'Like what?'

'A wife, a home, some loving, some kids maybe.'

'I'm not ready for that, Jimmy. I'm only twenty-two next month.'

'When *will* you be ready for that?'

'Who knows? Next year, maybe. Or the year after.'

'Do the others mean that much?'

'No.'

'Do you like any of them better than Tony?'

'I never go with them twice. I've told him that. They don't mean a thing. They're not interested in me except for bed and it's the same for me.'

'So Tony's a bit ahead in the race for Siobhan Nolan?'

'Sure he is.'

'Why?'

'God knows. I guess I like him in a funny sort of way. He's kind. He cares about me. I'm not just a screw.'

32

'He's not phoney, kid. Not the way you mean it.'

'How do you know?'

'I just do. Leave it at that.'

'You're not just a guy about tourists, are you?'

'That's a rhetorical question.'

'What's a rhetorical question?'

'A question where the person already knows the answer.'

She laughed, and then said softly, 'D'you want to do it to me?'

'That's another rhetorical question.'

'It isn't. I don't know the answer.'

'You do. The answer's always going to be the same whoever you ask. So the answer is yes, I do want to. But I ain't going to all the same.'

'Why not?'

'Because it would make Tony unhappy and he's unhappy enough right now.'

'He wouldn't know.'

He looked back at the big brown eyes. 'People in love always know. You'll know when your turn comes for that.'

'You're a funny fella, Jimmy, aren't you?'

'In what way?'

'How old are you?'

'Thirty-seven.'

'You talk like my old dad. But he's going on fifty.'

'I take that as a compliment, little girl.'

She smiled. 'It is.'

'You'd better go and find Tony and see if he wants to go back or stay another day.'

'I'll have to go back today anyway.'

'OK, see what Tony says.'

Petrov was torn between the few extra hours with the girl on the journey back and the peace of the small town. But when the girl promised she'd see him the next evening he stayed. They drove her to the station on the far side of the town. When they were back at the hotel Petrov was restless, and Lawler suggested that they walk down to the river bank. Petrov seemed to like the river.

They crossed the footbridge to the Boat Club and walked up-river to the small islands opposite the Golf Club. The Avon was much narrower there and they sat on the bank watching the brown cygnets with their proud parents struggling to get out of the river on to the far bank.

'Is there a reason why it's called the Avon? Does it mean something?'

'It comes from *afon* which is the Welsh for river.'

'Welsh is from Wales, yes?'

'Yes. The Avon ends up in the River Severn in Gloucestershire on the borders of Wales. I suppose you could class the Avon as a Welsh river if you were a Welsh nationalist.'

'When we are back in London maybe you take me to see the Karl Marx mausoleum.'

'Sure. It's not actually a mausoleum. Just a grave with a statue on top. A plinth and a sculpture of his head.'

'His body is not preserved for people to see?'

'No. I'm afraid not.'

'Is there no respect at all for him in this country?'

'Why should there be?'

Petrov shrugged. 'He was a great man. He changed half the world.'

'For God's sake, Tolya. Genghis Khan changed half the world. You've lived in a Marxist state. And you didn't like it.'

'Ah yes. But that was men, not Marxism.'

'It always *is* men. That's why Marxism doesn't work. Marxism and all the other isms would be great if it wasn't for the fact that people are people. Karl Marx was typical.'

'How was he typical?'

'He was typical of the very class he hated. The petty-bourgeois. And as a man he was both a hypocrite and a first-class bastard.'

Petrov smiled. 'You're just prejudiced, Jimmy. How was he a bastard?'

'You ought to be able to tell *me*. Haven't you read about him? Didn't you have lectures about him?'

'Of course, but you can't imagine the Politburo allowing

anything to be said which criticized him or his life.'

'All his life he lived on money squeezed out of other people. His father, his mother, Engels, anybody he could plead poverty to.'

'That's nothing. He lived in poverty.'

'Rubbish. The poverty was because he spent money like a drunken sailor. He had various inheritances that could have kept his family for years but he always moved to a better house and the money went in weeks. When Engels was just a salesman and lived very frugally he sent Marx money every week. He got no thanks for it. When Engels became well-off in his old age Marx got seven thousand marks a year from him. He had at least a hundred and fifty thousand marks from Engels. His father even borrowed money to send to him.'

'OK, he was bad with money.'

'He was bad with people too.'

'Who?'

'His wife. He ruined her health and gave her a dog's life. He had an illegitimate son by their maid whom he refused to acknowledge and left everybody with the impression that it was Engels's son.'

'So what was he good at?'

'He was a historian. A historian of capitalism. Nothing more.'

'But he worked hard at all that.'

'OK. He worked hard, but he didn't do any good for humanity, or the Russians.'

'There were rumours in Moscow that Shakespeare was homosexual. What do you think? Is it possible?'

Lawler laughed. 'You can't even things up by making Shakespeare a queer. Nobody knows. There are theories that the sonnets were written to men not women. But scholars are always putting two and two together and making five.'

'If somebody could prove that he was homosexual what would happen?'

'He'd sell it to the *Sunday Times* or the *Observer* for fifteen thousand. He'd write a book. It would be in all the papers and a couple of weeks later it would have been forgotten. Come on, it's getting cool. We'd better get back to the hotel.'

The walk seemed to have done Petrov some good. He was so relaxed and talkative that in his bedroom after dinner that night Lawler took the plunge.

'Are you still worried about me, Tolya?'

'In what way?'

'Like you said the other night, that I might do you some harm.'

Petrov took a sip of his whisky and said softly, 'I've not made up my mind. You could be waiting until you get your orders.'

'Do I look like a killer?'

'No. But killers seldom do look like killers outside the KGB.'

'Do you miss the Soviet Union?'

'Of course not.'

'What *do* you miss?'

'Russia.'

'What in particular?'

'The first time I realized that I was homesick was a few weeks back at a football match. It was just a friendly match. Arsenal versus Moscow Dynamo. My lot won.'

'Which is your lot?'

Petrov smiled. 'Exactly. That's what made me homesick. Dynamo won. But I realized they weren't mine anymore. I cried in the taxi on the way home. Not for a football team, but for silver birches and Leningrad, vodka and *zakuski,* and God knows what else. Not that any of it is better than what you have here, but just that those things are in my blood. In Moscow I didn't have to work things out. I knew the rules. They're like the weather or breathing. I was used to them. In a way I lived in a very small pond, a privileged pond maybe; but here, I'm swimming in an ocean. I have lots of new freedoms but all the same I'm a prisoner. In Moscow I had almost no freedoms, but I did not feel a prisoner.' Petrov smiled. 'When all are prisoners the jailers are free men.'

'What could we do to make you happier, Tolya?'

'Stop asking me questions about KGB.'

'Silvester thought that you were quite happy to co-operate.'

'I was, but not now.'

'Tell me why.'

'You remember story of Scheherazade? She tells a story every night to delay her execution.'

'Yes.'

'I realize one day that I am Scheherazade, and before very long I have no more stories left. And then . . .' Petrov smashed one hand into the palm of the other.

'What suddenly made you think that?'

'My information about KGB operations in UK and United States is very useful to your people. They want it all very much. But what I know is like toothpaste in a tube. The tube starts full and fat, then day by day a little more is squeezed out. It takes a long time but one day the tube is empty and flat. And then it's thrown away.' The brown eyes looked at Lawler. 'I want to keep some paste in the tube. I don't want to be thrown away. The paste left in the tube is my insurance policy. It's what Silvester and the others want most. It's what KGB were doing in last two years and what they are doing now. So I decide not to talk so easily, so quickly.'

'But when you've brought them up to date you'll be looked after. A place to live. A pension, or a job. You'll be secure.'

Petrov smiled. 'Either you are very innocent, my friend, or you see me as a fool. What security is there for me?' He shrugged with his hands wide apart.

'I'm sure Silvester would give you a lump sum of money right now, and more when you have brought them up to date.'

'You are capitalist, James. You think money is security. I was KGB. For me security is being alive. You cannot guarantee that, neither can Silvester.'

'What made you decide to stop co-operating, Tolya?'

'I already told you.'

37

'No. You don't understand. One day you were co-operating and the next day you decided not to. Why *that* particular day?'

'Because on that day I realize my position.'

'But why on that particular day? Why not the day before, or the day after?'

Petrov's eyes looked keenly at him and then the Russian shook his head.

'That's part of my insurance too.'

Lawler stood up. 'It's time we went to bed, Tolya.'

Petrov nodded. Then, smiling, he said, 'Is there girls to find in this town?'

'You mean tarts?'

'Yes.'

Lawler laughed. 'There's bound to be somebody who obliges the locals but you'd have to live here for months to find out who. You'd better save yourself for tomorrow night with Siobhan.'

'Is OK she stay with me at your place?'

'Sure. Unless you'd rather go to Ebury Street,'

'No. Is OK at your place if you agree.'

'Of course I agree. By the way, where did you meet her?'

'She was with another girl in pub – "Bricklayer's Arms". I talk to them and make date with Siobhan.'

'What does she do for a living?'

'She is actress in TV commercials. Earns good money when there are jobs. I think maybe she also get money from her family.'

'Sleep well.'

'And you.'

The next day Lawler took Petrov to see Anne Hathaway's Cottage. They walked there and back, and had an early lunch. They were coming off the M1 at Hendon by four o'clock.

Lawler dropped Petrov at the girl's place and then drove back to the King's Road. There were a few letters on the mat and he picked them up without looking at them. He dialled the number for Cooper who transferred him to Silvester.

'What news, James?'

'It's going slowly, Adam. I think that's inevitable in the circumstances.'

'What circumstances?'

'He's genuinely scared that when we've finished de-briefing him we shall knock him off.'

'Surely you can reassure him on that score?'

'It'll take more than blue eyes and soft words, Adam. He's been in the business a long time. He knows what goes on.'

'But we need what he's got. We need it desperately.'

'I think something happened to put the wind up him.'

'Like what?'

'I've no idea. Have you got tapes and transcripts of his de-briefing?'

'Of course.'

'All of them?'

'Yes.'

'Is it obvious when he stopped co-operating?'

'I don't remember. I should think it is, more or less.'

'Could you have it checked?'

'Yes. I'll check it myself.'

'Could you come back to me when you've done it?'

'Yes. I'll work backwards but it will take a day or two.'

'I'll be at the flat for the next few days. After that I'm taking him down to Dover and Rye.'

'Why there?'

'The white cliffs of Dover and all that.'

'I hope it works.'

'So do I.'

And on that note of no-confidence Lawler hung up. As his coffee cooled he looked through his mail. The top one had a Barclay's Bank look about it and he could see through the transparent window of the envelope that it was his statement. He tried to guess what his balance would be. It must be just over £2,000, say £2,250. However carefully you worked it out your balance was always much less. So halve your guess. Call it a round thousand and you'd be safe. He opened the envelope and looked at the last figure.

39

It was £72. The next item was a postcard with a printed message that informed him that the Restaurant d'Or was under new management, and would value his custom. A larger buff envelope enclosed a magazine from the Intelligence Corps depot at Ashford. And the last letter was from his solicitor. Not really his solicitor, but a friend who was advising him. It was typed, except for his name and the signature, which were hand-written.

Dear James,
    I have done a bit of checking which only confirms what I told you. So far as Sarah is concerned you are on to a beating to nothing. The law says that the father of an illegitimate child has no rights of any kind beyond being sued for maintenance. The law also relieves you of any responsibilities. I know this was not your objective, but that is how it is.
    The mother has all the rights. She can decide the child's name, its nationality, its domicile, its residence (I explained the difference when we spoke). The fact that the mother is feckless and irresponsible, lives with a crook, and is virtually an alcoholic, makes no difference in the eyes of the law. Even if it goes as far as physical cruelty to the child or gross immorality you would have no standing. The child would be taken into care by the Local Authority.
    I very much regret having to pass on this news. It is undoubtedly unfair and unjust, but it *is* the law. And as I told you, the courts are there to administer the law, not justice.
    The Salvation Army might be able to help if ever you were able to supply grounds for their concern. They're not so dumb as they look.
    If you're wise you'll close this particular door because there is nothing you can do. When Sarah is of age (16 years) she will be free to see you if she wishes. They may have kept all news of you from her, but in my experience young people frequently want to meet the lost parent no matter what lies have been told.
    It's a sad, sad story and you have my sympathy (Rosie's too of course). It may seem harsh, but my advice is to forget it all. Children *do* survive, and banging your head against a brick wall will do nobody any good, least of all you. J is a 24

carat bitch and the man will sooner or later end in the nick.
Yours affectionately, Phillip

He folded the letter up slowly and slid it into his jacket pocket. It was odd how people's criticisms of Joanna always made it worse. The criticisms were always wrong. She wasn't a bitch. She was weak, and feckless, and an alcoholic. But she wasn't a bitch. Women said she was a bitch because she was beautiful. Men said it because they didn't understand. And because it sent his mind rushing to her defence it always brought it all back. There was almost nothing good to remember but it *had* all happened. He had survived, but that was no consolation. All of it sickened him.

Slowly, very slowly, and only subconsciously aware of what he was doing, he unpacked his bag.

He phoned Petrov before he turned in but there was no answer. He dialled the girl's number and there was no answer there either.

5

HOLLAND 1936

The grey-faced man lay with his head turned to one side as his eyes looked at the woman sitting beside his bed. He was propped up, almost sitting, by four thick pillows, and his bright red lips were rimmed with a vivid blue. Although his breathing was quick and shallow his narrow chest barely moved.

The room was dark from the drawn curtains, but a thin line of golden sunshine lay across the foot of the bed, and the soft, faint sounds of voices in the street barely disturbed the quietness of the room.

The man's name was Albert Behar, a Dutch Jew with a British passport that was partly a reward for his service with the British Army in World War 1. The phosgene he had inhaled during a German gas attack had left him with the laboured breathing and the blue rim round his lips.

The house on Spengensekade in Rotterdam had been his home for ten years. But once his illness was terminal they moved to Scheveningen for the fresh sea air. He had two daughters and one son, and they were a close and happy family.

His wife, the woman beside his bed, knew that at best he had only a few months to live. He was only forty-six and although she loved him dearly she no longer prayed for him to live. He was going to die and she knew. And so did he.

In fact he had only weeks to live. When peritonitis set in it was the beginning of the end. He died two weeks later in April 1936.

In those last weeks he had struggled to talk. About how they should live, and what she should do. What seemed to concern him most was the fate of his fatherless son.

CAIRO 1938

The man in the white cotton suit, and the boy, clambered down from the number 8 bus and waited for the shuttle-bus to turn. Henri Curiel would have been more comfortable travelling in his almost new Daimler, but for the sake of the boy they had made the trip from Cairo to the Pyramids by bus. Young Georges Behar had to get used to the fact that when he eventually went back to Rotterdam there would be no money for cars at all, let alone Daimlers.

Henri Curiel was an Egyptian Jew, and wealthy. He was the boy's uncle; and his wife, the sister of the boy's mother, had taken the boy under her wing when his father died. She and her family, including the boy's mother, felt that he needed the influence of a man in his life.

He paid a guide for two small folding seats and they sat together in the evening sun. They spoke French together as a change from speaking English.

'So what do you think, young Georges?'

The boy sighed and hesitated as he looked at the man.

'I think, Uncle, I prefer the Sphinx.'

'Tell me why.'

'The Pyramids are very big. But the Sphinx is beautiful. Like a cat in the sand.'

Henri Curiel smiled. 'Very good. Very good. She is beautiful, despite her poor broken nose and—'

'How did she lose her nose?'

'They say it was from the artillery when Napoleon was fighting here in Egypt.'

They sat silently together for several minutes and then the man said, 'They say that one hundred thousand men laboured for twenty years to build the Great Pyramid. What do you think of that?'

The boy smiled. 'Maybe in those days it was sensible but it seems to me a waste of time.'

Curiel laughed softly. 'And I agree with you. It was a waste of time. There should be better things for men to do.'

The boy looked at him. 'What is a Marxist, Uncle Henri?'

'Why do you want to know?'

'Ahmed says you're a Marxist.'

43

'Who's Ahmed?'

'A boy at school.'

'Who's his father?'

'Anwar Fawzi.'

The older man's brown eyes looked intently at the boy's face.

'Tell Ahmed Fawzi that he is a fool. Tell him that with my compliments.'

The boy was silent.

'D'you understand, Georges? You tell him.'

'Yes, Uncle.'

'Has anyone else said anything like that?'

'No. But they said I was a British spy.'

Curiel laughed. 'How old are you?'

'Nearly sixteen.'

'You tell them that your father was a war hero. He was awarded the OBE. You must have seen it. And the Legion of Honour. He was on Field Marshal Haig's staff. If anyone says it again I want to know his name.'

'Why don't Egyptians like the British, Uncle?'

'Because the British Army occupies Egypt. We are ruled by the British.'

'Is that bad?'

'It's imperialism. Nations should be free to work out their own destinies. You won't understand, boy. But just you remember. Your father was a brave man. A hero. He was British, but he was a good man.'

Henri Curiel took a taxi to Sharia Sheikh Rihan that night, and then walked towards the Nile, eventually turning into one of the streets behind Shepheard's Hotel.

The beggar who sat at the gate that led to the courtyard held out his thin claw-like hand and Curiel gave him two piastres as he walked by. The heavy door to the house was guarded by a large Nubian with a heavy stick, but when his one good eye recognized Curiel he hurried to open the door. Inside, Yehia Souidan was waiting for him, and they went to his quiet study.

They talked for two hours in voices that were low but

44

passionate as they argued. It was Curiel who was most vehement.

'It has to be done, Yehia.'

'I have known him all my life, Henri. He means no harm. I am sure of it.'

'He may mean *no harm but he does harm. His son tells people that I am a Marxist. It's impossible. People's lives are at stake.'*

'I could warn him, Henri.'

'Yehia, Yehia, what good can that do? It's too late already. Who knows who else he has told?'

Souidan shook his head. 'I don't have your conviction, Henri. I want what you want, but slowly, peacefully.'

Curiel smacked both his hands on his thighs in exasperation. 'A slow and peaceful revolution, Yehia? And of course we can have a slow and peaceful war afterwards.' He shook his head. 'You disappoint me. You frighten me.'

Souidan looked at Curiel's face as he stood up.

'What are you going to do, Henri?'

Curiel looked at him with anger. 'I'll do what has to be done, but remember tonight, my friend. Because Moscow will remember too. It won't be long.'

And Curiel walked angrily from the room and the house. It was past midnight when he reached Sharia el-Muiz Lidin Allah. He rang the bell at the silversmiths' workshop and waited in the silent street.The blind man who eventually came to the door gently touched Curiel's hand and the half-sovereign that lay in his palm.

In the small back room he waited patiently with the old man while the old man's grandson fetched the two young men. Curiel gave them their instructions, and three golden sovereigns each from the purse on his canvas belt. They were surprised and faintly amused that he insisted that the body should go in the Nile. The traditional last resting place of police informers. They wondered briefly what Anwar Fawzi, a rich merchant, could have told the police to warrant such an end.

HOLLAND 1940

By midnight the whole of Rotterdam was burning. Twenty-six thousand houses had been destroyed by the Luftwaffe in two hours of indiscriminate bombing. The city was virtually undefended so there was no resistance. The small Dutch garrison in Rotterdam had refused to surrender and the bombing was the Nazis' response. And in that single attack thirty thousand civilians had been killed or wounded. The Dutch government surrendered that night to avoid further useless slaughter.

Catherine Gertui Behar and her two daughters were still at the house in Scheveningen on the day the Germans invaded. On the advice of an English friend she abandoned all her possessions and, with her two daughters, made her way to the Hook of Holland. They were taken aboard one of the three Royal Navy destroyers sent to pick up the Dutch royal family and those members of the Dutch government who had been able to make their way to the Hook. Her son, George Behar, still at high-school in Rotterdam and living with his grandmother, had had to be left. All communication with Rotterdam had been cut.

He had made his way through the rubble and ruins and raging fires to his grandmother's house at the edge of the city. It had been hit, but two rooms were still standing. The seventeen-year-old boy and the arthritic old lady had slept that night amid the rubble under the stairs.

The following day young George Behar had walked into the city to try to buy some food. The whole of the centre of Rotterdam had disappeared, and in the ring of the suburbs the fires still raged, the roar as they burned as frightening as the flames themselves. The stench of burnt flesh hung over the city, and wounded women and children lay unattended, those who were conscious pleading for help. But there was no help to give. The hospitals that were not already rubble were still burning.

It was dark when he got back to the ruins of the house, an iron-hard loaf his only booty. The two Gestapo men were waiting inside. A neighbour had reported that he was a Britisher to the round-up squads searching for aliens and

46

suspects. He spent that night and the next two months in an internment camp near Alkmar north of Amsterdam.

On the sixty-third day of his internment, his eighteenth birthday, he escaped from the camp and made his way to his uncle's house at Warnveld in Gelderland. Twice the Gestapo had come searching for him and he moved to a safer hiding place on a farm.

LONDON 1943
The man on the other side of the table pushed the two buff files on one side and tore off the top page of his notepad. A Field Security sergeant stood by the door.

'My name is Captain Holmes and I want to ask you some questions. Please relax, and if you want to smoke, please do.'

He pushed across an open tin of Army ration 'Gold Flake' and a box of matches.

'First, your name?'
'George Behar.'
'Where were you born?'
'Rotterdam, but I'm a British subject. My father was British and I have a British passport.'

The officer nodded and tentatively touched one of the files.

'You say in your statement that you worked with a Dutch Resistance group. Where did it operate?'
'In Limburg and Gelderland.'
'How old are you?'
'I'm twenty.'
'What did you actually do yourself in the Resistance group?'
'I was a courier. And I helped receive SOE parachutists.'
'You say a British intelligence officer told you about the escape line. What was his name?'
'It's in my statement.'
'What was his name?'
'Child. Commander Child.'
'How did you come to know him?'
'He was a friend of my father.'

47

'You say in your statement that the Gestapo had put a price on your head. How do you know that?'

'I saw the posters with my photograph and my name. My cover name.'

'What was your cover name?'

'Max van Vries.'

'Why did you choose that name?'

'I don't remember. I think I just liked the sound of it.'

'You said in your statement that your mother and your two sisters came to England as soon as the Germans invaded Holland. When was that?'

'The Germans invaded the Low Countries on the tenth of May. My mother and sisters left on the eleventh.'

'Why didn't you leave with them?'

'I was in Rotterdam, they were in Scheveningen. Commander Child told me that he had advised them to leave immediately. He took them to the Hook and vouched for them himself.'

'Do you know where they live in England? The Dutch embassy has no record of a family named Behar.'

'Why should they? We are British, not Dutch.'

The captain took a photograph from one of the files and slid it across the table.

'Do you recognize that person?'

'Yes. It's Commander Child.'

'And that photograph?'

'It's a lady named Renée. I don't know her other name.'

'How did you know her?'

'I was sent by the escape line to see her in Lyon. She was something to do with the United States Consul there.'

'What can you remember about her?'

'She had only one leg.'

'Have you been interrogated before you got to England?'

'Yes. In Gibraltar.'

'Who interrogated you?'

'I think his name was Major Darling. They called him Donald.'

'Why did you come to England apart from getting away from the Gestapo?'

'To fight the Germans.'

Holmes noticed the flash of anger at even the vague hint that he was escaping from the enemy.

'What had you in mind as your activity?'

'I am at your disposal. I have experience and talents that could be used.'

Holmes pushed the files together and stood up.

'We'll talk again tomorrow, Mr Behar.'

In fact they had 'talked' every day for three weeks and two or three times a week for a month after that.

Holmes opened the file and read the top sheet again before he looked around the table. There was another Intelligence Corps officer, a Special Branch representative, an officer from the Immigration Office and a FANY secretary.

'George Behar. Aged twenty years four months. He doesn't know it but he came down Guerisse's "Pat" escape line. I don't think there's any problem. He is British. His father was British. Awarded an OBE in fact. He did work with a Dutch Resistance group. We've checked and can confirm all this. He didn't do as much as he would like to think he did, but what of it? Very much resents being under suspicion. A touch self-important but he's only a youngster.

'Child confirmed advising the mother and him. Gives him and them a good write-up. Only two problems. There's no trace of the family being over here, so maybe they went on to Canada or the States . . .'

'We've traced them, Frank.' It was the Special Branch man who interrupted. 'She changed her name to Blake when she came over here. She and the girls are living on a farm near High Wycombe. Said she changed her name to be more English. Nice woman. No adverse information.'

'Did you tell her he was here?'

'No. But she identified the photograph.'

'Well, it seems like we can release him.'

'You said there were two problems.'

'Ah, yes. I sent a signal to Darling in Gib and he's got no record of interrogating a George Behar or a Max van Vries.'

The Special Branch man shrugged. 'It isn't that

important, is it?'

'I suppose not. I'll fix for him to be released tomorrow and provide him with an identity card and ration book et cetera.'

He reached for another file and said, 'Now this one is a real stinker, it's the Belgian from Liège and . . .'

George Behar, now George Blake, and living with his mother and sisters, was bitterly disappointed at his reception in England, and even more disappointed that after his release there was so little interest in employing him. Early in November 1943 he joined the Royal Navy as an ordinary seaman. A few months later his superiors, having finally realized that he spoke fluent Dutch, French and German, as well as English, recommended him for a commission. Early in 1944 he was commissioned as a sub-lieutenant in the RNVR.

Eventually he was transferred to the Dutch section of Special Operations Executive and finally as an interpreter to SHAEF HQ. In the official photographs of the German surrender to Field Marshal Montgomery on Lüneburg Heath Sub-Lieutenant Blake is standing beside the Field Marshal. Shortly after he was posted to Hamburg on intelligence duties Queen Wilhelmina of the Netherlands awarded him the Order of Nassau, Fourth Class, and George Blake was a happy young man.

6

Lawler sat in the soundproof room, the headphones around his neck as Silvester fitted the big spool on the tape recorder.

'This tape goes from March first to the thirty-first. My guess is that he started back-tracking on the seventeenth or maybe the sixteenth. It's hard to tell. Listen for yourself. The second tape is from April first to the fourteenth, which was when I realized we weren't getting anywhere. I'll be in my office for the rest of the day.'

Lawler put the headphones over his ears and pressed the button on the tape recorder, pulling the notepad and pencil towards him. He listened for a few moments and then reversed the tape back to the fourteenth.

Petrov was describing the layout of the Soviet Embassy building in Kensington. SIS had meticulous drawings, and details of every brick in the embassy buildings, so they would merely be double-checking Petrov's memory and truthfulness. He wouldn't be expected to be strictly accurate because he had never worked at the embassy beyond a few flying visits of a day or two at a time. He was doing quite well and Lawler pushed the tape on. It was three hours later and Petrov was covering the details of the radio equipment at the embassy. He was going strong when the interviewer called it a day. The interrogator's voice registered the fifteenth of March as a Sunday and no inter-view, and the tape rolled until the interrogator's voice registered the date as the sixteenth. He was taking Petrov back over the embassy stuff. There were two sessions for that day. An hour in the morning and seventy minutes in the afternoon. They were still on the embassy and Petrov was still responding, but at minute forty-one there was a noise as if somebody had touched the microphone. The

51

interrogator said, 'Sorry,' and carried on. But from that interruption Petrov's replies were vague. Facts and details that he had already given were diluted. After ten minutes the interrogator switched to Russian, but Petrov's answers were positively evasive. If you hadn't been waiting for it, listening for it, it could have been evaluated as tiredness. But even the voice was slightly different. Harsher, tighter.

Lawler marked the spot on the tape from the LED display and moved the tape back.

Half an hour later in Forensic he looked at the zigzags on the long paper chart as the audio man stood beside him. The man pointed with a pencil to the chart.

'The big peaks and troughs last about a second. The interruption is the part between the two vertical red lines. To the left of that you can see the voice waves. The dotted line is the mean pitch in cycles. The other two lines in chain dots are the peaks and troughs. The same on the right-hand side. But you can see the change. The pitch is a consistent ten to twelve cycles higher and the peaks and troughs are smaller.'

'What's all that mean?'

'It means the pitch of his voice went up and his voice range was more restricted.'

'And?'

'He was either ill or scared.'

'There couldn't be any other reason?'

'Only one.'

'What's that?'

'Some men's voices do that when they are highly aroused sexually.'

'You mean thinking about sex?'

'No, it would have to be more than that. He'd have to be very near the point of orgasm.'

Lawler half-smiled. 'I don't think Tony Reid's likely to arouse those kind of pressures.'

'Is the guy a queer?'

'No.'

'It's impossible to be sure what caused it without more data but I'd say he was scared.'

'Thanks. Will you shred the chart for me?'

'It's over there, you can do it yourself, the flat yellow button on the panel.'

After shredding the chart Lawler signed the two tapes into the audio archives and went up two floors to General Archives and checked the catalogue. He made out a slip for Blake, G., signed it and passed it to the girl.

She came back with the brown folder tied with pink tape.

'There are four files. This is number one. It's got the index. You can have one at a time. There are seven pages extracted and you need a department head's signature for those.'

She gave him the docket to sign and the key to a vacant reading room.

They were in one of the new interrogation rooms. The décor was more *Architectural Review* than Foreign Office Gothic. Rumour had it that somebody had authorized a study by one of the redbrick university psychology departments into 'The Relationship between Response and Environment in Conflict Situations' and that the six new interrogation rooms were the result.

There was a table in the centre of the room. Swedish and stark, in teak, with two straight-backed chairs on each long side. A curved arrangement of settee modules took up one corner faced by three leather armchairs. A well-grown *Monstera deliciosa* in a large clay pot stood in one corner and the colour scheme was pale and dark browns. There were no windows and no visible hardware of recorders and microphones. All that was dealt with now by a miniature hand-control operated by the interrogator and using remote radio control instead of wires and plugs.

Lawler sat waiting for Reid, and as he waited he used the hand control to listen to the tape again and again. Then he saw the green light go on over the door and he pressed the entry button.

Tony Reid was one of SIS's most experienced interrogators. In his late forties, he looked more like an antiquarian bookseller or a schoolteacher than an intelligence officer, and that was part of his success. He specialized in long-term interrogation, where it was necessary to build up a relationship with the subject. They played examples of his tapes for students at the training school in Surrey. His technique was only used when it was necessary to unwind a mass of information from a man's memory, or to lead an unco-operative and aggressive subject to the stage where he would at least talk. Only top subjects got the Reid treatment.

He sat down opposite Lawler, pushing his glasses back up his nose.

'I gather from what you said on the telephone that you've got some query about the Petrov material.'

'Yes. Was it you who first noticed that Petrov had stopped being co-operative or was it Silvester?'

'So far as I know it was me. But I reported on it to Silvester.'

'How long have you been talking to Petrov?'

'Nearly three months, off and on.'

'Did you feel that it happened slowly or quickly?'

'It was quite marked.'

'Did you have any feeling as to why it happened?'

'No, not really. We had been going over material we'd gone over several times before, so it wasn't the subject matter that put him off as far as I could tell.'

'I've listened to the tapes and I think I've spotted where his attitude changed, but I'd like your opinion. I've got the tape concerned set up for you to hear.'

Reid leaned back. 'Go ahead then.'

Lawler ran the tape for the fifteen minutes before the interruption and fifteen minutes after, with a few minutes of random material twenty numbers further on. Reid asked to hear one portion again before he put up his hand.

'You can't really be precise on these things but I'd say you're about right.'

'I had a voice pattern done, and his voice is higher-pitched and restricted after that noise. Audio say it's a typical fear pattern.'

'Have you talked to Petrov about it?'

'No. I daren't be that direct.'

'What's Silvester's view?'

'He thinks Petrov wants to go back.'

Reid shrugged. 'They all do at some time or another. It generally passes in a couple of days.'

'Do you remember that particular interview?'

'No. I'm afraid not.'

'What do you think the noise was? The interruption?'

'I'd say a knock against the microphone bracket. Subjects sometimes give it a knock if they start gesticulating. I do it myself sometimes. If I happen to knock it with a pencil it sets up a howl, so it must have been a hand.'

'So you must have been using one of the old rooms?'

'I was. By that stage he didn't seem to need cosseting. Maybe I was wrong.'

'Did you have any theory about why he suddenly dried up?'

'Not really. They do that sometimes for a couple of days if it's a long interrogation. I'm quite happy normally when it happens.'

'Why, for heaven's sake?'

'It means they've got pangs of guilt about what they've been telling me.' He smiled. 'And that usually means they've been telling me the truth or they wouldn't feel guilty. Is there anything more I can do for you?'

'I don't think so. Thanks, Tony.'

Lawler checked-in the radio-control unit and headed for the flat. He knew that he would have to edge back into it again sometime with Petrov.

He got tickets and took Petrov and the girl to the Festival Hall, and in the interval they walked out to the upper landing to look out across the Thames. The lights were already on in the buildings on the far bank and there was a cosy glow from the cabin of a tug hauling a string of coal barges down-river. It was as the first interval bell pinged its early warning and they turned to go back that Lawler saw the man watching them from the far side of the foyer. It was the man he had seen on the bench in Royal Avenue. Petrov hadn't noticed him, he was walking ahead with the girl and there was no reason anyway why Petrov should recognize the man. But as Lawler looked at him the man turned his face hurriedly, pretending to be interested in the traffic on the river. As Lawler followed Petrov he wondered why the man should be so concerned that he had been seen. They were, after all, part of the same set-up.

The second half of the programme was Ashkenazy and the Rachmaninov Third, and the magic brought such prolonged applause that it seemed likely to keep the young man bowing and smiling until midnight. André Prévin smilingly persuaded him back to the piano and Ashkenazy played them variation 18 of the Rhapsody on a theme of Paganini. Honour was served, and the audience were delighted with their 'bon-bon'.

The girl was spending the night with Petrov in Lawler's flat, and Petrov was in good humour as they sat around drinking wine. They were on the third bottle when the phone rang. It was Silvester.

'Any progress, James?'

'We're all just about to turn in.'

'He's with you?'

'That's right.'

'You can't talk?'

'Right again.'

'D'you need to talk, maybe later?'

'Yes.'

'You know my home number?'

'Yes.'

'I'll stay up until you call me.'

'OK. Sleep well.'

It was over an hour before Petrov took the girl to his room, and Lawler waited for another hour before he let himself out into the street.

The King's Road was empty as he walked up to Sloane Square. The late-night coffee van had gone, and the taxi rank was empty. The first telephone kiosk had been vandalized and the second stank of vomit. He propped the door open with his foot as he dialled Silvester's number.

Silvester answered at the second ring.

'Hello.'

'It's Jimmy. Sorry to keep you up. But Petrov and his girl are at my place. He's there most of the time now.'

'What's the problem?'

'Who are you using to keep an eye on us?'

'Pleasance and Travers.'

'Pleasance is the big blond fellow, yes?'

'He's about five-eleven. He was with you when you were doing that job at St Albans.'

'And Travers?'

'He's much older. Early fifties. Tubby. Medium height. Wears glasses.'

'So who's the youngish guy in jeans and denims with the long hair?'

'No idea. He's not one of mine.'

'He's Special Branch, I'm sure. I've seen him somewhere before.'

'Why are you interested?'

'He's tailing us.'

'How many times have you seen him?'

'Twice.'

'Could be coincidence.'

'Once outside my flat and tonight at the Festival Hall.'

'I'll check if maybe somebody has stood in for Pleasance or Travers but I'd raise hell if they had. You and Petrov are restricted.'

'Do we have photographs of Special Branch surveillance men?'

'Yes, but they may not be bang up to date. They used to be up-dated every month but I don't know how often they do it now.'

'Who looks after them?'

'Photo Registry.'

The photographs were pasted on cards in alphabetical order and Lawler had checked Bridges and Bridger. There was a Bridges but no Bridger, and the Bridges face was nothing like the one he wanted. He started back at the As and checked each card, and he had got as far as Kingsley when the name came back to him. It was Ridger not Bridger and he went through the cards. There was a pink removal card under Ridger. Paul Endicott Ridger. 'Card temporarily removed'.

He took the card across to the duty clerk.

'How do I get to see this card?'

The girl looked at the pink card and then back at his face. 'It's issued out to Special Branch Personnel for up-dating.'

'How long does that take?'

'About two days usually.'

'When did this one go out?'

The girl turned the card over and pointed.

'Gosh. It went out ten days ago. Should have been back long ago.'

'Can you phone SB Personnel and check when it will come back?'

'Hang on. I'll see what they say.'

She walked away to the plastic phone hoods and he watched her as she dialled a number. She was three or four minutes on the phone and when she came back she was frowning.

'Sergeant Glass says the card is withdrawn but I've not had an official notice about it.'

'Do they often withdraw cards like that?'

'Not unless the guy's ill for a long period or he leaves.'

'No other reasons?'

She shrugged. 'Only for security reasons, and there's not been more than a couple of those since I've worked here, and that's over three years.'

'Do you have files on SB Personnel?'

'I don't know. Archives might have them. We're only photographic here.'

'Thanks.'

'You're welcome.'

He was walking up to Silvester's office when Dyer came out of the small conference room.

'Hello there, James. Nice to see you. Come and have a cuppa in my office.'

Lawler liked Dyer. He affected a rather casual manner but there was a sharp, intelligent mind behind the smiles and the easy-going style.

'I can't stay long, Richard. I was just going up to see Adam.'

'Is he waiting for you?'

'No. But I've only got ten minutes.'

Dyer's girl brought them coffee. The real stuff, from the private and unauthorized Cona.

Dyer took off his jacket and hung it over the back of his chair before he sat down. He was brushing imaginary dust from the seat of his chair as he spoke.

'I gather you're doing something very special for Silvester.'

'I'm pretty busy, yes. What happened to Oberon?'

'Oh. Pigeon-holed. There wasn't time to brief someone else. Maybe they'll let me have you back before too long.'

The shrewd but smiling eyes looked across at him awaiting an answer, but he didn't respond. He knew Dyer was just fishing. Probably just to give him the chance to annoy Silvester.

Dyer reached out for another cigarette, and when it was lit he said, 'Any progress about the little girl?'

'Afraid not. There's nothing I can do. It's just a shambles. A write-off.'

'Must have upset you a lot.'

'I'm trying to get used to it.'

'It can't be easy. I'm sorry.'

Dyer stubbed out his cigarette half-smoked and reached for another.

'How's your present operation going?'

'No comment, Dickie. You know me better than that.'

Dyer grinned. It was bad form for departmental directors to quiz anyone from another department. And it was bad security too. Lawler was surprised and embarrassed that Dyer should step over the line.

'Where did you learn your Russian, James?'

'At Cambridge, and I did a refresher at Coulsden.'

'Is it good?'

'It gets me by.' Lawler stood up. 'Do you speak Russian?'

Dyer laughed. 'Not a word. That's not true. *Da, Nyet* and *dos vedanya* and something some bastard told me meant "I love you", and was, in fact, very rude and very specific.'

'See you soon.'

'Of course. Pop into Cadogan Square any time you feel like a bit of company. Parties can be laid on at five minutes' notice. Orgies take longer – up to half an hour.'

'Love to Mandy and the girls.'

'They'll appreciate that, James. They really will.'

Lawler was no longer in a mood for talking with Silvester. Even the glancing reference to Joanna had been enough to put him down.

He walked to Waterloo Station and took a taxi to Sloane Square. He bought a copy of *The Gramophone* at the W.H. Smith shop and as he was waiting for the lights to change at Sloane Street, on an impulse he turned down Lower Sloane Street and walked through the narrow side street behind the Duke of York's HQ to St Leonard's Terrace and the far end of Royal Avenue. He walked slowly up the centre of the avenue along the line of plane trees. When he was almost at King's Road he stopped. An old lady with a dog on a frayed rope sat alone on the wooden bench. In the far corner by the Drug Store two teenage lovers stood kissing and cuddling. A nanny with a pram stood watching the traffic as she jogged the sleeping baby. There was no sign of the watcher.

He waited for a break in the line of cars and started to cross the road. An impatient red bus drove him back to the pavement and it was then he saw him, standing just inside the big glass doors and windows of Tesco's, a wire basket swinging loosely in one hand. He was wearing a plaid shirt and denim trousers, his face raised to look up at the window of the flat, unaware that he was being observed. Lawler glanced up briefly at the flat windows. Siobhan Nolan was standing there, looking down at the shoppers, and Petrov's face was just visible over her shoulder. When he looked back in the store the man had gone. He thought he saw him in a group of people waiting to cross the road but when he hurried over the man had a dark skin and a Zapata moustache. Lawler went into the store, walking between the displays, up and down, his eyes looking at every face. There was no sign of the man.

He stood as if he were looking at the shelves of tinned fruit trying to make up his mind. Then he turned and walked slowly out of the store, down Royal Avenue to the telephone kiosk by the Royal Hospital. Cooper was off duty and the duty-officer gave him Silvester's number. He was at the Travellers' and the porter fetched him to the phone.

'Silvester.'

'I'm using a call-box and I'm out of coins – can you call me back?'

'What's the number?'

Lawler gave him the number, hung up and waited, to the obvious annoyance of a woman who was pacing up and down, impatiently waiting her turn. Then the phone rang and it was Silvester.

'What is it, James?'

'You remember the man I told you about? The one I thought was tailing us?'

'Yes.'

'He was at it again and this time it was quite obvious that he was watching my flat.'

'Were you able to trace him?'

'I've got his name. He's Special Branch all right. But his photo card had been withdrawn to Scotland Yard. They are normally returned in two days. It had been out for ten days. I got the clerk to check when it was coming back. They said it was withdrawn and they didn't know when it would be returned.'

'What's his name?'

'Paul Endicott Ridger. Born 7 Jan 1946.'

'Just a minute, I need a pencil.'

There was a pause and then Silvester came back on the line. 'Paul what was it?'

'Paul Endicott Ridger. Born 7 Jan 1946.'

'You're quite sure that he's the guy concerned?'

'Yes.'

'And you're quite sure he's tailing you?'

'Absolutely sure.'

'Do you think he's seen our friend?'

'Our friend and his girl were at the window. He may not know who he is but he couldn't fail to have seen him.'

'I'll see what I can find out. Leave it to me.'

'OK.'

It was nearly seven when he got back to the flat. Petrov and the girl were in their room. He switched on the radio so that they would know he was there. It was the news on Radio 4. The Russians had launched eight Cosmos satellites from one rocket. As he sat in the leather armchair he wondered if the time hadn't come for him to resign. What he was doing seemed so utterly futile. SIS was a kind of dream world that nobody outside it would believe. You survived by being so involved in its intricacies that you had no time to think about yourself. And the strange thing was, that it was your own life, your private life, that became unreal, as if you were an actor playing a part. SIS seemed somehow safer than the outside world. They were almost like monks from some silent order, speaking only in their own special language that was not for normal mortals. Fighting the good fight in silent dedication. But acting as companion and protector to Petrov seemed to epitomize the futility of his work. He had made some progress in his relationship with Petrov. So what? A Russian defector with vague thoughts of going back was looking a bit more cheerful. And if they were lucky, sooner or later he would start co-operating again. Which was fine except for one fact. Despite his cheerfulness the Russian was still convinced that they were intending to kill him. In the meantime Lawler was sitting in the pale evening sunlight, alone and depressed.

He washed and changed and walked down to the Royal Court Hotel. He ate alone and it was nearly midnight when he got back to the flat.

The girl had left and Petrov was sitting in the living-room

in his bathrobe, a half-empty bottle of vodka on the floor beside him. His face was flushed and his hand trembled as he poured himself another drink. He held the bottle up to Lawler.

'You drink with me, Jimmy?'

'No thanks, Tolya. I'm going to bed.'

Petrov lifted his glass. '*Na zdrovye.*'

'*Na zdrovye.*'

'You been planning how you kill me, Jimmy?'

Lawler sighed. 'I told you, Tolya. Nobody's going to kill you. Nobody *wants* to kill you. Nobody has any reason to kill you.'

'Not yet, my friend, not yet.'

'What does that mean?'

'You wait till I have told you all you want to know. Then you kill me.'

'Why should we do that?'

Petrov reached down for the vodka bottle and filled his glass again. Lawler realized that it wasn't the first bottle for Petrov. He wasn't yet drunk, but he was well on the way. Petrov sat looking back at him without answering.

'Why should we want to kill you, Petrov?'

'I told you is same as the man you call George Blake.'

'We didn't kill George Blake. He was tried in court. He confessed. He was sentenced to imprisonment and he escaped.'

'You are naive, my friend. A child. A fool. Or you think *I* am a fool.' He banged his fist on his chest and his eyes blazed as he shouted the words. 'Not with me you play those games.'

'I don't understand what you mean.'

He saw the swing of Petrov's arm but the vodka stung his eyes. Very slowly he fumbled for the box of Kleenex and took a tissue to wipe his face. And all the time he kept his eyes on Petrov.

Lawler said very quietly, 'I think perhaps somebody else should help you, Petrov. I'm obviously making things worse.'

Petrov shrugged. 'It makes no difference to me, Jimmy,

who they fix to kill me.'

'I'll talk to Silvester tomorrow morning and arrange for a replacement.'

'Why they choose you for me, *tovarich?*'

'Because I speak some Russian and some German.'

'Is plenty of your officers speak Russian and some German. It must be more than that.'

Lawler sighed. 'Silvester said that he thought we were like one another.'

'In what way?'

'A bit romantic and emotional.'

'How old are you now?'

'Thirty-seven.'

'And how old me?'

'Forty-three.'

'How you know?'

'I saw it in your file.'

Petrov leaned back half-smiling. 'What does it say in my file?'

'You know I can't discuss that, Tolya.'

'You got father and mother?'

'Yes.'

'What does he do?'

'He's a writer.'

'Not either for me. No father, no mother.'

'What happened?'

'He was officer in engineers' regiment. I never hear of him again. My mother died in Leningrad during German siege.'

'Was she killed?'

'A land-mine on the hospital.'

'How old were you?'

'Fourteen, fifteen, I don't remember.'

'What happened to you?'

Petrov shook his head vehemently, tears on his cheeks. He waved his hand as if he were cleaning a window, washing things away.

'I not talk about that.'

Lawler leaned forward. 'When Silvester briefed me

about you he said that he was worried that you wanted to go back to Moscow. He wanted me to make you feel at home here in London. He couldn't possibly want you killed or he wouldn't do all this. It would just happen. You know that. Give me one possible reason why Silvester should want you killed.'

Petrov shook his head. 'I say no more. You must know what I mean.'

'Do you mean that you never said or hinted to Silvester that you wanted to go back?'

Petrov shrugged. 'Of course I say that. Two, three times maybe.'

'But you don't want to go back?'

'Is not possible for me to go back.'

'So why did you suggest it?'

'To test him. To see how he react.'

'And how did he react?'

'He fix these games with you.'

'Why do you think he did that?'

'So I go on talking, and when he has all he wants then . . . pouff! They fix me. You do, or they do.'

'Who's they?'

Petrov just stared back at him and the hand on his knee was trembling. He stood up slowly, staggering slightly as he bent to put his glass on the table. His eyes were half-closed. At the door of his bedroom he turned and looked back at Lawler.

'I think maybe they make fool of you, Jimmy. They don't tell you.' He smiled. A shrewd, knowing smile. 'Maybe you better find out about Blake or they end up to kill you as well as me.'

'Goodnight, Tolya. Try and sleep.'

Petrov closed the door behind him without replying.

7

HAMBURG 1945

He booked the German into the jail and put the things he had collected into a large buff envelope. Everything except the keys to the flat. He wanted to search the flat thoroughly, but on his own with the German that hadn't been possible. The German was a big strong man despite his one arm. And an Obersturmbannführer der SS was a good haul for one night.

Outside the jail he sat in the open jeep. It was a warm night with a bright moon that emphasized the heaps of rubble and the skeleton shapes of what remained of the buildings of Hamburg. It was August 1945 and Sub-Lieutenant Blake took his duties as an intelligence officer seriously. There were many of his colleagues who thought, and sometimes even said, that he took his duties far too seriously. He ignored their slipshod attitudes. He knew what had to be done. He knew what the war had been about, and they didn't. They saw their time in occupied Germany as a time for self-indulgence and making money on the black market.

He looked at his watch. It was just past eleven and he decided to go back and search the flat while it was fresh in his mind. The tip-off had come from the SS man's wife and he had almost decided to ignore it. But duty is duty, and if information came in it should be used, whatever the source and whatever the motive. He started the engine and headed back to the house by the Grossmarkthalle.

It was one of the few remaining old houses that were still standing. The windows had all been blown out and were boarded up, and there were tarpaulins fastened across half the gaping roof. It was well after curfew, and there was silence everywhere, except where a broken pipe dripped water, and rats scuttled stealthily in the rubble. There was still the smell of rotting corpses in the air.

He took his torch and the paraffin lamp from the back seat of the jeep and crossed the road to the house.

The electricity would have been switched off at eleven in all buildings except those occupied by troops and Military Government, and he played his torch over the door until he found the lock. As he opened the door he saw a door close at the far end of the corridor. He went slowly up the stairs to the second floor, and to his surprise there was a faint bar of light at the bottom of the door. He took the pistol from its holster and held it in his left hand as he slid the key into the door lock and turned it slowly. He threw the door open. The pale light came from a British army paraffin lamp on the table, and a girl was standing naked with a glass of beer in her hand. A sergeant with RAOC flashes was sitting in a wicker arm-chair. For a moment all three of them were silent and then Blake recovered from his surprise and walked over to the sergeant.

'Where's your AB64 part 2, Sergeant?'

The sergeant put down his empty glass, fished in his battle-dress pocket and pulled out the brown book. Blake turned over the pages and read them carefully before handing the book back.

'You know it's an offence to fraternize with Germans, Sergeant.'

'It was just a drink, sir.'

'How long have you been here?'

'About twenty minutes.'

'You'd better get back to your unit and thank your lucky stars I'm Royal Navy not Military Police.'

The sergeant stood up, put on his forage cap and left.

Blake turned to look at the girl. She was very young and very pretty, long-legged and big-breasted and obviously unconcerned at her nudity. But her half-smile turned to surprise and fear when he spoke in German.

'What's your name?'

'Heidi.' And she smiled back at him, nervously.

'Heidi what?'

'Heidi Voss.'

'Where did you get the beer and the lamp?'

'They were given to me.'

'By whom?'

'The sergeant gave me the beer and a captain gave me the lamp.'

'What was the captain's name?'

She shrugged. 'I've no idea.'

'Where did you meet him?'

'At the officers' club. I'm a waitress there.'

'You live with the SS officer?'

'No. I don't know any SS officer.'

'Klaus Horstmann.'

The surprise was genuine. 'I didn't know he was a soldier.'

'You'd better get dressed.'

She looked surprised. 'You can do what you want for cigarettes.'

'Is that what you do at the officers' club?'

'They come back here with me.'

'How old are you?'

'Seventeen.'

'And how long have you been sleeping with men for money?'

'Since May. Since the occupation.'

'Why don't you get a job?'

She shrugged. 'There are no jobs. I can't do anything except this.'

'How much do they pay you?'

'A packet of cigarettes. Twenty cigarettes.'

'And you let them have sex with you for that?'

'Yes.'

He stood looking at her and she mistook his look for lust and smiled back at him. 'You can have me all night if you want.'

He shook his head slowly, and said quietly, 'I'm ashamed. I'm ashamed at what they do. It's terrible. Unforgivable.'

'They need a woman, it's nothing more. They're just men.'

'Men don't treat women like that. They're scum.'

'Don't you sleep with girls?'

'No.'

68

'Are you married?'

'No.'

'How is it you speak such good German?'

And even that minor probing of his intelligence background brought him back to earth.

'The SS man is under arrest. He won't be back.'

She nodded and he abandoned his intended search. As he stood at the door he said, 'Will you be here tomorrow morning?'

'Yes. Until eleven. Then I go to the club to serve lunch.'

'If I have time I'll bring you a carton of cigarettes. Two hundred. Not for sex.'

'For what?'

'To make up for the others.'

And he closed the door securely as he left and went back to his quarters.

Despite being heartily disliked by his Royal Navy colleagues Lieutenant-Commander Blake had been noticed by officers of MI6, and while his colleagues were only counting the days to their demobilization, George Blake was recruited to help, in a minor role, the counter-intelligence operations against the Russians in the British Zone. He worked hard and zealously and, although his colleagues found his intensity and single-mindedness an embarrassment, he was recommended for a home posting to take a Russian Language course at Downing College, Cambridge. As always, he did outstandingly well.

His 'P' file assessment noted that he lacked personality and had more the air and appearance of a junior clerk. A nonentity rather than an intelligence officer. But a section field operations officer had scrawled in red ink — 'So what? This is exactly what we want.'

The Foreign Office was more used to finding a home for mild eccentrics than the Royal Navy, and when he came down from Cambridge in 1948 George Blake was posted as His Britannic Majesty's Vice Consul to the Legation in Seoul, the capital of the Republic of Korea.

8

KOREA 1950

The film was the English original with sub-titles. It was Carol Reed's The Third Man, *and the audience was silent and rapt. The camera closed in on the hands on the zither, and then the sound track groaned, and the image on the screen flickered and finally faded. There was a murmuring from the audience and a few people made for the aisle, to be suddenly illumined by the bright white light on the screen. The loud-speakers crackled, and then a tense voice, breathless and high-pitched, spoke in Korean. All soldiers were to report immediately to their barracks. The message was repeated three times and then the house lights went up. There was no panic but there was pushing around the doors, and frightened faces. It was Sunday, 25 June 1950 and the North Koreans had crossed the thirty-eighth parallel into South Korea. The Korean War had started.*

George Blake waited until the cinema was almost empty and then walked back to the Legation. There were crowds in the streets and already there was the sound of distant gunfire, and as he passed the Toksu Palace he saw soldiers formed up at the side of the road being harangued by an officer.

Captain Holt, the British Minister, was already burning secret papers and the two of them stayed up all that night preparing for the worst.

Four days later Seoul was occupied by the North Koreans, and despite the looting and destruction, time was found to attack the British Legation. Men wearing the red arm-bands of the People's Militia and carrying automatic pistols surrounded the compound. On that first day they only looted the building and took away the Legation cars. Captain Holt, Consul Owen and Vice-Consul Blake spent the next two days in the stripped Legation wondering what

70

their fate would be. Holt rehearsed his piece about international law and territorial rights without much hope of being heeded. There was no electricity and therefore no communication with the world outside. And no news of what was happening outside. The battery-driven radio could only pick up Korean stations and none of the three men could speak Korean.

It was early in the morning two days later when the police vans drove into the compound and an hour later amidst shouting and confusion all the Legation staff were bundled into the vans, under arrest. They were driven to the large house on the outskirts of Seoul that had been taken over by the North Korean Security Police. Outside they could hear bursts of machine-gun fire and the crack of exploding grenades. Commissioner Lord of the Salvation Army and a Roman Catholic priest, Father Hunt, were brought in a few minutes later.

Captain Holt asserted the Legation staff's diplomatic status in vain, and a rough and ready interrogation by their captors began. It was interrupted by the small-arms fire around the house, and eventually the questioning stopped when several South Korean police officers were brought in. They had been viciously beaten up, their legs broken, and blood was pouring from their ears and mouths. They gave no signs of fear or pain as they were violently interrogated, and half an hour later they were taken out and shot.

The North Koreans seemed to have lost interest in the diplomats but a few days later they were pushed into a truck and taken to Pyongyang, the Communist capital. In the camp at Pyongyang they were joined by other European civilians. By then the Americans were pushing back the North Korean army and the treatment of the civilians in the camp became harsher. They were moved on to the town of Man-po on the River Yalu on the Manchurian border.

On 20 October American forces captured Pyongyang. Then the Chinese army came into the war, and the civilian prisoners were moved from one town to another, and the mood of the guards became ugly. At the end of October the internees started on a forced march. They were warned

71

before they set off that those who collapsed would be shot, and that their corpses would have to be carried by the survivors, and the nightmare journey started. Disease, wounds, exhaustion, starvation and cold took their toll, and the victims were dealt with mercilessly. Across mountain passes in blizzards men stumbled exhausted as they carried corpses on their backs, and the only gesture of mercy from the Communists was that they sometimes shot those who fell exhausted at the side of the road. About a hundred people had died or been shot by the time they arrived at their destination, the village of Chung-Kang-Djin. The morning after their arrival the guard commander ordered physical exercises as a punishment for bad behaviour on the march, and another dozen deaths were added to the toll.

A few days later they were moved to a larger camp at a nearby village, Hadjang. It already housed a variety of civilians and American and United Nations' prisoners of war.

The camp commandant at Hadjang was known as 'The Tiger'. Ruthless and energetic, he turned the camp into a camp for the dying. With temperatures sometimes falling to seventy degrees below freezing the cold itself would have been enough, but when dysentery, meningitis and gangrene were added, then death was a commonplace. Out of seven hundred and eighty American PoWs, four hundred and sixty died in Hadjang, and the proportion among the civilians was roughly the same.

When prisoners were seriously ill 'The Tiger' had them moved to a line of wooden huts where they were left alone to die. Vice-Consul Blake had his share of dysentery and frost-bite, but Holt and Consul Owen were seriously ill. Blake nursed them both, and argued and pleaded that they should not be removed to the death-huts. The two diplomats were so near the point of death that they had no knowledge of what was happening. George Blake survived, day by day, and despite his weakness he struggled to help the helpless and protect the dying from the guards. His haggard, white face was given a touch of defiance by his faintly jaunty beard. His attitude to his captors was a strange mixture of aggression and politeness.

In this camp without hope, food, medical care or mercy, the Communists mounted their first attempts at indoctrination of their prisoners. The lectures by the barely literate and simple-minded North Korean political officers were almost a welcome relief to the sick, half-starved prisoners whose minds were still alert. The indoctrinators were no match for the tactics of their victims, who argued skilfully with far more knowledge of Marx and Lenin than their captors. Some hackneyed quotation of Marx or Lenin that was used to make a point was often thrown back in their faces with a counter-quotation that exposed their real ignorance of Marxism and the revolution. But all this amateur indoctrination programme ended in the autumn of 1951. The diplomats and certain other key prisoners were removed to a farmhouse at Moo-Yong-Nee where indoctrination was to begin in earnest.

The leader of the indoctrination team was a Russian whom the prisoners christened 'Blondie'. He was obviously well-educated and spoke fluent English, and one by one he interviewed them alone as the start of his task of persuading them that the Communist system was a superior way of life. Convincing a group of intelligent Europeans who were experiencing first-hand the effects of Communism made his task hopeless from the start. The prisoners welcomed the interludes of conversation but were scornful of the attempts to persuade them towards the Communist line.

The Russian, Gregori Kuzmich, had served on the staff of the Soviet ambassador to Canada and later at the embassies in London and Washington. His knowledge of the Western way of life was first-hand and extensive, and his English was faultless.

Because George Blake spoke Russian he seemed an obvious target for Kuzmich's arguments and he listened, as he had to, to the iteration of the massacre of the Red Indians by the settlers, Dickens quoted as an authority on living conditions in Britain, and the general discrimination against

Negroes and coloured people. But it took more than Oliver Twist *to convert intelligent Europeans to Communism.*

On 20 March 1953, without any explanation, the three British diplomats were taken to Pyongyang. The journey took nearly two days by car, and en route they were able to see the destruction wrought by the war. From Pyongyang they were taken to Antung, Peking, Moscow, and finally they were handed over to the British authorities in West Berlin. After a couple of days' rest they were flown to the RAF airfield at Abingdon, Berkshire where they were given a hero's welcome. But it was 21 April 1953, and the public were rather more interested in the gruesome details being revealed in Bow Street Magistrates' Court about John Reginald Christie and how he had murdered his wife and several other women in the house at 10, Rillington Place.

Captain Holt was knighted, but his captivity had broken his health. He retired in 1956 and died four years later. He told many people in those last years that he owed his life to the loyalty and nursing of George Blake.

9

They had stopped for a meal at Hindhead and it was just past three o'clock when they turned off the Portsmouth road at Petersfield. Buriton is a small, quiet village in the shadow of the Downs that leads nowhere and links no roads. Its Norman church and the manor house are its only landmarks.

The Lawler cottage was the only building in the lane near the edge of the village. It was long and narrow, its small wooden windows in typical Sussex style set in the thick stone walls that had once housed the village inn. Set on the Hampshire/Sussex borders, its thatched roof and general neatness declared its Sussex influences. It sat at the edge of the village green, below Butser Hill and the forest, and there were blackberries in the hedge and golden samphire between the stones.

Edward Lawler was sitting in the old-fashioned garden at a round white table and he stood up smiling as he saw his son and his two companions. As his son made the introductions they could hear the piano inside the cottage, and 'Moon River' merged into a Schubert song that spoke of evening stars.

Chatting, the four of them went into the cool of the cottage, through the quarry-tiled kitchen to a large room with an oak strip floor. The Blüthner boudoir grand was in the far corner and flowers were everywhere. In vases and pewter pots they frothed their colour around the room. Old-fashioned flowers. Campanulas, lupins, wallflowers, sweet-peas and phlox, not artfully arranged, but overflowing from their containers in every direction. The black-haired woman who was walking from behind the piano held her arms out to her son and kissed him on the mouth. Then she turned to be introduced, smiling at Petrov and impulsively kissing the girl.

'It must be Kerry or Cork,' she said.

The girl laughed. 'It was Cork, but Dublin the last few years.'

'Well, bless you wherever it was, at least I get the chance to see my boy.' She looked at Petrov and then at her son, and turned to the girl as if the men weren't there. 'My God, they look so miserable the pair of them, what on earth have they been up to? Putting the world to rights I suppose, as per usual.' She took the girl's hand. 'Come on. You can help me do the cream.'

Edward Lawler turned to Petrov. 'Can I help you with your bags, Tony?'

Petrov looked embarrassed. 'Is no trouble, Mr Lawler.'

'I'll get them, Dad. Are my friends at the back upstairs?'

Lawler senior said, 'That's right, Jimmy. There's flowers in the lady's room and a bottle in your friend's.'

James Lawler smiled at his mother's tactful insistence on the niceties.

When Mrs Lawler and Siobhan brought in the high-tea they all ate and talked until the room was almost dark. James Lawler watched his mother and father work their magic on Petrov and the girl. They treated them as old friends, and the Russian and the girl responded. Arguing about politics and literature, the two women joined forces against the men.

It was nearly midnight when Petrov and the girl went upstairs and Lawler sat with his parents, drinking a last cup of tea. And it was Edward Lawler who made the first comment.

'What's he afraid of, Jimmy?'

'Who?'

'Don't kid me. Your friend Tony. He's scared as hell.'

'What makes you say that? I've never seen him so much at ease.'

'Maybe. But there's a terrible tension there. Is it the girl?'

There were a few moments of silence and then Edward Lawler said, 'I think we'd better not probe anymore, Mother. It's not our business anyway.'

James Lawler said quickly, 'Tell me what you think of him, Father. I'd like to know.'

'He's not a friend of yours, is he? Not a real friend.'

'What makes you think that?'

'When we were talking and arguing he never once turned to you for support. Once he'd got used to us he changed from being very withdrawn to being almost . . . I don't know quite how to describe it . . . authoritarian, peremptory . . . something like that. I'd say he's a man who's come down in the world. A rich man or an important man who hasn't got used to having no money, or influence, or whatever it was.'

'What does he need to put him right?'

His father shrugged. 'Who knows? Time, for one thing. He speaks very good English for a German . . . or whatever he is . . . but he hasn't settled down here yet. He's tense, alert, constantly looking for a second meaning to anything that's said. But once he was talking he forgot all the caution and was full of his own opinions. Almost aggressive.' He looked at his son. 'He's not a journalist, is he?'

'No.'

'Something to do with your work?'

James Lawler turned quickly to his mother. 'He wants to marry the girl. Would that help, do you think?'

She shrugged. 'Who can tell, dear? Who can tell? It might work for him but I doubt if it would for her.'

'Why not?'

His mother sighed quietly. 'She's a sunny girl and he's a dark cloud. You could end up with either a silver lining or a thunderstorm. I'd say the storm. She obviously likes him. He's intelligent and attentive. But he needs her. He's hanging on to her like a drowning man to a life-belt. She knows it too. She's not Irish for nothing, you know.'

'Is she the marrying kind?'

'Oh sure she is. But she's the kind who'll want to look around. And what about you? How are you managing?'

'I'm getting by.'

'What's that mean?'

'There's nothing I can do, Ma. I've got no rights in law.'

'You've got responsibilities all the same.'

He sighed. 'I know, but I've got no way of affecting the situation.'

'Have you spoken to her?'

'She won't speak to me.'

'She's a foolish girl, but it's not her I'm worried about. It's little Sarah.'

'There's nothing I can do.'

His mother shrugged and shook her head. 'I'm surprised at you, Jimmy. I grieve about that little girl in that set-up.'

'So do I. It haunts me.'

His mother looked at him for a moment, and reached out her hand to cover his. 'I'm sure it does, my love. And you haunt me. If I sound harsh it's really only me railing against fate.' She sighed. 'I wish I had some magic wand to put it all right.'

'And what would you wish?'

Her grey eyes looked at his. 'You're right of course. There's nothing to wish for. Nothing could be right.' She stood up. 'It's time you were in bed. Both of you.'

The next morning when Lawler went downstairs Petrov was already up, sitting at ease on a high stool in the kitchen, watching his mother shelling peas. He nodded briefly at Lawler and went on talking, and Lawler froze as he heard him speaking.

'. . . and in all Moscow bakeries is always a fork so you can test that the loaf is fresh. And in GUM I go for meat. You go to the cashier for a twenty *kopek* receipt, wrap a *treshka* in the receipt and you get one kilo of best meat . . .'

'What's a *treshka*, Tony?'

'A three-rouble note. Two pounds sterling.'

'Well now . . . ' and Mary Lawler turned to look at her son. 'What breakfast would you like, Jimmy?'

'Just a coffee, Ma. We'll have to get on our way.' He turned to Petrov. 'Where's Siobhan?'

'Still asleep. I wake her, yes?'

'OK.'

When Petrov had gone Mary Lawler turned with raised

eyebrows. 'You've got a problem there, James.'

'Tell me.'

'He wants a background. Parents. Wife. Children. He wants to have been married for ten years already. He wants the security of a set of long relationships. He's a sad man waiting for a miracle. He's desperate for it to happen soon. He'd like to go to bed tonight and wake up tomorrow in someone else's life.' She stood with her arms on her hips. 'Somebody's taken away his soul. Is it your people, whoever they are?'

'No, Mother.' He shook his head. 'It's not us. Maybe we added the last straw, but it's just the result of his life.'

She looked at him, her eyes wet with unshed tears.

'And is that going to be the result of your life ten years from now?'

'No. I don't think I'll ever have his problems.'

'He told me what he was.'

'So I gathered. Did he say more?'

'He spoke about this man Blake who escaped from prison.'

'What did he say?'

'He said he'd warned you but you didn't understand. He said he was scared.'

'Of what?'

'He didn't say.'

And then Petrov and the girl were coming through the sitting-room with his father.

They had a snack before they left, and as he drove back to London Petrov and the girl slept in the back of the car. Right up to the time to leave Petrov had been like a child on holiday. Laughing and talking, with the girl obviously impressed by seeing him in such an unaccustomed mood. But Lawler felt lonely and depressed as he drove in silence like the captain of some ghost ship, a *Marie Celeste* on its aimless circling of the oceans. What the hell did Silvester expect him to do? It was a hopeless, doomed exercise, that probably only a psychiatrist could solve. Provided he had ten years to do it in.

He dropped Petrov and the girl at her flat. They were

going out for a meal and then coming round to his place for the night.

The phone was ringing as he threw his case on the bed. It was Silvester.

'Been trying to get hold of you. Thought you must have fled the country.'

'I was only away for a night, for God's sake.'

'You sound touchy. Anything wrong?'

'No. Not really. It's just wearing. And it's slow progress.'

'Have you made any progress?'

'Yes. I took him down to my parents with the girl. He made himself really at home.'

'Well, take your time. We need the bastard, but I'll leave it to you to decide when he's ready to carry on.'

'Did you check up on Ridger?'

'Ridger? Who's Ridger?'

'The Special Branch man who's been tailing me.'

'Oh yes. It must have been coincidence. He resigned from SB four weeks ago.'

'What's he doing now?'

'The record says he's training as a computer programmer at some commercial training school. Paid a fee of four hundred quid. Passed an aptitude test with a high rating. I should forget him.'

'What was his last address?'

'Somewhere in Croydon.'

'So why is he hanging around outside my place right now?'

'Are you sure?'

'Of course I'm sure, and he didn't look shifty when I looked at him either. He just stared back like he didn't give a damn.'

'Maybe he's got a girl-friend near you. Or perhaps he's moonlighting for some private agency. Divorce stuff maybe.' There was a pause. 'You don't think it could be Joanna, do you?'

'She hasn't got the money for those capers. Apart from that what interest could she have? I'm not married to her.'

'Could be some crazy scheme to check on your life-style

in case you applied for custody of Sarah.'

'For God's sake, she knows I haven't a chance in a million.'

'You never know, Jimmy. She's pretty way out. Bear it in mind anyway.'

10

Petrov came back to the flat mid-morning, tense and irritable. When Lawler asked him what was the matter he threw a small box on to the coffee table. It rolled like a large dice and there was gold lettering on one of its sides.

'Look at it,' Petrov said aggressively. 'Look at it.'

Lawler picked it up and realized what it was. He opened it carefully. In a velvet-lined case there was a platinum engagement ring. Two small diamonds set on either side of an opal. Lawler guessed that it must have cost well over a hundred pounds.

He looked at Petrov. 'What happened?'

Petrov shrugged. 'I give her ring. Ask her to marry me. She say no.'

'Just that?'

'We have bloody row, she says she is finished with me.' He shrugged again. 'Is all over.'

'What was the row about?'

'That she say no again.'

'Did you try to persuade her to change her mind?'

'I tell her she is a bitch.'

'That wasn't very bright. What did *she* say?'

'That I am a phoney. No family. I don't belong here. I don't really have a job. I make bad husband and bad father.'

'And what did you say?'

'I say is better be phoney than a whore.'

'That must have gone down well.'

'Is true. No? She's just a *baralka*.'

'What do you want to do?'

Petrov shrugged. 'God knows. You tell me.'

'Do you really want to marry her, Tolya, or is it just something that's got fixed in your mind?'

82

'Of course I want to marry her.'

'Would you marry her if she was a Russian girl and you were both in Moscow?'

'Would be no problem. In Moscow I am senior officer in KGB. She would marry me first time I ask.'

'But *would* you ask her if you were in Moscow?'

'Yes.' He nodded to give an emphasis that somehow didn't ring true.

'Do you want me to go and talk to her?'

'Why?' Petrov sneered. 'You want excuse to sleep with her?'

Lawler bit back the words and said, 'So far as I'm concerned she's your girl, Tolya. But you and I had better talk first.'

'OK. You talk.'

'How about we start by levelling with one another?'

'What does that mean?'

'We speak the truth. We say what we really mean.'

'OK. You start.'

'We need the information you can give us. All of it. And we need it quickly so that we can take action. In return for this we pay you a pension. We can discuss the details before you talk if you want. We'll find you a house. Give you a new cover identity. Give you protection if you want it. And we'll meet all reasonable demands.'

Petrov sat silently for several minutes, looking at Lawler's face as if there might be some sign that proved his sincerity. Some psychic litmus paper that went blue for loyalty or truth. When Petrov finally spoke Lawler sensed that there was an actual change in their relationship. As if the weeks of random, pointless friendliness were actually having some effect. Not much, but some. But it could be that the question that Petrov put to him represented no more than curiosity.

'Tell me about the girl in the photograph.'

'Why that, Tolya?' But Lawler didn't say it resentfully.

'I want to know about you. You said they put you with me because we're like one another. I don't see that at all.'

'How do you see me?'

83

'I'd say you were efficient at your job. A loner. You give the impression of being a nice guy. Friendly, sympathetic and so on, but underneath it all I'd guess you were very tough. You don't seem to have many friends. That could be because of your work, or it could be because they find you out.' .

'Which of those things doesn't apply to you?'

'None. But I'm not sure if I was in Moscow and you had come over that I would care all that much so long as you did what we wanted. If you stopped co-operating we'd try and get you back on the railway lines, but if it didn't work I guess I wouldn't shed tears if you ended in the Gulag. So why should you be any different?'

'I don't think I am, but what you described isn't really the scenario we've got here.'

'Why not?'

'You were co-operating. Suddenly you stopped. There's obviously a reason. All I'm trying to do is find out that reason and put it right. Silvester thinks that you might be missing Moscow, that you want to go back. You tell me that you miss some things, but that you definitely don't want to go back. That makes sense. If I was suddenly transposed to Moscow there are things that I should miss, so I understand all that. But I don't think that you stopped co-operating for that reason.'

'What do you think the reason is?' Petrov's eyes were half closed with concentration as he waited for an answer.

'I can only tell you the truth.'

'So tell me.'

'The truth is that I have no idea. Not the faintest, thinnest clue. But if you'll tell me what it is I'll put it right, whatever it is.'

Petrov closed his eyes for a moment, then opening them he said slowly, 'If I did really want to go back who would make the final decision?'

'The Section heads concerned with the Soviet Union.'

'Who are they?'

Lawler hesitated for only a moment. 'Silvester, Mason and Dyer.'

'What does Mason look like?'

'About five-seven, stocky, black hair plastered down. A slight Scottish accent. Generally wears tweed jackets and drill trousers. A bit untidy looking. Doesn't smile much and . . .'

'What's Dyer look like?'

'About the same height as Silvester. Five-eleven or six foot maybe. Medium build. Fair hair, blue eyes. Always well dressed. Neat, easy going, friendly. That's about it.'

'And what would their answer be?'

'I'd bet on it being "no", unless you had some really exceptional reason.'

'What if one of them strongly supported my request?'

'You mean Silvester, I suppose. It could make a difference. Possible but not probable.'

'And when they had said "no" what would happen to me?'

Lawler looked embarrassed. 'You'd lose a lot of freedom. I'd guess they would put you in some comfortable house under permanent guard. You'd get whatever you wanted. Food, female company, the odd trip out under escort, but you'd be a prisoner. A very comfortable prisoner.'

'Why all the trouble? Why not liquidate me?'

'For obvious reasons. These things filter out. They always do. Any KGB or GRU man thinking of coming over would think twice if he thought that might be his fate. What you did to Sneddon got about, and I'd guess it did you a lot of harm.'

'Did you know Sneddon personally?'

'Yes.'

'You didn't see his defection to us as a possible attempt at a plant?'

'Not in Sneddon's case, no.'

'Why not?'

'Sneddon didn't work in the field, he was basically a historian specializing in the Soviet Union. He was used as a sort of "devil's advocate" in evaluating Politburo and KGB moves. I wouldn't have classed him as pro-Soviet but he was a sympathizer. He saw the good as well as the bad. He knew more about Marxism than most Marxists do. He just thought the Soviet Union was no longer Marxist. He was very useful to us. And I suspect he was very useful to your people when he defected.'

'We could never decide. We couldn't understand why he came over if he wasn't committed. So in the end the hard-liners won the day.'

'Were you one of the hard-liners?'

'Yes.'

For a fleeting second Lawler was revolted, before he realized that it represented a break-through. It was a piece of honesty that Petrov would recognize did not endear him. He was too experienced to think otherwise. Lawler was also aware that temporarily their roles were reversed. Petrov was the expert and Petrov was the interrogator. It was Lawler who was being weighed in the balance, as friend or foe.

'Tell me what's worrying you, Tolya.'

Petrov smiled and it was the first time Lawler had seen Petrov smile since the visit to his parents.

'No. You tell me about the girl in the photograph.'

Lawler sighed and took a deep breath. 'Her name is Joanna. Joanna Calthrop. She's about twenty-seven. We lived together for nearly six years. We've got a daughter named Sarah. She's three years old. Joanna went off with someone else about three months ago.'

'Why didn't you marry her?'

'She's already married.'

'Why didn't she get a divorce?'

'He's rich and influential, and he still loves her in his own peculiar way. He wouldn't divorce her and I think Joanna kept him as an insurance policy. A bolt-hole she could go back to if all else failed.'

'Why did she go off with another guy?'

'It's a long story. And very boring.' He sighed. 'And very sordid.'

'Tell me.'

'Does it really make any difference, Tolya?'

86

'I think so.'

'When I first met her she had left her husband about a year before. She was lively and pretty and she was on drugs and hard liquor. She was mixing with some of the wildest specimens of the so-called upper classes that you could find. The kind we used to send to the colonies with a family pension provided they never came back. The people who supply the gossip columns with their juiciest material. Some of it too juicy even for them. We shacked up together and I calmed her down. She was off the drugs, and one whisky a day was enough.

'That lasted about three years and by then we had Sarah. Then I had to do a two-month stint in Washington and they came with me. Some creep from the Brazilian embassy latched on to her, and in a matter of days she was back into the smart set and drugs. By the time we left I was getting flak from the embassy, and SIS brought me back to London. They read me the riot act but they were sympathetic. What she got up to in London didn't matter so much. It got worse and worse and I was no longer able to influence her. She was charged with drunken driving and then she left with a man who runs an antique shop. He receives stolen goods and is suspected of financing a drug-distribution operation. She lives with him in Kensington. That's about it.'

'Do you love her still?'

'No. I sometimes feel sad for her. And sometimes I loathe her. But I love the little girl.'

'Why don't you take the little girl back?'

'It's not possible. I don't have any legal rights because we were not married.'

'But you have influential friends, surely they could bring pressure?'

'I'm afraid not.'

'And this makes you sad about the small girl, Sarah?'

'Yes. It's my fault that she is in bad surroundings.'

'The mother's responsibility too.'

'She isn't a responsible person.'

'Does she care for the child?'

87

'In a way she does. But not the right way. She sees her as a decoration. A possession.'

'Was the woman – Joanna – good to you before she started drinking again? Did she love you?'

'No. She didn't love me. She needed me at the time. She isn't really capable of loving anybody. She's neurotic. She pretends very well. And you can pretend that it's love for a time. If you want to pretend.'

'And you pretended?'

'Yes. I'm afraid I did. It was stupid of me.'

Petrov sat looking at him, and the Russian looked older, more mature, more in control of himself. As if the retailing of someone else's misfortune and foolishness had made him wiser.

'And what you going to do now?'

Lawler smiled wryly. 'Nothing, just soldier on.'

Petrov nodded. 'He was right, your Silvester. We are a bit the same. We got no stake in the world.'

'Is that what you want, Tolya, a stake in the world?'

'Yes.'

'Is that the problem?'

Petrov shook his head vigorously. 'No. That's not the problem.'

'Tell me what it is. Maybe I can solve it.'

'Did you read the file on Behar . . . on Blake?'

'I went through the summary. I didn't see any relevance to your situation.'

'Maybe you should read the file, not just the summary.'

'There are four files. Thick ones.'

'So. Maybe you should read four thick files.'

'Why don't you save me the time and just tell me?'

'Because of two reasons. If I tell you, you will not believe, and if I tell you I would be dead in a few days.' He paused. 'And now I am sure that you would be dead too.' He leaned forward, his face earnest and his eyes alert. 'This what I tell you about Blake is nothing to do with what you and I do now. It is not nice and cosy and friendly, it's part of our other life. Remember what I say. When you read of Blake you are back in business of espionage. Is not a game, that part of our talk. When I speak of Blake I speak as colonel in KGB, not a man with a crazy Irish girl-friend in a strange country. Is about living and dying. You and me. I was not colonel because I was stupid or afraid. You know that. You ask Silvester of my record.'

'I'll do what you say, Tolya. Do you want me to talk to Siobhan?'

'If you think you can do any good, yes.'

'I'll talk to her anyway.'

11

George Blake was granted indefinite sick-leave to recover
from the debilitating effects of pneumonia, dysentery and
vitamin deficiencies. Most days he lay in bed reading at his
mother's house in Reigate. There had been talk at the
Foreign Office of an OBE but the idea had been dropped.
MI6 had already broken a major security rule when they had
recruited him. Only natural-born British subjects of natural-
born British parents were recruited to the Foreign Office let
alone its secret service. And while George Blake had been in
Korean prison camps Burgess and Maclean had defected to
Moscow. The security screening of civil servants had
become a continuous issue in both Parliament and the press.
The less attention received by Blake the safer his position
would be. They had no doubt of his loyalty. He had proved it
conclusively all through his career, and his recent courage
and loyalty in the prison camps were even further proof.

When he had recovered he was posted to Queen Anne's
Gate, the HQ in London of SIS. And it was there that he met
his first and only love. She was a secretary who worked for
him. A gentle, pretty, intelligent girl, the daughter of the
Foreign Office's Russian language expert. It was a strange
courtship, typical of the diffident man who so often said that
he wanted no responsibilities away from his job. He owned
no furniture, no flat, no car, not even a radio, but it was
obvious that he loved the girl. When they talked of marriage
he tried to put her off. How could he keep her properly? He
was half-Jewish and barely used to the life and customs in
England. He was shortly to be posted to Berlin. But on 23
September 1954 George Blake married his pretty girl, and
his superiors were quietly pleased. A secret agent in Berlin
who was married was far more secure than a single man.

It was a white wedding at Marylebone's parish church,

and was attended by many officials and secretaries from the Foreign Office. They honeymooned in the South of France. On the marriage certificate he gave his name and his father's name as Blake not Behar. When they returned to London he found that he was not to be posted to Berlin until the following April, and the couple lived with his mother in her flat at Baron's Court.

BERLIN 1955

The girl bent down to switch on the electric fire and stood up slowly, her hand on her faintly convex stomach. She was four months pregnant and she sat down slowly in the armchair and reached out to switch on the radio. She turned the volume down and listened to the music from RIAS Berlin. It was a repeat of a Bert Kämpfert concert that had been given in Cologne.

She looked across at her husband as he sat at the table. He was studying a street map and a handful of photographs. He looked so young, and yet so determined. Intent on what he was doing, like a child with a new puzzle, determined to succeed. Because she had worked at Queen Anne's Gate she knew the kind of work that he was doing. Not very precisely, but well enough to wonder why he chose to do it. He didn't seem like any of the other SIS men she had met when she worked at Queen Anne's Gate. They weren't all like one another but they had something about them that marked them off. A self-assurance, an air of confidence, even a sense of humour. But her George had none of these things. When they met new people they tended to patronize him and she sometimes felt guilty that she understood their attitude. She had overheard somebody describe him as a nonentity and she knew what they meant. It wasn't just his quietness and diffidence but his appearance and attitude: he was so self-effacing, more like a salesman in some old-fashioned department store. But his superiors seemed to be well pleased with their puritanical and conscientious recruit. He was a good husband. He cared for her, helped with the housework, and did the shopping when it meant driving across to East Berlin. Once or twice a month he took her out *for a meal or a concert. He was frequently out until the early hours of the morning, but that was just part of his job. She had no fears about other women, and that was more than many British wives in Berlin could say. He looked younger than his years despite his rather earnest face, but often, when she said some endearment to him, his face would light up, his eyes sparkling as if his mind was coming back from some-where far away.*

Gillian Blake was happy with her husband, and happy at the thought of having a child. The flat in Platanen Allee was in one of West Berlin's pleasantest suburbs.

George Blake parked the car in the car park at Olivaer Platz and walked to the corner of Duisburger Strasse and Konstanzer Strasse. The van was already there. As he walked towards it the driver flashed the lights twice, very briefly. When he was level with the back of the van he knocked on the door, and when it opened he went up the two metal steps and the door closed behind him.

The three soldiers were all in civilian clothes. He knew them all. The lieutenant and the sergeant were from Security Signals, and the third man was the SIS liaison officer with the BfV. It was he who spoke first.

'They've given us clearance, George. Carte blanche *and no questions asked. He's been on net already tonight.'*

Blake nodded and turned to the lieutenant. 'Have we got tapes of tonight's traffic?'

'Yes. It was high-speed and we haven't got equipment for reducing it here. We'd like his set for examination until you need it for evidence.'

'I'll be taking him to the villa.'

'The car and the driver are round the corner. We can get them round in seconds when you want them.'

'Is he alone?'

'So far as we can tell.'

Blake looked at his watch. It was ten minutes to eleven. He looked at the lieutenant.

'I'll go up now. Give me five minutes and then ring. Two long and a short. I don't think he'll give any trouble.'

92

The air was hot and heavy inside the building and he walked slowly up the stone stairs to the top floor. The door facing him had a visiting card in a brass holder that said simply Paul Kretski: Geigenbauer - *violin maker*.

He already had a key. One of his men using the cover of meter reader had seen to that. Outside the door he stood quite still, closing his eyes for a moment. Then he slid the key into the lock and opened the door.

The man stood there, a look of surprise on his face, a small metal file in his hand as he turned from filing a cello bridge held in a small vice on a wooden bench.

'Herr Kretski?'

'Who are you? What's going on? How did you get in?'

'Are you Paul Kretski?'

'Yes. But I don't—'

'Please sit down.' Blake nodded towards a wooden chair and hesitantly the man sat down. His hand was trembling as it rested on his knee and there were beads of perspiration on his upper lip.

Blake looked at him. 'Where's the radio?'

The man pointed at the small Telefunken set. Blake shook his head.

'The other radio. The short-wave radio.'

'Are you a policeman?'

'Where is the transmitter, Herr Kretski?'

'What would I want with a transmitter? I repair violins and cellos, not radios.'

'You're wasting my time.' Blake said it in Russian, and it was as if the man had been struck. His face was white, his mouth open, and his body was shaking violently. For a moment Blake thought the man was going to faint. Then the bell rang and he walked to the door, still keeping his eyes on the man.

When the three other men came into the room the man groaned involuntarily.

'Where is the transmitter?' Blake still used Russian.

The man shook his head slowly. He was too scared to speak. Blake sighed, and sat down and waited.

It was ten minutes before they found the transceiver. It was

93

in a drawer under a commode at the side of the single bed. The two Grundig TK 20s were in the wardrobe. The Security Signals lieutenant looked as pleased as if he had just won the Irish Sweep. He tried not to say anything but in the end he gave in.

'*It's a Mark 7 Sigma. A real beauty.*'

Blake nodded and turned to the man.

'*You'll be coming with me.*'

The man stood up. He had regained some of his composure. Blake pointed to the door and followed the man down the stairs. The BMW and the driver were waiting outside.

'*Why were you in direct touch with Moscow?*'

'*Those were my orders.*'

'*Why direct to Moscow? Why didn't you just pass the information to the KGB in Karlshorst?*'

'*Only Moscow could answer that.*'

'*When did you last hear from your wife and daughter?*'

'*I got a letter last week.*'

'*What was the postmark?*'

'*Dresden.*'

'*What did she say?*'

'*She said she was receiving the money every month and had been paid half in hard-roubles. And the apartment was to be decorated.*'

'*Why don't you telephone her in Moscow?*'

'*All telephones to the Soviet Union from West Berlin are monitored.*'

'*You could phone her from the safe-house in East Berlin.*'

'*I don't know such a place.*'

*Blake sighed and looked at a card. '*You were there on the third and fifteenth of last month. You were photographed going in and coming out.*'*

'*Tell me what you want. I need to sleep.*'

Blake pushed across a packet of cigarettes and a lighter and watched the man as he lit the cigarette and inhaled. He never threatened or used violence. He just kept on and on. Going over the same questions again and again before moving to some new line of questioning.

'Why did you stay in Smolensk after the war was over?'

'I had no choice, I was still a prisoner of war. If I stayed and worked I could be released.'

'Where did you meet your wife?'

'She was a secretary of the company which obtained the special woods for my work.'

'Why did you become a Soviet citizen?'

'I was there. My wife was Soviet. My work was there.'

'Where did you get your radio training?'

'In Moscow.'

'Where in Moscow?'

'At MVD headquarters in Dzerzhinski Square.'

'In your messages last week you said that there would be workers' risings in East Berlin next month. Did they ask for information on that subject?'

'They said I should join the Union and go to meetings and inform them of what was discussed.'

'You did that?'

'Yes.'

'What response did you get?'

'It was then I was given the briefcase with the US dollars and told to give them to Otto Kellner of the Transport Union.'

'Did you get a receipt?'

'Yes.'

'Where is it?'

'I posted it as I was instructed.'

'Where to?'

'To an address in Warsaw, I don't remember the details.'

'Who brought you the dollars?'

'I told you. A Russian brought me the money. I don't know his name.'

'Was he MVD?'

'I think so.'

'Where did you meet him?'

'I told you. Café Keese in Bismarck Strasse.'

'What was the password?'

'No password. I carry a violin case and a piece of music.'

'What music?'

'Sag' beim Abschied leise Servus.'

'What did the Russian look like?'

Kretski closed his eyes to think. He spoke slowly and hesitantly. 'Tall. About one metre eighty. Thin. Brown eyes. Quite good-looking.'

'How old?'

'Very young. Early twenties, maybe twenty-five. Very sophisticated.'

'Did you speak Russian or German?'

'Both.'

Blake showed his card to the Volkspolizist as he was stopped just past the Brandenburger Tor and ten minutes later he pulled up near the Friedrichshain Hospital. He walked for ten minutes to the safe-house and rang the code on the bell. Two long and one short. It was several minutes before the door was opened. He felt a sudden flash of anger that it was the girl. She was wearing a dressing-gown that revealed most of her naked body and she yawned as he spoke to her.

'Where is he?'

'Asleep.'

He pushed her to one side and went up the broad stairs two at a time. As he switched on the light the man asleep in the bed didn't stir. He shook him awake and the man rubbed his eyes, shielding them from the light.

'For God's sake, Georgi. What is it?'

'Kretski's blown, Tolya. Finished. You must pass it on immediately.'

'How do you know? How can you be sure?'

'Just give Moscow the message. I can't stop.'

It was dawn when he let himself into the flat in Platanen Allee.

12

BERLIN

Alwyn Bowden peered over the top of his heavy-rimmed glasses, his bushy eyebrows raised in judicial enquiry.

'You realize that there's no come-back, George, if you refuse. You're doing a good job and we're quite happy to let you carry on doing it. But you've got exceptional qualifications for extending your usefulness. It's up to you entirely.'

George Blake looked back at him, his willingness, his enthusiasm, written on his face.

'I'll take it on, Mr Bowden, if that's what you want.'

'You realize that you will be running considerably more risk than you are at the moment. There's your family to consider. I want you to take a couple of days to think it over. Don't be over-keen, or over-persuaded by me.'

Bowden stood up, pushing his glasses back up his nose. A habit that had been much mimed in the days when he had taught at Eton before he was drawn into MI6's operations.

'You did well with Kretski, George.' Bowden smiled. 'Our friends in East Berlin are going to be very peeved when they realize we've got him in the bag.'

'He didn't put up much resistance. But he's worried about his wife in Moscow.'

'Yes, of course he is, they'll take it out on her. What have you got in mind?'

'I thought we might suggest a deal. He co-operates fully. Names, addresses, safe-houses, drops, and we let him loose. He's pretty harmless, and he's talked.'

'Could be. Sound him out. No commitments but dangle it around a bit. See if he takes the bait. Give me a call in the next few days. Take all the time you need before you decide.'

'Right, sir.'

When his superiors at SIS, who operated what was coyly called the External Affairs Division at the old Olympic Stadium in Charlottenburg, suggested that George Blake should penetrate the Soviet intelligence organization in East Berlin in the guise of a double agent they were providing him with a perfect cover for his treason. For George Blake had been an agent of the Soviet intelligence services since he was a young man.

In the early days when, as a teenager, he acted as a courier for the Communist-run Resistance group in Holland, he had been spotted by a shrewd Dutch Communist and subtly and slowly drawn into a more positive commitment. His flight from the Gestapo had been genuine, but by then he was already committed to Moscow. It was several years before he was used beyond small tests of loyalty, but from the moment he was posted to Hamburg he was a Soviet agent under instruction.

His capture in Seoul had been a blunder made in ignorance by the North Koreans, but it had necessitated a complicated scenario to preserve his cover as a loyal SIS officer. The Soviets took a risk in releasing the small group that included Blake several months before the armistice was signed, and many months before other prisoners were released. The risk paid off, for nobody had thought to analyse why that small group should receive such privileged treatment. There had been other clues that SIS overlooked. Small but definite clues, whose overlooking might have indicated laxity or further treason, to a more suspicious agency.

There was a rough circle with a vertical line through it in pink chalk on the fence of the cemetery and Blake drove to the KO department store in East Berlin. Kaufhaus des Ostens was used extensively by Allied personnel, and if his car was noticed in the car park it would be assumed that he was at KO like all the others, for fresh fruit and vegetables. Although buying goods in East Berlin was frowned on by the Allied authorities it was considered a good thing to buy *fruit and vegetables to save importing scarce supplies from West Germany. He bought their usual weekly requirements and put the two cardboard cartons on the back seat of his car where they could easily be seen.*

Ten minutes later the taxi dropped him by the ruins of the church in Becher Strasse. From there he walked to the book-shop. He bought the second-hand copy of Vom Winde verweht *and walked through the bead curtains to the corridor. The door at the far end opened as he raised his hand to knock. The Russian stood aside as he walked in.*

'I've got no more than twenty minutes,' he said as he flopped into the soft armchair.

'Moscow have gone berserk about Kretski.'

'Tell them not to worry.' He smiled. 'I'm going to fix a deal and release him.'

'How in hell can you do that?'

'They never knew who he really was. They knew he was something, but he stuck to his cover story, and I didn't probe beyond the superficial stuff.'

'My God, they'll be relieved.'

Blake smiled at him. 'I've got better news than that.'

'Tell me. I need some good news.'

'I've agreed to be a double agent, my friend.'

The Russian frowned. 'I don't understand, Georgi.'

'My masters want me to penetrate the Soviet intelligence organization in East Berlin. I have been ordered to offer my services to the MVD.'

The Russian sat down slowly. 'You're joking.'

'I'm not, I assure you.'

'Why did they choose you? Do you think they're suspicious? Do you think it's a trap?'

'You underrate me, Tolya. I speak German. I speak Russian. I'm an experienced operator. And I'm going to be very successful as a double agent.'

'Georgi! This is fantastic. But Moscow won't believe it. It's too good to be true.'

'I come carrying gifts and expecting a reward.'

'Go on.'

'The date planned for the workers' rising in East Berlin is

June the seventeenth. It will start in Marx-Engels Platz with the railway workers. Another group will come from Alexander Platz station.'

'Can you give us names?'

Blake smiled. 'I can, but I won't. Warning is enough. If you stop it happening I should be blown in hours.'

'And what do you want from me?'

'A nice low-grade agent who's working for you and isn't very important. What have you got?'

Anatoli Mikhailovich Petrov walked over to the small freestanding metal safe. He brought out a small cardboard box and laid it on the settee beside him. He flipped open the lid and went slowly through the white cards. Twice he took out cards as he went through them. He picked them up and read both sides of each and then slid one back in the box.

He turned to look at Blake. 'I'll have to clear this first with both Karlshorst and Moscow.'

'What are you offering?'

Petrov read from the card. 'Fräulein Ursula Schmidt, aged twenty-nine. Works as a typist at an RAF base. Provides copies of secret and top secret documents on RAF and USA fighter-bombers and their equipment. She gets one thousand two hundred marks a month from us. She has two German associates. They don't do much but I could throw them in.'

'Why are you ready to throw her away?'

Petrov scratched his chest and smiled. 'We've got the manuals and detail drawings for all current fighter-bombers from another source. We don't need her any longer.'

'She'll do for a start.' Blake stood up. 'I want at least three new dead-letter drops or I shall get my lines crossed.'

'I'll contact you through the man at the reception desk at Hotel am Zoo. You've used him before, haven't you?'

'Yes. But I don't like using him.'

'Why not?'

'He's crooked, and what's more he looks like it.'

Petrov laughed. 'We've got him under control. We've got

some photographs that would surprise his wife. He'll behave.'

It was five months before Fräulein Schmidt was tried. She and her two helpers were sentenced to just over four years, and George Blake, whose bona fides *as an agent were never in doubt, had established himself with MI6 as a successful double agent.*

It was shortly afterwards that Blake was given an assistant. He was warned never to meet him at either the Olympic Stadium offices or at his own home. Horst Eitner, codenamed 'Mickey', was a tough professional.

13

Lawler spent the whole day reading the first two of the Blake files and by mid-afternoon he had had enough. He phoned Siobhan Nolan and she agreed to see him, but she sounded very reluctant.

He had never been inside her flat before and he was surprised. In contrast to the happy-go-lucky girl the flat was furnished and decorated with elegance. The large, square living-room was floored with cork tiles. The walls were pine-boarded and spotlights from an aluminium strip were the only lighting. Cushioned seating lined three walls, and on the fourth wall were bookshelves and a row of framed prints of French Impressionists.

Siobhan Nolan looked more Italian than Irish in a white dress with large red poppies around the skirt. She looked amused at his obvious surprise.

'Well, what did you expect, pigs in the parlour and potheen in the kitchen?'

'It's beautiful, Siobhan. It really is.'

'And me?'

He smiled. 'And you're beautiful too.'

'You're allowed to sit down. D'you fancy a whisky?'

'That would go down well.'

She poured him a large whisky from a bottle of Jameson Ten Year Old, and handed it to him.

'There. Get that down ye, and stop looking so bloody miserable.'

She sat down on a big leather pouffe alongside him, looking at his face as she sipped her whisky.

'And ye've come to tell me what a lovely husband he'd make, yes?'

Lawler sighed. 'I thought we could talk about it.'

She crossed her long legs. 'What did he tell you?'

'He said that he bought you an engagement ring, asked you to marry him, you refused him, and then you both got pretty angry with one another.'

'Did he tell you *why* he bought the ring?'

'Yes. It was an engagement ring.'

'Was it hell.'

'What was it then?'

She looked down at the shiny toe of her black court shoe, and it was several seconds before she looked back at his face.

'It's not really fair to tell you. It would spoil things between you and him.'

'How could it do that?'

Her soft brown eyes looked at him. 'He told you a lie about why we had a row. And he told you a lie about why he bought the ring.'

'Tell me.'

She shook her head. 'No. It wouldn't be fair. God save him, he needs all the support he can get. But he can't get it from me.'

'I thought you liked him. You told me you did. You said he cared for you, that it wasn't just sex.'

'I know. And I do. But let's just leave it at that.'

'Has he done something to offend you?'

She hesitated then said, 'No. But there's no way we could marry. It would be crazy.'

'Is it something to do with you being a Catholic?'

'No. It's because I'm me and not somebody else. Nothing more than that. But it wouldn't be good for me and it wouldn't be good for him.'

'Will you see him from time to time?'

'I'll see him any time he wants, provided he never talks about love or marriage. We can be friends. He can still screw me, but that's as far as it goes.' She looked away from him towards the window and he saw again, vividly, how beautiful she was. And it caught him unawares as she turned her head quickly to look at him. 'There's something I *had* better tell you.'

She looked at him as if she were expecting a sign of

approval. He nodded and she said, sighing, 'He told me his background. What he's doing here.'

'All of it?'

'How should I know?'

He closed his eyes, slowly shaking his head. 'Jesus God,' he whispered. 'You know what this means?'

'No.'

'It means you have to be screened. Sign the Official Secrets Act and be under surveillance.'

She shrugged. 'I'll sign anything they goddamn want. What's signing?'

'You don't understand, kid. You'll be under continuous surveillance. Twenty-four hours a day.'

'Send me pretty ones, that's all I ask.'

'Don't joke, Siobhan. It's serious. What made him tell you? He must have been out of his mind.'

She said softly, 'He is out of his mind, Jimmy. He's scared you're gonna kill him. He says you've done it before, or your people have.'

'Nobody's going to kill him, Siobhan. It's just become an obsession.'

'He says he's seen the guy who'll do it or arrange it.'

'Where? Who?'

'He wouldn't say any more. He said they might kill me too.'

'That's rubbish, Siobhan.'

'He said you didn't understand because it's your people who are involved.'

He stood up slowly. 'Let me take you out for a meal.'

She smiled. 'I'm going to like being under surveillance.'

'Don't joke about it, sweetie. You're going to hate it.'

Adam Silvester's flat off Curzon Street looked like an annexe of the Reform Club. Masculine, leathery, and expensively gloomy. There were plenty of books, but in closed glass-fronted bookcases, and there were stuffed fishes in their natural surroundings in glass cases. And Silvester himself looked distinctly formal, even in his dressing-gown and slippers. There were drinks on the

104

bamboo table. In decanters, not bottles, and carefully arranged on silver coasters.

Lawler had broken the news, but Silvester obviously believed in first things first, and he held the whisky up to his nose and then the light before he sipped it.

'What have you got in mind, James?'

'I want to persuade her to come and stay permanently at my place with Petrov until I've got things sorted out.'

Silvester sat down heavily in what was clearly his own personal chair.

'Do you think you *can* sort them out?'

'It's going to take longer than I thought.'

'That's no answer. *Are* you going to be able to get Petrov back in line?'

'I don't know.'

'Do you feel you've made any progress at all?'

'Yes. But every time I get over one hurdle there always seems to be another. And there's always this phobia about Blake in the background.'

'How carefully have you looked into the Blake case?'

'I'm about half-way through the files.'

'Any clues as to what he's on about?'

'Not a thing. It just doesn't hang together. He escaped from Wormwood Scrubs and that's that.'

'It might pay you to have a word with Special Branch liaison.'

'About what?'

'It was an IRA man who helped Blake escape. I've forgotten his name but he was in the Scrubs part of the time that Blake was there. He got his pay-off from the Soviet Embassy. There might be something there.'

'I'll check it out.'

'You do that.'

'I'd better have copies of your chap's surveillance reports on my place just in case I miss something.'

'You can phone Carter and he can read them out to you.'

'Nothing new from your side?'

Lawler noticed the momentary hesitation but put it down to Silvester having other things on his mind.

'Nothing of any importance.'

Silvester stood up and Lawler took the hint and left.

Lawler took them down for the week-end to his parents and the magic seemed to work again. Petrov chopped logs and trimmed hedges, shelled peas and sprayed pesticide with venom on the greenflies on the roses. And Siobhan Nolan and his mother regaled one another with amiable banter laced with quotations from Somerville and Ross and Oscar Wilde.

Petrov and Lawler walked in the fading sunlight around the edge of the cricket field and up the slope that led to the forest. On a fallen tree-trunk they sat looking across to the village.

'I'm more than half-way through the Blake files, Tolya.'

Petrov turned to look at him. 'What year are you up to?'

'About 1955.'

'And what have you discovered?'

'Nothing that's relevant.'

'What about Curiel?'

'The uncle in Cairo?'

'Yes.'

'But he was a child when he was there.'

'What about Paris?'

'When?'

'Nineteen fifty-one onwards.'

'There's no mention of his uncle apart from the time he spent with him in Cairo after his father died.'

'What about his prison sentences?'

'Whose?'

'Curiel's. That's why he moved to Paris. Farouk put him in jail because of his Moscow connections. And Nasser put him inside again and then expelled him for organizing Arab revolutionaries. When he was expelled he went to live in Paris.'

'But that's Curiel, not Blake.'

Petrov gave a short laugh. 'Blake was in touch with him all the while. He went to see him in Paris in 1952.'

'You mean he was Blake's contact?'

'For a short period he was, and Curiel was the one who passed the money to get him out of your prison.'

'Do you know where Curiel lives now?'

'He doesn't, my friend. In 1961 the French put him inside for collaborating with the Algerian FLN guerrillas. He was a contact later on for the terrorist Carlos, and the Japanese Red Brigade. A rightwing terrorist group called Delta shot him at his home in May last year. Half an hour after they killed him a Paris news agency got an anonymous telephone call. The caller said that the KGB agent Henri Curiel, a traitor to the country which had taken him in, had ceased all activity that day.'

'Curiel was never mentioned in the files apart from the time Blake spent with him in Cairo as a child.'

'Do you believe me now?'

'Believe what?'

'Believe that you don't know why I think they could kill me.'

'There's no connection, Tolya. Maybe there were things we didn't know but the fact *is* that he got away.'

'The fact *is* that either your people didn't know what was going on, or somebody in MI6 was covering for him.'

'You mean Philby?'

'No. It wasn't Kim. I *can* tell you that.'

'Do you know more?'

'Of course I do.'

'So tell me. Why play games?'

'I'm not playing games, *tovarich*. I'm making sure I stay alive. Making sure you protect me because of what you want to know.'

'You don't trust me?'

Petrov laughed softly. 'I don't trust anybody.'

'Can you give me any more clues?'

'Just one.'

'What's that?'

'Your people assumed that Blake was turned while he was with the North Koreans, yes?'

'Yes.'

'Well, read the files again, but this time read them

knowing that he always was working for the Soviets.'

'From when?'

'From when he was the courier in Holland before he came to England.'

'Are you sure?'

'Absolutely sure.'

'How can you be sure?'

'Work it out, my friend. Work it out.'

14

BERLIN 1956
The people in the block of flats at Platanen Allee were all British officers and officials and their families. All except one. The exception was a man who lived alone. There were people in the block who had never seen him and were not even aware of his existence.

He was seldom seen out and never alone. Rumour said that he was recovering from a nervous breakdown, and the young men who walked with him were doctors or psychiatrists. There was no name on his door panel. Although they were not obvious there were steel shutters at his windows, high-security locks on his doors both inside and outside, and a special alarm system connected to an office in the Olympic Stadium that was manned twenty-four hours a day. And his constant companion was a German Shepherd dog that had been trained by RAF dog handlers.

The British Commandant, General Sir William Oliver, KCB, had given the security instructions himself. Only seven senior men knew the man's real identity.

'Twenty Gauloise.'
The girl looked up quickly.
'We don't stock Gauloise. I'm sorry.'
'What do you recommend?'
She opened a drawer and put a packet of cigarettes on the counter. He saw the figure seven in red ink on the corner of the packet and looked back at the girl.
'I think I'll try somewhere else.'
She nodded and slid the packet back in the drawer as Blake left the shop. It was inconvenient and unreasonable, but the red ink meant that it was an emergency. And 'treffpunkt' seven meant the S-bahn station at Pankow.

Petrov was already there when he arrived. The girl must have phoned him. The Russian ignored him as he walked past and then went back into the area by the ticket office, through a door marked 'Privat'.

Petrov was sitting on the battered old desk, one leg swinging casually as Blake walked in.

'I'm due at a meeting in forty minutes, Tolya, what is it?'

'It's Bialek. Moscow insist that we pick him up as soon as possible.'

'But he's been over there for nearly three years. He will have already told them everything he knows.'

'Those are Moscow's orders.'

'When are you going to do it?'

'I'm putting three two-man teams in there with different cars. Round the clock. Every day until we've got him.'

'I can't help you. I'm never there.'

'Does he know you? Would he recognize you?'

'Yes. I check with him most days.'

'At particular times?'

'No. When it happens to suit me.'

'What do you do when you visit him?'

'I check the rooms to see that he's not under duress, and that's about it. We exchange a few words about the weather. He's in a constant state of fear for his life.'

'I've worked out a plan but I need your co-operation.'

'Tell me what it is.'

The man's grey eyes looked at him for a moment without recognition, unfocused and unseeing. Then, as the dog growled he said, 'Ah yes. Come inside.'

'I'll come in after you've been for your walk. Mr Leavis says it is OK for you to take a short walk provided you take the dog with you. He's been delayed but he'll be along later.'

The man nodded. 'I'll get my coat.'

'I'll call in later this evening,' Blake said, and walked slowly along the corridor and up the stairs to his flat.

He took off his jacket as he walked into the bedroom, across to the windows. But it was already too dark to see anything much in the street. It was almost an hour before the

110

telephone rang and the girl's voice told him that the interview had gone well. Fifteen minutes later the phone rang again. The duty officer's compliments and he should report immediately to the General's HQ and ask for Colonel Squires.

General Sir William Oliver, KCB, had presided over the meeting himself. He made no attempt to hide his anger. There were only five others there, and they were informed that Robert Bialek had been attacked by two men and bundled into a car as he turned the corner from Platanen Allee into Leistikow Strasse. An investigation had already started. The West Berlin authorities and the press would not be informed, and the men at the meeting were warned that they themselves would be interviewed.

Robert Bialek had been better known as Lieutenant-General Bialek, Inspector-General of the East German Volkspolizei. He had defected to the West in 1953. Previously in charge of the SSD, the State Security Service of the East German government, he was the most important non-Russian defector who had ever come over to the West.

The British government and their Commandant in Berlin lodged protest after protest with the Soviet authorities who blandly denied all knowledge of Bialek's whereabouts. After prolonged and violent interrogations in the headquarters of his old command he had been put to death.

BERLIN 1956
Ivan Serov was its first General when the MVD became the KGB in 1954, and his visits to East Berlin became more frequent during the next year. East Berlin had become both a prime source of incoming intelligence and one of the principal launching posts for Soviet agents being filtered into the NATO countries. There was also an eighteen-year-old girl who lived in an elegant flat near Karl Marx Platz who, although she never visited the SSD headquarters on Normannenstrasse, was on its payroll as a senior secretary.

It was on one of these visits early in 1956 that Serov took the opportunity of informing Petrov of his promotion. He stood up behind his desk and leant over to shake the young man's hand. It was only the third time he had actually met

Petrov but he was familiar with his name and his successes.

'Sit down, Captain.' And Serov pointed to the chair in front of the desk. When Petrov was seated Serov took a small cardboard box from his briefcase. He smiled as he pushed it across the desk. Printed on the lid were the words 'Starshi Komandnyi Sostav'. When Petrov hesitated Serov said amiably, 'Open it.'

As Petrov took off the lid he saw the pair of shoulder-bands. Gold braid and a five-pointed star between two red stripes. The insignia of a major. When he looked back at Serov the General was smiling.

'A present from Moscow. Congratulations.'

'Thank you, Comrade General, I . . .'

Serov held up his hand. 'It is effective back-dated to January 6. But to business. Tell me about your SIS man. How reliable is he?'

'Completely, Comrade General. He is providing us with top-grade material.'

'You said in your report that you were concerned that he would be working with the man Eitner. Why?'

'Eitner has changed sides so many times. He worked for Gehlen, then the British, and now he works for us and the British. I don't like two double agents coming together. Especially when neither of them knows that the other is working for us. It makes life too complicated. And between them they know too much.'

'Do you think there is some trap being set by the British?'

'I don't think so, Comrade General. The information they give to Blake to pass on to us still comes through. It would be enough to satisfy us in continuing the game. But what Blake provides himself is invaluable. He's on our side. I trust him implicitly. He is a dedicated Party man.'

'Well. We can only leave it to your judgement. But keep to the rules, young man. They may be tedious but they are for your protection as well as ours.'

Petrov stood to attention before he turned and left the room.

The West Berlin suburb of Rudow lays no claim to either

fame or beauty. It lies along the border with East Berlin and is heavily built up with workers' apartment blocks. It is in the US-controlled sector of Berlin, and the US Air Force had built a forward radar station close to the border, behind the barbed wire entanglement erected by the East Germans. The radar installation faced directly across the border and only Rudow cemetery and the broad expanse of Schonefelder Chaussee separated the Americans from the Soviets.

When an additional building was to be erected on the radar site it was US Army engineers who carried out the work. The foundations obviously provided special problems, for there were large numbers of men employed on the site for several months. Fortunately it was summer, and the summer of 1955 was a typical Berlin summer. Dry and sunny. The new building was completed by July and was in use by the middle of the month.

It was in January 1956 that Blake was escorted to the radar station by a major from US Counter-intelligence. The warm air as they went down the steps inside the new building was tainted with the smell of oil and electrically induced ozone, but once they were inside the security doors of the tunnel itself the air-conditioning took over.

The tunnel was almost nine metres underground and 600 metres long. The US major found his British colleague rather subdued as he pointed out the technical niceties of the operation. The operation was code-named 'Operation Gold' and it tapped all telephones used by the Soviets and East Germans. Not only those covering Berlin, but the cables linking East Berlin with all other East German cities, with Warsaw, Moscow and Red Army headquarters at Zossen. Tape-recorders, telexes and printers lined the tunnel, cut off in lengthy modules and guarded by security doors and locks, and US marines.

The US major was used to conducting VIPs around the installation and was used to their amazement and enthusiasm for its sheer effrontery and technical ingenuity. After all, beyond the half-way point you were actually in the Soviet Zone, and way back in Dahlem hundreds of typists and translators were handling the mass of information that flooded in daily from 'Operation Gold'. But his British colleague was silent for most of the inspection. He asked a few very shrewd questions but was light on praise and admiration. He seemed to take it all for granted. But the Texan major took the coolness in his stride. It was obviously an example of British phlegm.

Horst Eitner was the same age as George Blake but that was virtually their only similarity. Horst Eitner was a born opportunist. Once a small-time Nazi, he regarded himself now as a 'good German', on the side of the angels, a born-again democrat who merely cashed in on the West's need for information. He was a man who saw himself as a bon-viveur but who, in fact, merely wanted Berlin night-clubs, bottles of champagne and lots of pretty girl-friends. Oddly enough the puritanical Blake and the extrovert Eitner got on well. Blake was amused by the man's vulgarity, and vaguely envious of his happy-go-lucky outlook on life. And Eitner saw Blake as the cool operator who knew exactly what he was doing and was never diverted by anything. Instinct told him that Blake was a man who knew all the tricks and would stand for no nonsense. Unlike Eitner, he wasn't just in it for the money and excitement. Blake was never excited.

Eitner knew Blake only as Max van Vries, a Dutchman working for the British. He knew nothing of Blake's background, not even that he was married. He assumed that Blake's only home was the separate room that he rented in one of the side streets off Bismarkstrasse. Eitner had a small flat in Wieland Strasse in Charlottenburg, not far from Blake's real home. He lived there with his pretty young wife Brigitte, and Blake was a frequent and welcome visitor to their home. Eitner had no suspicion that Blake worked for any intelligence organization apart from the British, and Blake had no idea that Eitner had any contact with the Russians.

Blake used Eitner to ferret out low-level acts of espionage by West Germans in the pay of the Russians. Telephone operators who passed on lists of military phone numbers, middle-aged women who smuggled out classified documents for a few dollars and a little loving by some KGB leg-man. Blake himself was occupied with much bigger game.

In mid-April 1956, Bulganin and Khrushchev paid an official visit to Britain that ended in disaster for MI6. The massive Soviet cruiser Ordzhonikidze *brought them to Portsmouth Harbour. The Prime Minister, Sir Anthony Eden, set much store by the visit and the opportunity it presented of moderating the cold war. Two months earlier Khrushchev had denounced the policies of Josef Stalin. Both Britain and the US had hopes of easing the mounting tension with the Soviets.*

It would have been difficult to plan an action that could do more damage to the political talks than the action planned by a small group in MI6. Even if it had succeeded the prize would have been barely worth having.

It was rumoured that the Ordzhonikidze *had a hatch in its hull for laying nuclear mines, and a hurried and totally inefficient operation was put together in a matter of hours for a frogman to surreptitiously examine the cruiser's under-water hull. The very nature of the plan excluded using a Royal Navy diver, and to the political insensitivity was added the stupidity of calling on the expertise of a swash-buckling, middle-aged frogman who had been used for similar risky enterprises in the past. Lieutenant-Commander Lionel Crabb was a brave but reckless man whose taste for adventure frequently over-rode his good judgement. The night before the operation, with amazing indifference to even elementary security precautions, he booked into a Portsmouth hotel, giving his true name and address in the visitors' book, and stayed there for the night.*

The next day he slid into the cold waters of Portsmouth Harbour and was never seen again alive except by the Red Navy look-out who spotted him a hundred yards from the cruiser.

When, twenty-four hours later, Crabb had not returned, the conspirators feared the worst. But their fears had not imagined just how bad the worst would be. The Russians' delight at foiling the attempt was matched only by their anger

115

at the crude abuse of hospitality and diplomacy. They carried out similar operations themselves on foreign warships in their harbours, but even they were not inept enough to indulge in such exercises when top-level inter-government talks were involved.

The British newspapers headlined the Soviet protests, and the roar of the Prime Minister's anger echoed through Whitehall for months. The Portsmouth police hastily tore out the offending page of the hotel's register only hours before the first astute journalist came looking for it. The fact that it was missing was almost as conclusive evidence as if the page had been left. It also excluded any possibility of a cover story being contrived to suggest that it was a piece of private enterprise or a practical joke. It is illegal to remove a page, or delete an entry, from a hotel register, and the police were not likely to provide cover for mere practical jokers or gung-ho ex-Royal Navy officers. The Prime Minister took his revenge on MI6 a few months later when he made the head of MI5 the new boss of its old rival, MI6.

On the day the Soviet leaders returned to Moscow Blake contacted Petrov and arranged a meeting for that afternoon.

They stopped talking, and Blake stood up slowly and hesitantly as the black horses with plumes on their heads crunched majestically down the gravel path pulling the hearse behind them. A couple of old black Mercedes limousines carried the mourners towards the far corner of the cemetery. Petrov had stayed sitting on the bench, impatient and irritated. As Blake sat down Petrov turned to look at him.

'How can I promise what others will do when I don't know what it is all about?'

'All I'm saying is that it's dangerous to tell you, and it's only worth the danger if they use it quickly.'

'That's for Moscow to decide. You know that.'

'Will you put it direct to Moscow, not through Karlshorst?'

'Why, Georgi? Those are my channels. I can't go behind their backs. Why should you want me to?'

'Because Karlshorst will look fools. They might just cover it up.'

Petrov sighed heavily. 'I can't help that, my friend. I've got my orders, and they apply to you too.'

Blake looked at the lean handsome face, then closed his eyes to concentrate on his dilemma. When he opened them Petrov's eyes were still on his face.

'There's a tunnel under the zone border in Rudow. From the radar station. It's nearly 600 metres long. They have been tapping all the Soviet and East German telephone traffic night and day for nearly seven months.'

'The zone frontiers are mined, Georgi.'

'The tunnel is almost nine metres underground.'

'Is the source reliable?'

'The source is me. I've seen it.'

Petrov stared at him silently, absorbing the information. It was several minutes before he spoke. 'My God. You're right. Heads will roll at Karlshorst. I see what you mean.'

'After the frogman thing last week this could be a fantastic exposure. Actually in the Soviet Zone.'

'Where does it finish in our Zone?'

'In Alt-Glieneke opposite the Rudow cemetery.'

'How many people have seen it?'

'Quite a number, but they were all top brass. They wouldn't be suspect because of their rank. It would be taken for granted that they wouldn't even have the opportunity to contact your people. Or the know-how.'

'The Americans will swear they know nothing about it.'

'You can show the journalists the equipment. It's mainly British and still has the manufacturers' plates on it.'

Petrov put his hand on Blake's knee. 'I'll work it out, Georgi. Leave it to me. They'll be very grateful to you. I wish there was something we could do to reward you. Isn't there some damn thing you want? We can lodge it in Geneva. Anywhere you want.'

'I've never done any of it for cash and I never will. I do it for Moscow and the Party. And for no other reason. You know that.'

'If ever you want to come over you only have to say. You

would be honoured publicly for your dedication. Every privilege you wanted, for you and your family.'

'Just preserve my security, Tolya, that's all I ask.'

'We'll do that, my friend. Never fear.'

Colonel Ivan Kotsyuba brushed his thumb across the microphone and when the speakers responded he raised the microphone on its stand. He looked around the well-lit hall and was pleased. There were just over a hundred journalists present, and permits had been issued for eight television crews to film the press conference. He spoke English with an American accent and German with a Russian accent but nobody would fail to understand the importance of his announcement. He smiled and held up his hand.

'Ladies and gentlemen. Thank you for attending this press conference at such short notice. As you will all know, for years the Soviet Kommandatura have protested continuously to the other occupying powers in Berlin concerning the provocative and dangerous operations of British and American espionage organizations in the city of Berlin.

'As you also know, our protests have been either denied or ignored. The Western press, including many newspapers represented here this morning, have suggested that our protests are no more than propaganda. Some of the more "revanchist" journals have claimed that our protests at best were evidence of paranoia on the part of the Soviet authorities.

'When my assistants contacted you early this morning they asked if you would allow for two hours of your valuable time to be made available for the press conference. I think that some of you will wish to give even longer to this story when you realize its significance.

'We have issued you with numbered cards as you came in. They indicate your seats on one of the seven buses that are waiting for you outside. The journey itself takes twenty minutes, and that will give you time to study the press-kits which are waiting for you on the buses. Photographs have been included, but you are at liberty to take your own *photographs at the site. Thank you again for your attendance.'*

Kotsyuba repeated the speech in German, then smiled, switched off the microphone, and nodded to his assistants to open the doors and guide out the silent journalists.

The press-packs included a six-page commentary on 'Operation Gold', a dozen different photographs of the tunnel, including close-ups of the equipment showing the British manufacturers' name-plates, and photo-copies of over twenty press articles where the US or British governments denied Soviet allegations that West Berlin was being used as an espionage base by Western intelligence services against East Germany and the Soviet Union.

Every journalist who walked through the tunnel knew that this was a Soviet propaganda victory. The Americans and the British had been caught with their pants well and truly down. After Whitehall's vain efforts to deny any part in the Crabb affair there was nothing that would explain away this shambles. It was obviously the story of the year, and they treated it as such. In Whitehall, Washington and Berlin, American and British spokesmen refused to rise even to a 'No comment'. Despite the seriousness of the exposure the press's own feelings were mixed. There was a lurking admiration for 'Operation Gold'. It had a touch of the KGB's own handiwork about it. It was cheeky, but its exposure was a major propaganda defeat for the West, and that was how it was treated editorially. The Russians opened the site for conducted tours and a hundred thousand East Berliners were shown 'the war-monger's listening post'.

The British in the Olympic Stadium, and the Americans in Dahlem, spent weeks studying the old lists of visitors to the tunnel. There were nearly two hundred names when the builders and installers were included, and they knew that there was no hope of the investigation to find the traitor being fruitful. For almost a week George Blake had been seconded to the team evaluating the list of British visitors.

15

The King's Road flat was far from ideal for three adults, especially when their relationships were so fragile. But Siobhan Nolan made life more tolerable for the three of them. She tactfully left Lawler and Petrov alone when she sensed that they needed to talk, and she was even-handed with both men. She still slept with Petrov, but there was no longer any element of being possessed emotionally. At twenty-two she mothered them both.

Petrov was still sound asleep as Lawler and the girl ate breakfast together. She wore a towelling bathrobe that was both cosy and revealing, and she sipped from a glass of fresh orange-juice, held as a child would hold it, in both hands.

'How long will this go on, Jimmy?'

'I don't know. I suppose it depends on me. I'm not being very bright. But I'm trying to put two jigsaws together at the same time and half the pieces of both of them are missing.'

'Why *is* he so scared?'

'Like he told you. He thinks we've got some plan to kill him.'

'Have you?'

'Of course not. There's no reason why we should. He's been helping us. All we ask is that he goes on helping.'

'What about the people up above you? They might think differently.'

'Why should they? They wouldn't gain anything by wiping him out.'

'But people do get killed in your kind of business, don't they?'

'Maybe.' And Lawler concentrated on his boiled egg. When he looked back at her face she put down the glass.

'He's a very mixed-up sort of fellow, you know. Whatever his work was in Moscow it's left him very insecure.'

'Go on.'

Her big eyes looked back at his face as if she were looking for something. Some indication of his mood. Eventually she said softly, 'I'd better tell you what the ring and the row was all about.' She waited for a response but he didn't reply. 'Do you know about the Polish girl?'

'What Polish girl?'

'The one he married.'

'That's about all I do know. I gather they were divorced and she went back to Warsaw.'

'That's one way of putting it. He was crazy about her. He didn't want to divorce her. They gave him the choice. Either he divorced her or she'd be treated as a dissident, prosecuted publicly, and sent to the Gulag. And that would mean that he would lose his KGB job and have God knows how many black marks on his record. The day they faced him with this he pleaded for time and they took that as a sign that he wasn't going to toe the line. When he got home that night she'd gone. They'd already arrested her. The neighbours told him. He never saw her again. He knew that he had no choice. He divorced her so that she would be released and shipped back to Poland. He never recovered from that. He had thought that the work he had done would be protection enough for her indiscretions, and when he found that it wasn't he started thinking about defecting.'

'How was that part of your quarrel?'

She shrugged. 'I guess I was stupid. He used to call me Maria sometimes when we were making love. It happened that day, and like an eejit I said something disparaging about him and her. He hit me and then it was for real. We both said things that were vicious. You'd have to love someone a hell of a lot to forgive them. He went out and bought the ring to make up for the quarrel. He asked me to marry him and when I said no there was another flaming row and he stormed out. I don't love him, I just like him. And he doesn't love me, he's "in love" with me and that's very different. He knows it and I know it, and the sooner

121

we can go our own ways the better.'

'You think he loved the Polish girl? Really loved her?'

'Oh yes. I've no doubt about that.'

'Would it make a difference if I could get her over here?'

'He'd do anything you want if you did that. Anything.'

'That's the first ray of sunshine I've had since I started on this wretched exercise.'

'Can you do it?'

'If she's willing to come, yes.'

'How long will it take?'

He smiled. 'Who's the lucky man?'

She frowned. 'I don't understand.'

'Who are you rushing off to?'

She shook her head, smiling. 'You're just scared you'll have to start cooking your own breakfast when I've gone.'

'Maybe.' He looked across at her. 'What kind of man *do* you really want?'

She put her head on one side, thinking, and he was aware of her slender neck and the line of her shoulders. Then she shrugged.

'I'll know when I meet him.'

'Why did you leave Dublin?'

'Boredom.'

'What about your parents?'

She smiled. 'Snap. My father's a writer. My mother teaches piano. You'd like them. It seemed odd at your house. They're different people but the atmosphere is the same.'

'Tell me.'

She laughed. 'Relaxed, warm, concerned. Like lying in a bath when the water's just warm.'

'Do you miss them?'

'I didn't at first, but I'm beginning to. Knowing our mutual friend has taught me a lot. Makes me count my blessings.'

'Would you like to go down on your own to my parents for a few days?'

'Would your people let me?'

'Yes. And my parents like you a lot. You'd be restricted

to the cottage of course. But you'd be safe there.'

'Would that suit you better than having me hanging around the flat?'

'No. I'd rather have you here.'

'Why?' And she was smiling.

He shrugged. 'I like having you here. You're the one bit of sanity for him and for me.'

She smiled. 'He's going to be so pleased. I hope it all works out for all of you.'

'I think maybe you've brought us all good luck.'

She stood up. 'I'd better rouse the sleeping beauty and get myself dressed.'

Silvester sat listening without comment as Lawler repeated his conversation with Petrov. When he finished Silvester looked away, towards the window. He sat in silence for several minutes before he turned his head again to look at Lawler.

'Just let me recap. We get his wife out of Poland. He marries her again. In return Petrov continues his co-operation. Is that it?'

'Yes. Plus the guarantee of a house and a job or a pension.'

Silvester looked at him. 'Doesn't make sense to me, James.'

'Why not?'

'According to what he's told you he was scared of being sent back to Moscow, so he pretends that he wants to go back just to see what our reaction was. Right?'

'Yes.'

'Then he says he's scared we're going to knock him off when he's told us all he knows. Yes?'

'Yes.'

'So where's the logic in this deal? What's to stop us from still knocking him off after he's told us all he knows? If he thinks we'd kill him, then why shouldn't we kill him anyway? If that's our inclination we aren't going to be put off just because his wife's around.'

'According to him he's got another piece of information.

123

A kind of insurance policy.'

'What is it?'

'A further piece of information.'

'About what?'

'I don't know, but he says that once he's told me that there won't be any chance of his being killed.'

'D'you think this bugger's sane?'

'Yes. I think he's been over-wrought but he's sane enough.'

'Maybe this has all been the wrong tack. Maybe we should have put him through the mincer and *made* him talk. All this playing games only encourages him to go on with it.'

'I don't think so, Adam. It's been my fault as much as his. My brief was to smooth him down. I've only partly succeeded but I think I'm nearly there.'

'This stuff about the Egyptian, Curiel, did you grind it out of him or did he volunteer it?'

'I suppose I could say he volunteered it. He wanted to show that I didn't know the real story of Blake. And he implied that if it wasn't on our files then SIS didn't know vital facts, or was covering them up.'

'Why should anyone want to cover up any facts? And those facts in particular.'

'I don't know, but he implied that I would understand when he told me this additional thing.'

'D'you believe him?'

'Yes.'

'Why?'

'We can check up on Curiel. If he's right then he does know more than we do about our own man.'

Silvester bent down and loosened his shoe laces, sliding the black brogues off his feet and flexing his toes.

'I'll check up myself.' He looked up at Lawler. 'If he's right I'll agree to the deal, if he's wrong we'll change our tactics. Agreed?'

'If he's wrong I think we should discuss it again anyway.'

'How would you deal with his ex-wife?'

'I'd get Houghton to trace where she is and then I'd go over myself. I'd have to talk to her. She may not want him now. If she does, then I'll put a team together and get her out.'

'D'you speak Polish?'

'No. But she speaks fluent Russian.'

'I'll check on the Curiel business with Paris, and then get in touch with you.'

'How long will it take?'

'I should get an answer some time tomorrow.'

Silvester's secretary had phoned mid-afternoon. Silvester wanted to see him at five. At Century House.

Lawler sat in Silvester's outer office for nearly an hour before the secretary indicated that Silvester was ready to see him.

Silvester was talking on the phone and pointed to a chair. When he hung up he pushed a heap of files to one side and leaned forward with his arms on the table.

'I've checked with Paris, and I've just checked with Cairo. That's why I had to keep you waiting. He's absolutely right. Paris confirmed what he said, and Cairo have just confirmed too. You can go ahead with the deal.'

'OK.' Lawler stood up but Silvester waved to him to sit down again.

'I've checked Blake's files and you're right. There's not a word about any of this. There are no pages missing, the numbers run consecutively without any breaks. I can't believe we didn't check. It's so elementary, and it would have stopped Blake ever being recruited. It's going to lead to a full-scale enquiry. Is there any chance of persuading Petrov to tell you the rest of the story right now?'

'I don't think so. I think he'd see it as an attempt to avoid the bargain. But he'll talk when I've got his wife back. If I succeed, that is.'

Silvester was silent for what seemed a long time. Then he said, 'Let me know what facilities you need for the trip to Warsaw. And I want you back soonest.'

'D'you feel it will be satisfactory for Petrov and the girl to go down to my parents while I'm away?'

'If that's what you want. But make proper provision for

them to be under discreet surveillance.'

'Right, sir.'

16

BERLIN 1956-59
A token of Moscow's appreciation came to Blake via Horst Eitner. Petrov had given Eitner the lead to two Soviet agents who were considered expendable. It served Moscow's own purpose too. It would embarrass Adenauer himself, his party and his government.

Viktor Schneider was an ex-SS officer who managed to evade prosecution as a war criminal, and became manager in the office of the official news-sheet of Adenauer's Christian-Democratic Party. Apart from passing low-grade political intelligence to the Russians, Schneider added one last piece of effrontery to his record by establishing the Party office as a dead-letter drop for Soviet intelligence networks in West Germany. The British handed over the embarrassing details to the Adenauer government who ineptly failed to keep the details from the press. Blake's seniors complimented him on his investigation and discretion, and from that point onwards Blake was responsible for almost the whole of MI6's Berlin network. In addition he had access to files and dossiers on all the Allied networks in East Germany. He was considered now as an expert on Soviet intelligence and politics, and top-secret papers from the Foreign Office and the Cabinet were available to him. The briefings and requests for information from Moscow that Petrov passed on to him had gradually swung from military intelligence to political intelligence.

Slowly the Soviet Union was applying more and more pressure to the Western powers, and in November 1958 Khrushchev publicly demanded that all troops should be withdrawn from Berlin. This demand, if it had been accepted, would have pulled back the American, British and French troops two hundred miles from Berlin, leaving the city surrounded by twenty or thirty Soviet divisions. Strategically it was never a runner, but Britain's new Foreign Secretary Selwyn Lloyd was not entirely opposed to the idea, provided 'real' safeguards for Berlin's freedom could be wrung from the Russians. Dulles, for the Americans, flatly refused. Through George Blake, Moscow knew every detail of the Allied disagreement.

In January 1959 the Kremlin pressed for a four-power conference that would include the East German government. When Moscow issued a further threat of a six-month limit for discussions or the Soviets would take unilateral action, it looked like the prelude to war. Macmillan and Selwyn Lloyd went to Moscow to try and break the log-jam. Khrushchev refused to see them after the initial reception ceremony, claiming that he had toothache. They cooled their heels in Moscow for eleven days, and the diplomatic snub was open and undisguised. The world waited to see what the West's reaction would be to such open pressure.

The four Foreign Ministers met in Geneva in May, and when the Western plan was put forward Gromyko rejected it out of hand. He didn't even read it. There were observers at the conference who suggested that he looked as if he already knew the details of the plan. As the news gradually filtered back to Moscow that the West was prepared to resist, the Russians eased off the pressure. A proposed meeting in Paris was put into cold-storage and no further meetings took place. Once again Moscow had been able to adjust its stance because it knew in advance what its adversaries had decided to do.

It was in February 1959 that Petrov had received new instructions regarding George Blake, and he had sent him a message to fix a meeting that evening at the Humboldt University.

There was light snow falling as Blake got out of the taxi at Marx-Engels Platz and walked back down Unter den Linden to the university. Petrov was waiting for him in the main hall, and they walked through various halls to a long corridor. Petrov took him into a room at the far end. It was *obviously some professor's private interview room. Comfortably furnished but small.*

'Are you in a hurry, Georgi?'

'Not particularly, but I want to be back before curfew.'

'D'you want some food?'

'Let's talk first.'

Petrov sat down, and Blake could see that he was in a state of some excitement. The Russian obviously had something important to say.

'Serov was in Berlin yesterday. I had two hours with him, mainly about you.' Petrov looked at him, hesitating before he went on. 'They want you to ask for a transfer back to London.'

'Why?'

'They think you will be even more useful there. They're giving me promotion and are sending me back to Moscow.'

'Congratulations.'

Petrov smiled and nodded. 'In fact double congratulations. I'm getting married.'

Blake put out his hand and Petrov grinned as they shook hands.

'They may not agree to a transfer for me, Tolya. And apart from that it won't be so easy in London.'

'We'd give you a top-grade controller, and all the help you needed.'

'Tell me something, Tolya. I'm very suspicious about one of my contacts. Either he's playing games with the CIA or he's playing games with you. I want to know which.'

'Who is he?'

'His name's Eitner. Horst Eitner.'

Petrov smiled. 'Horst Eitner. Code name Paulus. He's playing games with me.'

'Does he know about me?'

'For God's sake, no. There's not half a dozen people all told who know about you. He gives me reports about you. He still believes your story that you're a Dutchman free-lancing for the British.'

Blake nodded. 'Who's the lucky girl?'

'Polish. Eighteen years old. Very, very pretty. Lively.

She's great. I wish you could meet her.'

'Maybe I will. You could bring her to London.'

Petrov shook his head. 'They would never allow that. One of you always has to stay. It's a kind of insurance. You know how it is.'

'Anything else?'

'You'll make the application?'

'Yes. It's time I was leaving Berlin. But there may be difficulties.'

But there were no difficulties. Blake was a valuable MI6 officer, and his stint in Berlin had been long, successful and wearing. And they could use his talent and experience equally well in London. Blake returned to London two months later in April 1959.

SCOTLAND 1958

Flight-Lieutenant Andrews wasn't drunk, but it would be fair to say that he looked just a little bit tipsy. He stood swaying very gently, the pewter tankard held high.

'And the last toast to all you chaps. You'll be leaving for London tomorrow. An optional forty-eight-hour leave pass in the bright lights and then home. The sweat is over, so "cheers", gesundheit, skol, à la vôtre, salut, and all that jazz.'

Flight-Lieutenant Andrews was a veteran of passing-out parades and celebrations at the Royal Navy Fleet Air Arm base at Lossiemouth in Scotland. Every three months they came. An officer attached for training from each of the NATO countries.

Willing hands guided him back to his chair and ten minutes later they were all singing 'Auld Lang Syne'. The foreigners had all been coached in the words for the last ten days.

Andrews walked with his room-mate across the tarmac towards the huts. It was the first week in October, but even in Scotland the summer still held. The sky was a dark blue and the stars were so clear that they looked almost artificial.

'Are you going to take your two days in London, Heinz?'

The big German shrugged and grinned. 'I think maybe I do.'

130

'Where will you be posted to in Germany?'

'Is not posting for me. I go back again to Bremerhaven.'

Andrews pushed open the hut door. The light was already on. He sat down heavily on the bed and reached for the bottle of whisky and the glass. When he had poured a drink he offered it to the German who shook his head. Andrews took a swig of the whisky and put down the glass.

'What happened to you at Pensacola?'

'What does it say in my file?'

'Severe reprimand, but allowed to continue flying instruction.'

'I crashed a plane.'

'Jesus. What happened?'

'I was coming in for a landing on a carrier. A seagull hit the screen and I came in too low. Hit the water. Broke both legs, one arm and ruptured my spleen. The court of enquiry awarded me a severe reprimand.'

'On what grounds?'

'On grounds I was already too low in approach.'

'What did you do before Pensacola?'

'Was crew on US minesweeper in Bremerhaven.'

'Says on your file you got a university degree.'

'Sure. Engineering degree from Jena.'

'Is that where your folks live?'

The German's eyes looked at him. 'Why you ask that?'

Andrews reached for the glass. 'Just never heard of Jena.'

'I was brought up in Jena.'

'What sort of a place is it?'

'Is famous for Zeiss, and university.'

'Why's the university famous?'

'Hegel and Schiller taught there.'

'Great.' Flight-Lieutenant Andrews scratched his jaw. 'You know the drill for tomorrow. You get your pass and pay from the flight-sergeant, and there's a unit bus to the station at ten-o-five.'

'OK.'

'You'd better get some sleep. I'm going for a pee.'

Flight-Lieutenant Andrews went for a pee. He also made a brief telephone call to Edinburgh.

131

BREMERHAVEN 1958

The clanging of metal on metal echoed and reverberated in the big hangar despite the open doors. Trailing cables from overhead lines snaked down to lights clamped strategically on the fuselage of the fighter aircraft bearing the insignia of the newly formed navy of the Federal German Republic.

The two men who stood just inside the door watched for a few moments as the naval officer crouched down inspecting the leading edge of one of the plane's wings. Nodding to the mechanic, he straightened up and they walked over to him. His face was smeared with oil and he was wiping his hands on a piece of industrial waste.

'Lieutenant-Commander Ludwig?'

He nodded. 'That's me. What can I do for you?'

'I am Major Shelley, a British intelligence officer, and this is Herr Oberst König attached to the Federal German Ministry of the Interior.' The major coughed. 'Horst Heinz Ludwig, you are under arrest.'

'What am I charged with?'

'High treason.'

'You must be mad. I am an officer in the Federal Navy.'

'We are taking you to Hamburg where you will be formally charged.'

'I want to see my Commanding Officer.'

'He has already been informed.'

The big German stood there with his hands on his hips eyeing the two men.

'Can I make a phone call?'

'I'm afraid not.'

'Can I call a lawyer?'

'Who is your lawyer?'

Ludwig shrugged. 'OK. Let's go.'

The clock on the wall was ten minutes fast. It showed 12.10 but it was actually exactly midnight.

Shelley and the German sat at each side of the table.

'What did your father say?'

'He said that he and my mother would be in trouble if I refused.'

'Did he say what kind of trouble?'

'He said he thought they would be sent to a camp in Russia.'

'Why didn't you advise them to cross into West Germany?'

Ludwig sighed. 'They've lived in Jena all their lives. My mother has never been outside Jena, and my father had been once to Berlin. All their friends and relations who are still alive are in Jena. They would be lost anywhere else.'

'So you agreed to see the two men in Berlin. What were they like?'

'One was Russian pretending to be German, and the other was a genuine German. He had the code-name "Viktor", the other one used the code-name "Schultz". They said I should join the Bundeswehr and volunteer for flying duties.'

'Tell me about Chief Petty Officer Fritz Briesemeir.'

'I will talk only about myself.'

'Unter-offizier Briesemeir is already under arrest. He has told us what we want to know. Where did you first meet him?'

'When I was on the mine-sweepers at Bremerhaven.'

'And "Viktor" made you arrange a meeting between himself and Briesemeir in Berlin?'

'Yes.'

'What made you think "Viktor" was a genuine German?'

'He was a German. He had a slight accent but he told me he had served in the British Navy for two years. He was German all right.'

'And what about your sister Hanni?'

'I know nothing about her.'

'You know her husband Werner Jaeger?'

'I met him a couple of times.'

'They are both already arrested.'

Ludwig looked beaten and he shrugged helplessly.

'My God. What a mess.'

'How much did they pay you?'

'About six thousand marks in three years.'

'Briesemeir says he thinks "Viktor" had never been a sailor, at least on a ship, like he said. What do you think?'

'*There are men in all navies who never go to sea.*'

'*He also said he thought "Viktor" was a double agent who also worked for the British.*'

'*Maybe he did. How should I know? I was stupid, Herr Major, but I am not a spy. I gave information to save my parents.*'

'*Will you sign a full confession?*'

Lieutenant-Commander Ludwig nodded and bowed his head. It was two years before the group was tried and found guilty of high treason.

17

WEST GERMANY 1959
There had been another mention of the man code-named 'Viktor' when two messengers at the West German Ministry of the Interior had been arrested.

Willi Knipp and Joseph Paul, faced with a charge of high treason, had decided to confess. They admitted to having photographed at least three thousand documents from the ministry's offices. The security at the offices was almost non-existent, and in the lunch-hour they removed documents from the desks in open offices, even from despatch boxes, and took them to the rest-room and photographed them.

The Minox camera had been found in Joseph Paul's room, and after days of interrogation they admitted that they were working for a man who used the name Viktor. They met him in Berlin, and when they handed over the undeveloped film they would be paid a bonus in addition to the monthly retainer of five hundred D-marks. They swore that they had not been working for the Russians but only for Viktor, who they were sure was German and working for British Intelligence.

The West German authorities, aware that the total lack of security in at least one ministry would be exposed, had them quickly tried without the public or the press realizing what the charges were. Knipp got ten years' hard labour and Joseph Paul nine years. Understandably the information regarding the contact named Viktor was not passed on to the British.

George Blake never liked meeting his contacts in the Café Tanz in East Berlin. It had become almost a club for low-grade informers. There were always plenty of foreign journalists there. Journalists were as ready to buy tit-bits of intelligence as were the various intelligence services. Some of them even paid better, and journalists had no way of checking what they were told. And you didn't end up as a corpse in the Spree when you embroidered a story for a journalist.

But the Czech had insisted that they should meet at Café Tanz. Blake's objection wasn't on the grounds of security or cover — he could be expected to frequent such a source of information. He objected to being seen in such an amateur, low-grade set-up. But the Czech had promised the contact with Alfred Frenzel, MP, a prominent front-bench speaker in the Bonn Parliament for the opposition Social Democratic Party.

Blake looked slowly round the café from the table far back in the corner where the lighting was dim. The café was, as always, packed with people. A three-piece band was playing waltzes, interspersed with pop for the benefit of the couples dancing on the few square feet of dance-floor. Then he saw the Czech shoving his way between the tables. Blake wondered if Sowa was his real name. He knew that it was the Czech for 'owl', and Sowa did have an owlish look with his large, tinted spectacles, and his shock of grey hair. It was probably a cover name devised by some moron with a sense of humour but no sense of security.

Sowa pulled out a chair and sat down without ceremony, snapping his fingers to a waitress. He turned to Blake. 'What'll you have?'

'A Pils. A half.'

Sowa laughed. 'Safety first, eh?' And he turned and gave the order to the girl. Professionally, they talked of the weather until the girl had brought the drinks.

'Tell me about Frenzel.'

Sowa grinned. 'Hold on, hold on. Let's talk about me first. What do I get out of this?'

'Information.'

'And money, my friend.'

'No. Just information.'

'Oh come on, it's . . .'

'Just information, Sowa. If that's not enough then we'll

forget it. I can find other contacts to Frenzel.'

'Not like mine you can't. He's feeding out of my hand. I'm right in there.'

'It's still information or nothing.'

'Jesus. What about expenses?'

'OK. But not a retainer. The expenses will have to be accounted for.'

'What sort of stuff do I get?'

'You've got a man at your embassy in London. He uses the name Husak. I expect it's a cover name. He's assistant military attaché. Special Branch are going to pull him in and question him before they discover that he's got diplomatic immunity. They'll use it in the press.'

'When are they going to do this?'

'You've got about ten days to pull him out.'

'OK. What do you want to know about Frenzel?'

'First of all, is he Czech or German?'

'He started off as a Czech, but when Hitler invaded Czechoslovakia in 1939 he escaped to England and joined the Free Czechoslovak Brigade. Then he joined the RAF Czech squadron and was trained as a navigator. He flew on a lot of bomber raids and I think he was decorated.

'After the war he came back to Germany and claimed German citizenship. He became a trades-union official, and then was an influential member of the Social Democrat Party. He speaks fluent English, and was elected to the Bonn Parliament in about 1953. He's got lots of English and American friends in Germany.'

'What makes you think he'll play?'

'I know he will. He's got expensive tastes. He may be a Socialist MP but he likes the good life and he can't afford it.'

'What can he supply?'

'Top-secret stuff from any Bonn Ministry. Cabinet position papers and their British and American equivalents.'

'What would he want?'

'Money and pretty girls.'

'How much money?'

'At least three thousand marks a month.'

'That's crazy.'

'Look, Georgi. Even Adenauer himself couldn't provide you with better material. It's dirt cheap.'

'How much will your people chip in?'

'A third. Not more.'

'When can I meet him?'

'He's in Berlin at the week-end. How about Saturday night at the Hilton?'

'What time?'

'About eight.'

'I'll be there.'

'Can you fix him a girl?'

'That's more in your line than mine.'

'OK. I'll find a couple of girls but don't sit there looking disapproving. He likes a good time and you've got to go along with him. It's got to seem like he tells you things because you're his friend, and you pay him money because we're all pals together.'

'He must be pretty naïve if he thinks that.'

'He doesn't. It's just got to look like that. D'you want another drink?'

'No thanks. I'll see you Saturday night.'

In fact there had been no problem with Frenzel, and after the first meeting Sowa seldom joined them. Blake guessed that Sowa and other agents of Czech intelligence saw Frenzel separately. Frenzel made no secret of his liking for good food, drink and pretty girls, and the fact that Blake didn't participate made him all the more trustworthy in Frenzel's eyes. Although nothing was said, it was obvious that Frenzel accepted Blake as a British intelligence agent.

Some of the less important information that Frenzel passed him Blake passed to SIS, but the vast majority went straight to Petrov and Moscow. When Blake was posted back to London, Sowa was Frenzel's only contact, and his information went direct to Prague.

It was on the second meeting that Sowa's vanity overrode his training. Frenzel had accepted the reduction in his payments but he still lived expensively, and had taken a suite at the Hilton.

They were waiting for the two girls to arrive and sat drinking champagne. Frenzel fished out a speck of cork from his drink with his finger.

'Tell me, my friend. Why the hell did Georgi sometimes ask me for information about British Foreign Office policy communications with Bonn? Why should he be interested in what the British already knew?'

'Did you ever ask him why?'

'Only once.'

'What did he say?'

Frenzel smiled. 'Oh you know Georgi. Very obliquely, very diplomatically, he indicated that sometimes he liked to test my information against known facts.'

'Did you believe him?'

'I didn't think all that much about it one way or another at the time. If that was what he wanted and it came to hand, so be it.'

Sowa leaned back in his chair, balancing his glass on the rounded arm as he looked at Frenzel.

'There was more to our friend than you knew.'

'Tell me.'

'He was an actual British intelligence officer, you know. Official, authentic and recognized.'

'I took that for granted.'

'That wasn't all that he was, of course.'

'Go on.'

'He also worked for the Russians.'

Frenzel looked shocked. His hand shook as he poured out more champagne.

'Are you sure?'

'Quite sure.'

'Did he tell you that?'

'Of course not.'

'How did you find out?'

Sowa smiled. 'That I can't tell you. Just let me say that someone made a mistake. Let a cat out of a bag. Only a small cat, but enough for me.'

There was a knock on the door and Frenzel stood up and walked over to open it. The two pretty teenagers stood there smiling. *Frenzel stood aside and waved them in. He looked at the blonde one. 'And what's your name, sweetheart?'*

'Heidi,' she said, 'and this is Renate.'

'Lovely names. You come and sit with me, Heidi, and Renate, you sit with my friend.'

As the girls settled themselves Frenzel said, 'We must talk about that matter again some time.'

They never did. But Frenzel hadn't forgotten.

18

LONDON 1959

Blake checked the train times on the indicator then walked over to the book-stall and bought an evening paper. Gillian Blake was back at home now after the birth of their second son. They had a pleasant flat in a semi-detached house in Bickley in Kent, and George Blake, in his sober blue suit, with black brief-case and umbrella, looked exactly what he was – a commuter.

He was usually home by 7 p.m., catching the 6.24 train from Victoria to Bickley. But once or twice a week, generally Tuesdays and Fridays, he caught the 6.18 to Bromley South and changed trains there to get to the next station, Bickley. It seemed an unnecessary and inconvenient diversion to change trains when there was a direct service that took less time.

At 6.14 George Blake walked through the ticket barrier. It was the office-leaving rush-hour and the collector barely glanced at his season ticket. Most of the seats were taken already and Blake joined the men lining the corridor. Exactly on time the train left, lurching over the complex points system that served the big terminus. A lot of the men in the corridor were regulars, reading their newspapers or chatting as they leaned back against the compartment doors. Blake was at the far end of the carriage in the space near the toilets. The man who was watching Blake's reflection in the dusty window of the train wore a dark-blue raincoat and a brown trilby hat. He had a solemn, still face, red complexion and gingery eyebrows. He neither chatted nor read a paper.

When the train eventually stopped at Bromley South he was behind George Blake as he stepped down on to the platform. He followed Blake as he pushed his way through the crowds, saw him toss the folded evening paper into the

141

wire wastepaper bin, and then join the crowds waiting for the next train, the train to Bickley.

Blake got on the next train, but the man in the raincoat waited. The throng of commuters gradually cleared. It was nearly an hour before a middle-aged man in a tweed jacket stood by the wastepaper bin, turned casually to look at it and then picked out the folded Evening Standard; *keeping it folded he slid it casually into his jacket pocket, looked at his wrist-watch and walked slowly to the exit steps. The man in the brown trilby made no move to follow him. He knew who he was. But he wondered why the pick-up was so circuitous. It would be micro-film, and that could surely have been passed through a dead letter box in central London. Or perhaps the elaborate precautions meant that Blake was more important than he had thought. It could, of course, be an SIS procedure, but if it were, surely MI5 would have been warned to avoid wasting Special Branch's time. Since the defection of Burgess and Maclean the relationship between the two security services had gone from cold to icy, but he'd kept it in his notes in case it was ever needed. In fact, he checked Blake's Tuesday and Friday diversions for two months. The pattern was always the same except that on one occasion an elderly woman was the pick-up.*

BEIRUT 1960
Most Middle East countries referred to MECAS, the Middle East College for Arabic Studies, as the 'spy-school'. In the days when it was based in Jerusalem it had trained many British security officers including men from SOE. In 1958, after Suez, the Foreign Office realized that in the decade to come it was going to need many more Arabic speakers. The fact that many of them would be employed on intelligence duties was coincidental. But when Britain relinquished the Palestine Mandate and the state of Israel was created, Jerusalem was no longer a tenable base for MECAS. Despite pressure from all the Arab States MECAS was made welcome in the Lebanon, and new buildings were constructed in Shemlam just north of Beirut.

George Blake was entered as a student at MECAS in

September 1960. He and his wife and two sons were not resident, but lived independently in a pleasant house at the edge of Shemlam village.

The syllabus at MECAS in Arabic and Arab studies was the most concentrated in the world, and lasted eighteen months. Blake was a model student, and his ability to learn languages brought praise from the MECAS staff. He was due to stay for only nine months instead of the full eighteen. He had been told in London before he left that he was wanted for a special assignment when he had completed his training programme.

Far away from the intrigues of Berlin and even the normal demands of his life in SIS London, Blake gradually relaxed. His months in Shemlam were undoubtedly the happiest days of his life. When not absorbed in his studies he spent all his time with his wife and children. London, Rotterdam, Berlin, Korea, and the rest of the world, seemed a long way away.

WEST BERLIN 1960

Horst Eitner saw the scarf out of the corner of his eye and walked over to the shop window. It was real silk with a hand-painted pattern of big red poppies. It looked either French or Italian, and it looked very expensive. There was no price tag on it. The luxury shops on the Kurfürstendamm were not for people who needed to ask the price. But Horst Eitner was doing well, he had never had so much money, and he had too much self-confidence to care about the customs and mannerisms of luxury shops. They were just shops, the same as any others. They merely charged more, and part of their appeal was that the goods they sold were recognizable as chic and expensive.

The scarf was nearly three hundred marks, and after checking it carefully for flaws he paid, and wrote out a note to be enclosed in the fancy wrapping.

He stood for a few moments in the sunshine on the wide pavement of the Kurfürstendamm. He looked at his watch. He was too early, she would still be sleeping, and she could be touchy when she didn't have her sleep. He crossed the road and walked up to Kempinski's. The café was crowded but his coffee and cakes came quickly. He left the table briefly and walked outside to buy a paper and a copy of Playboy at the kiosk in the street.

He had several coffees and he didn't read either the newspaper or the magazine. He did look at the Playboy centrefold. He thought Ushi was both prettier and sexier, and she wasn't out of focus either. At noon exactly, he phoned her. She was waiting for him already. He paid his bill and walked up to the cross-roads, turned right at Joachimstaller Strasse then across the street to Augsburger Strasse. He smiled to himself as he thought about Ushi Lange. She was seventeen, the prettiest girl he'd ever had, and there was nothing she wouldn't let him do. There was nothing she wouldn't let any man do, provided he paid her, but after the first two sessions Horst Eitner hadn't had to pay. Not in straight cash anyway. He'd picked her up seven months earlier at a club on Kantstrasse, and he was with her most days in the afternoon and early evening. She had to be at the club at nine. In the early days he didn't mind that on the back seats of cars, or the bombed buildings near the theatre, she opened her long legs for a series of GIs. He was the only man she took back to her place. He was special. She said so, and he believed her.

When she opened the door she was smiling, and again he realized how pretty she was. Brigitte was pretty, but she was fifteen years older than this girl. If it wasn't for Brigitte he'd be in clover. He could shack up with Ushi and between them they could make a fortune. His money from the Russians and the British, and Ushi's earnings must be fantastic. Berlin was full of well-paid troops, three military governments and scores of black-market barons, and she must earn more in a night than he made in a month. They could get a bigger flat and she could give up the club. He could get her all the men she could take. She could get him dozens of tit-bits of information that he could sell one place or another. But Brigitte knew too much to take any risks.

He watched as she unwrapped the present. She was delighted, and she wore it even when they got into her bed.

It was nearly seven o'clock before they got dressed again, and as she poured him a schnapps she said, 'Did you mean

144

what you said?'

   'I always mean what I say, kid.'

   She handed him the drink and sat down facing him.

   'Did you mean it when you said you love me?'

   'You know I do, or I wouldn't be here.'

   'I don't mean that kind of loving.'

   'Neither do I.'

   'What about Brigitte?'

   'What about her?'

   'Have you told her about us?'

   She saw the sudden fear in his eyes, and despite the warmth of the room and the schnapps she was suddenly cold. She had been stupid to imagine it could be more than it was. A guy who liked screwing her, who wanted to make it seem more. For his own sake, as well as hers.

   Eitner shifted in his chair. 'I didn't say anything about telling her, Ushi. I'd have to work out how to go about it. It wouldn't be easy.'

   She smiled a tight little smile. 'Forget it, Horst.' She stood up. 'I'll have to get fixed for the club. Are you coming tomorrow?'

   'Yes. Of course.' He looked at her and she was so young and beautiful. 'Let me think about it, kid. I just don't know how she would react.'

   'It doesn't matter. You didn't *ever say you'd tell her.'*

   'Would you marry me, Ushi? If I got a divorce.'

   She sighed. 'You know I would.'

   'I'd have to leave Berlin.'

   'Why?'

   'I can't explain. She knows things that could cause me trouble. I'd have to get out quickly.'

   'Where would we go?'

   'East Berlin.'

   'Why East Berlin, for God's sake?'

   'Leave it to me, kid. I'll work something out.'

19

Whenever they went to the park Petrov always took along his paper bag crammed with stale bread. He was an inveterate feeder of animals and birds. Notices at the Zoo not to feed certain animals he saw as man's inhumanity to the beasts of the field. It was not that he was an animal lover, but to him ducks and bread, elephants and buns, polar bears and doughnuts went together like Laurel and Hardy.

He sat now, tempting a couple of cantankerous drakes up to the bench. Eventually the bread was finished and Petrov crumpled up the paper bag and stuffed it into his pocket, as any good Muscovite would.

The wind ruffled a hank of his light hair as he turned to look at Lawler.

'Well, then?'

And Lawler smiled at the phrase and the accent. Petrov was an avid watcher of *Coronation Street* and was beginning to acquire a Lancashire accent.

'They've agreed, Tolya. No problems.'

'Do you trust them about this?'

'There's nothing to trust, *tovarich*. It's up to me. I've had permission to find her and bring her back. After that it's up to the two of you.'

'When are you leaving?'

Lawler smiled and put his hand on the Russian's knee.

'I've got to find her first. So I'll need your help.'

'You say what you want me to do and I'll do it.'

'Right. Her full name before she was married?'

'Maria Grazyna Felinska.'

Lawler took out his diary and wrote down the name.

'Are you sure she went back to Warsaw?'

'She was brought up in Krakow but the KGB insisted that she went back to Warsaw.'

146

'How old is she now?'

Petrov screwed up his eyes and counted out loud. 'Thirty-one, thirty-two, thirty-three.' He grinned at Lawler. 'Could be thirty-four.'

'Did she have a family in Krakow?'

'Some cousins or something. Her parents were dead long ago. But her father was mayor of Krakow at one time. The name will be known. It was a most respected family.'

'What about relations in Warsaw?'

'I don't know. Maybe she spoke of an uncle there.'

'What kind of work do you think she will be doing for a job?'

'She'll get a small KGB pension. They agreed to that to keep me quiet.'

'Would it be enough for her to live on?'

'Not really, and she would have to work to get her ration cards.'

'What was she doing when you met her?'

'She had some little job with a film production company. Continuity girl — something like that.'

'Have you got a photograph of her?'

Petrov reached inside his jacket and took out his well-worn wallet. He searched through it, pulled out a photograph and passed it to Lawler.

It was a half-length photograph of a girl, dark-haired with big eyes and a wide smile. It was a lively face, the face of a girl who knew she was pretty but didn't dwell on it. The high Slav cheeks emphasized the amused look in her eyes, and the openness of the generous smile. There was some writing across the bottom right-hand corner.

'What does it say, Tolya?'

Petrov sighed and without looking at the photograph he said, 'It says *"Ja ciebie kocham"*.'

'What's that mean?'

'It's Polish for "I love you".'

'She's beautiful, Tolya. Very much alive.'

Petrov shrugged. 'Too alive for the bastards in Moscow.'

'Let's get back, and I'll get the embassy in Warsaw seeing what they can find. Can I keep the photograph and get it copied?'

'Sure. I never look at it.'

'Why not?'

'Like I don't put my fingers in mincing machines.'

And as they walked back Lawler was aware that Petrov was silent and withdrawn. He was aware too of the extraordinary likeness between the girl in the photograph and Siobhan Nolan. It explained a lot, and he wondered if Siobhan had ever seen the photograph.

Lawler came out of Photographic with six damp prints of Maria Felinska and slid them into a buff envelope, marking it 'urgent' after he had addressed it to the Assistant Military Attaché at the Warsaw embassy. He passed the envelope to Admin for inclusion in the diplomatic bag.

Back in Photographic he collected the original and three copies for himself.

Two days later Silvester phoned. There had been a phone call for Lawler from Hooper at the Warsaw embassy. Would he return it.

It meant going to Century House, and he took a taxi to Waterloo Station and walked the rest of the way. It was probably an unnecessary precaution, because by now every taxi-driver in London knew that Century House was the new HQ of various officially non-existent organizations.

He booked a call for three o'clock, and waited in Silvester's secretary's office for it to come through. He was one of her favourites, or he'd have had strong hints that his own office was a more suitable waiting-room. But in his own office he wouldn't have had fresh coffee with three sugars.

Hooper came through at ten past three, and it was a good clear line.

'Your query, sir. There are nineteen of that name in the Warsaw telephone directory, and twenty-seven in the Krakow one. I've got two people ploughing through them but no link so far. There's one thin lead, and I'll be dealing with that this evening. He's a bit doddery. OK, sir?'

'Yes. Thanks for the speed and the effort. I'll be waiting for your call.'

'You've thought of the possibility that that might not be the name now?'

'Why shouldn't it be?'

There was a pause and then Hooper's voice wavered into the tune 'Here Comes the Bride.'

'Jesus. I wouldn't like it to be that.'

'It's only an outside chance, but looking at the pretty picture you sent me I'd say it's on the cards. Quite a doll.'

'Time's moved on since that was taken.'

'Of course. I'll call as soon as I've got reason to.'

'Even nil reports could help me sleep.'

'Right, sir. Cheerio.'

'Goodbye.'

Lawler had speculated on the possibility of the woman not wanting to see Petrov again. Or not wanting to leave because she was happy where she was. But it hadn't crossed his mind that the woman he always called Petrov's wife might now be somebody else's wife. Complete with family.

He turned to look at her. 'Which one would you take home?'

She smiled. 'Money no object?'

'Money no object.'

They were sitting on the bench in Gallery 28 in the Tate, and she didn't hesitate. 'The Pissarro. The snow one. I don't need to ask which one you would choose.'

'Which one, then?'

'The Millais. Ophelia.'

She laughed out loud at the surprised look on his face.

'How on earth did you guess?' He sounded almost annoyed. 'I didn't even comment about it when we were looking at it.'

She smiled. 'You know, you and Petrov are alike in many ways.'

'What ways?'

She shrugged. 'Neither of you hangs together properly. You're both romantics without acknowledging it. And

149

underneath you're both rather unpleasant. Ruthless, suspicious, cynical, and I wouldn't like to be a man either of you disliked.'

'Charming.'

'No way, boyo. Neither of you has got an ounce of charm but you're both quite honest, and I set store by that. And to a woman you're both as transparent as young boys. And women like that. It makes life easier for them.'

'And what's Millais' Ophelia got to do with all this?'

'It's romantic. Beautifully and gently painted. And the girl is young, and pretty, and innocent. Your idea of how girls should be. Nevertheless she *is* dead. Drowned. Lying in the stream. But that didn't sadden you. Although it might have passed through your mind that if you'd been there you could have rescued her.' She smiled. 'Don't look so shocked or insulted, whichever it is.'

He turned to look at her face. She was already looking at him. He opened his mouth to speak and changed his mind. He stood up and reached out his hand for hers. And as they walked through the gallery she slid her arm under his. She had said aloud almost exactly what he had thought about the painting. And he *had* barely been aware that the girl was dead. He saw just the beauty, and fleetingly thought that if he had been there he could have saved her. And he was hard enough not to want her to know how near the truth her barbs had been.

They walked down the gallery steps and crossed the road. As they leaned against the Embankment stone wall, looking at the boats on the Thames, he slid his arm around her, aware of her body and its soft warmth. The river was high and turgid, garbage and oil surging and falling from the wake of the passing ships.

'D'you miss Dublin and your people, Siobhan?'

'I do right now.'

'Why now?'

'You and Petrov. It's like another world. I can remember an engraving in a school book called *Orpheus in the Underworld.* Very detailed. Very dark and forbidding. Your lives are like that. It's like a terrible game. A sick game that normal people ought not to be mixed up in. It's like some crazy party where people go along dressed up as monsters, but the people who invited them aren't dressed up. They *are* monsters.'

'You think Petrov and I are monsters?'

'Yes.'

He was aware that she was watching his face, and almost without thinking he turned to look at her. She was so beautiful.

He sighed. 'I feel in need of a fairy princess.'

She smiled back at him. Indulgently. And then she put up her soft mouth to be kissed. He kissed her gently and then turned his face to look at the river. She said softly, 'Why haven't you made a pass at me?'

He shrugged. 'You're Petrov's girl. You belong to him.'

'Don't be so stupid, Jimmy.'

'What does that mean?'

'I don't *belong* to anyone. And Petrov hasn't made love to me since you agreed to get his Pole back for him.'

'I'm sorry about that.'

She laughed, her head thrown back. 'You really are the limit. What is there to be sorry about? The whole scenario was just like your game. Petrov screwed me because I'm pretty, because he likes screwing girls, and because he could pretend I was his wife. In his mind of course he'd put the reasons in reverse order. All part of the knight in shining armour fantasy. It wasn't me he was screwing it was a girl who, when he last saw her, looked like me and was about my age. But even *he* can't bring himself to tell me that. So he kids himself first, so that he can then try to kid me with an easy conscience. OK. I was kidded. But I don't mind. I understand. He wanted a momma and a wife, and a girl to screw. And I could only be one of those things. I didn't even know about his background. Nor about his wife, or what he was. I knew he wasn't what he pretended, but whatever he really was, it didn't matter to me.'

He looked back at her and the sun made her cheek look like a soft warm peach. 'You're very understanding, sweetie.'

151

She shook her head. 'I'm just a human being. You two inhabit your stupid world of cowboys and Indians, and I live in the real world all the time. You two are foreigners in the real world. Just visitors from outer space who don't know much about how real people behave.'

He saw tears at the edges of her eyes and it moved him enough for him not to pretend. 'I've wanted to go to bed with you from the moment I first saw you. But that was only because you were so pretty. I know you much better now and I'm not looking for a momma, I'm not sure about the wife bit, but I might be a problem.'

'How?'

'It would be more than just a screw for me.'

'Go on.'

'I'd like it to be real. That you were my girl.'

'I don't need gypsy violins.'

He smiled. 'You know me, Siobhan. I do.'

For long moments she looked at him, and then she said softly, 'Let's see how it goes.'

'Shall I tell Petrov?'

'It's up to you. He won't notice I'm not in his bed.'

'That's not true, kid.'

'Who was she?'

'Who was who?'

'The girl who sent you back into your no-man's land.'

'What makes you think there was such a girl?'

'Two things, my love. First of all it's very obvious. Secondly I read a letter to you from some lawyer. It was tucked into your desk. I saw the picture too. The one in the old-fashioned silver frame. The one you put behind the books.'

He sighed. 'I'll tell you when we know each other better.'

He saw the sudden anger in her eyes. 'You mean when you're sure I'm good enough you'll tell me about some tramp who cut your throat and threw you back in the water.'

'I didn't mean that at all.'

'What did you mean?'

'I meant that I don't know how to begin. Or what to say.

I tried to make it work but it was never on. I've never worked out why.'

'Forget it. I was stupid.' She kissed him and slid her tongue into his mouth, and his hand slid up under her arm to cup her breast.

20

Just like the girl had said, Petrov had been no problem. He brushed aside Lawler's halting explanations. All he wanted to know was why it was taking so long to trace his ex-wife. It had become an obsession now. Petrov wanted his wife for a score of reasons. She represented a time when his life had been good. She was his safety-net. The ready-made family, the dearly beloved, nostalgia, all that had been good. And underlying it all she would be the proof that they weren't going to kill him. When she was with him, and they'd negotiated the future, he would tell them what he had to tell. The things that would wipe out the threat.

It was two days later when Lawler got the call that Hooper in Warsaw wanted to speak to him. He ignored security precautions and took a taxi direct to Century House.

He had to wait an hour to get through, and he was tense and on edge as he heard Hooper's voice.

'What have you got?'

'Your friend's not in Warsaw. Not in Poland in fact.'

'What's that mean?'

'The old man *was* the uncle all right. But he's senile. It took a long time to get it all worked out. It means the person is positively identified as being alive. And I've got an address.'

'What is it?'

'I've put it in yesterday's bag. Should be your end tonight.'

'What's her situation?'

'It's there for you. It's not much. I suggest we leave it for now.'

'Is that all?'

'I'm afraid so.'

154

'Well, thanks.'

'Best of luck, sir.'

Lawler hung up and looked at his watch. Why had Hooper wished him the best of luck? He reached for the internal phone and dialled Foreign Office Admin and asked when the Warsaw bag was due. They were waiting for it now. It had arrived at Heathrow, had been cleared, and was on its way. He asked for his piece to be sent over straight away to Century House. It was midnight when the buff envelope arrived and he tore it open impatiently. It felt very thin. It was a single folded page and as he spread it open he closed his eyes for a second before he read it.

TO: J. LAWLER. LONDON HQ.
FROM: W. HOOPER. ASST. MIL. ATT. WARSAW EMBASSY.

MARIA GRAZYNA FELINSKA

INFORMATION FROM WOJTEK FELINSKI. UNCLE OF ABOVE. ADDRESS ON FILE HERE. (91409)

WHEN SHE RETURNED FROM MOSCOW SHE HAD DIFFICULTY IN OBTAINING A WORK PERMIT AND FOOD COUPONS. SHE WORKED FOR ABOUT A YEAR AS A CHAMBERMAID IN THE HOTEL BRISTOL-ORBIS IN ULITZA KRAKOWSKIE PRZEDMIESCIE. SOME TIME LATER, DATE NOT PRECISELY KNOWN, SHE WORKED AS CLERK AT THE TOURIST INFORMATION CENTRE, ULITZA KRUCZA, 16. AFTER SOME MONTHS SHE WAS TRANSFERRED TO AN ADMINISTRATIVE POST AT THE PALACE OF CULTURE AND SCIENCE, PL. DEFILAD. SHE WAS LATER EMPLOYED AT THE KRAKOW FILM CENTRE WORKING IN SOME CAPACITY ON TOURIST FILMS FOR ORBIS, AL. PUSZKINA 1. ABOUT ONE YEAR AGO SHE MOVED TO AN ADDRESS IN EAST BERLIN WHICH WAS GIVEN AS FRIEDRICHSBERGEN STRASSE 17. THIS INFORMATION CAME FROM A LETTER TO A FRIEND OF THE FAMILY. I HAVE SEEN THE ORIGINAL LETTER. SUBJECT APPEARED TO BE WORKING FOR A FILM COMPANY. ALTHOUGH

MR FELINSKI ONLY HINTED AT THE MATTER, IT SEEMED POSSIBLE THAT MISS FELINSKA OWED HER IMPROVED SITUATION TO HER RELATIONSHIP WITH A POLE OF GERMAN ORIGIN NAMED WALTHER KRAMER (NICKNAME BUBI). THERE SEEMS LITTLE POSSIBILITY OF CONFIRMING OR ADDING TO THE ABOVE INFORMATION WITHOUT DRAWING OFFICIAL ATTENTION TO OUR INTEREST. SHALL MAINTAIN LOW-KEY CONTACT WITH INFORMANT. MESSAGE ENDS.

Lawler sat in the almost empty group of offices trying to work out what to do. At least when she had been last heard from she wasn't married. But there was obviously a man in the picture somewhere. That was to be expected. But he knew nothing about her life or whether she had ever talked about Petrov. She had probably been warned by the KGB not to talk. It would mean going in cold and uninformed. But Berlin was going to be easier than Warsaw. A fifty-fifty chance against a forty-sixty chance. And there would be better back-up in Berlin. They could make some enquiries before he arrived.

He wrote out a message on the standard form and took it down to Coding. The big room was as busy as if it were midday. They checked it over and confirmed that it would be received in West Berlin inside the hour.

Back at the flat Siobhan was in bed, reading, waiting for him. She looked up, smiling. 'And how's the Peewit patrol done tonight?'

He sat on the bed and looked at her. 'It's bloody marvellous to come back to a smile. Especially at two o'clock in the morning.'

She laughed and pulled him to her. 'That's the most revealing thing you've ever said, my love. And for your information it's nearer three-thirty than two. D'you want a drink?'

He shook his head. 'I think I've traced his wife.'

'Where was she?'

'Can't say, sweetie. But it's good news.'

'Wake the poor bastard up and tell him.'

'Shall I?'

'Why not? He'll be delighted.'

And he was. Pacing up and down. Smiling at his private thoughts and insisting that they opened a bottle of Stolichnaya for just one drink each.

He was still drinking when Lawler and Siobhan went to bed, standing there smiling and happy, trying to get Radio Moscow on the radio.

The message from Silvester said that he wanted to see Lawler urgently, but when he arrived at Silvester's office he had been kept waiting for almost half an hour. It was seven-thirty before he was shown in and Silvester was just putting down the phone. He pointed to one of the chairs in front of his desk and walked round to sit in the other chair opposite Lawler.

'When are you leaving for Berlin, Jimmy?'

'The day after tomorrow. Facilities had difficulty booking me on a direct flight. I still might have to go via Düsseldorf.'

'Were you still intending that Petrov and the girl should go down to your parents?'

'Yes. I think they'll be OK down there.'

Silvester sighed and leaned down to undo the laces on his black brogues. When he straightened up he said, 'I want you to take both of them with you.'

'Why, Adam? They'll be in the way. And Berlin was Petrov's old stamping ground. Somebody might recognize him, for God's sake.'

Silvester looked at Lawler, as if he were trying to decide whether to tell him something or not.

'I think Petrov's in danger. Even the girl. And maybe you too.'

'I don't understand, Adam. What the hell's going on?'

'Something's cropped up. Even if you hadn't been going to Berlin I'd have wanted you out of London. Even out of the country.'

'Is this KGB?'

'I've been stupid, James. I've only just discovered how stupid. I'm not going to risk being stupid a second time.'

'Surely I can be told?'

'I can tell you part of it. I owe you that. But I can't tell you all of it.'

'Why not?'

'Because I'm not sure I'm right. If I'm wrong then there's no problem. I hope for a lot of people's sakes that I am wrong. I've told the Director but nobody else. He thinks I've stretched my theory much too far, but he agrees that we should behave for the moment as if I'm right. Nobody else is being told anything at all. When I analyse it myself I doubt my own theory. But when I go by instinct and experience then there's a faint chance that I could be right. I'm not intending to take any chances.'

'Has a threat been made?'

'No.'

'Is the Soviet Embassy making moves?'

'No.'

'What's the bit that I *can* know?'

Silvester looked down as he slid his feet out of his shoes and moved his toes, then he looked up at Lawler.

'I assure you it won't help.'

'It helped you, apparently.'

'Only because I've been around SIS for a long, long time.'

'I'd still like to know.'

'OK. The man Ridger. The one you thought was watching your flat. I put a check out on him. No priority. He was sacked from Special Branch for misconduct. I had him pulled in and questioned. The report was on my desk a week ago but I didn't read it until yesterday. He *was* watching you. He'd been paid to. He had no idea why, he just took the money and put in reports twice a day. Something in the report jogged my memory and I questioned him today, myself. What I got out of him was by no means conclusive. I'd had a wild, impossible thought. All I can say is that although what he had to say didn't confirm my idea, it didn't wash it out either. I'm having some other checks done. They could take months. Until they are done I'm taking precautions. That's all I'm going to say.'

'What precautions can I take?'

'So far as this is concerned, once the three of you are in Berlin there's no extra risk. But I've got a feeling I know what Petrov's piece of insurance is now. Part of it anyway.'

'What is it?'

'It wouldn't help you to know. And I could be wrong. So forget it. I've told Facilities to get the three of you on tonight's ten-thirty flight so you'd better get back and round up the other two. I've laid on a car to take you back to Chelsea and he'll wait and take you to the airport. The flights were over-booked but we've insisted on places tonight. The driver's got the warrants but you'll have to exchange them for tickets at the check-in desk. There won't be any problems.' Silvester stood up. 'If you look like getting Petrov's wife across and his girl-friend is going to be an embarrassment send her back and I'll take care of her at this end.'

'I'll see how it goes.'

'OK. Best of luck.'

Lawler hesitated, and then decided to say nothing about the changes in the trio's relationships.

'Who'll be my contact in Berlin?'

'Barlow. You know him, don't you?'

'Yes. We've worked together before.'

'I'll tell Barlow, and you phone my girl to let me know your flight number so you can be met.'

'Right, sir.'

Silvester nodded. 'It may not feel like it, Jimmy, but you're doing a good job. It is in my book anyway.'

As Lawler went down in the lift he wondered in whose book it wasn't a good job. Apart from his own.

They landed at Tegel just before midnight, but the airport was still busy. Joe Barlow, and a younger man who wasn't introduced, had helped them carry their bags to the waiting car.

When they turned into the driveway and pulled up out-

159

side the safe-house in Grunewald Petrov smiled. 'It's like going back to school. I've seen photographs of this place from every angle including from the air. I've seen drawings and notes of the internal layout, and once I even sat in on a discussion on how to blow it up.'

Joe Barlow smiled. 'We must have a chat about what you planned.' Barlow looked at them in turn. 'Do any of you fancy a drink or a meal? It's no trouble.'

But everybody voted for bed, although Lawler spent twenty minutes or so talking with Barlow.

'She's not at that address anymore, James. But we've traced where she is. She's living in a house by the river in Köpenick. But there's what looks like a big problem.'

'What's that?'

'The guy Kramer. He's a film director. Party member, influential, well-paid, and they live together. It was he who got her into better jobs. They seem to have a settled relationship.'

'What else do you know?'

'She works part-time at the studios as a production assistant. She's certainly worn well. Looks younger than her years. It's not going to be easy to get her away from all that. Not voluntarily anyway.'

'That's the only way it's going to be.'

'Let's talk about it after you've had some kip.'

It was a long time before Lawler slept. His mind was too full of his thoughts. Thoughts that were crowding in, uncontrolled, and uncontrollable, like people crowding into a subway. Petrov and Maria Grazyna Felinska, long, long ago, when all was well. Before a few public criticisms had smashed up their lives. Just a few words that sent them in different directions. Joanna, screaming drunk at a party, asking why the men were looking at other girls, and not at her. And coming back to the empty flat. The vision of Siobhan Nolan in bed with Petrov, her long legs spread wide, just as they were for him. Silvester and his little secrets. Petrov and his little secrets. And would anyone cuddle little Sarah when she was afraid or unhappy. Petrov, as happy as a love-struck adolescent, waiting impatiently for his love to fly to his arms. But what if his love was happy in her house on the river Spree? What the hell could he say to her? The first words, the opening sentence. What, in God's name, did you say? And back to Siobhan Nolan. Who knew more about him than he knew himself. What would she do to him? What form would her wound take? Asleep in the next room, safe in her self-knowledge. If Petrov went in to her even now, would she let him sleep with her? His eyes ached and burned as he tried to sleep, and not think, his body rigid and tense. Then suddenly, and silently, she was there, looking down at him, smiling, her hand reaching for his. She sat on the edge of the bed. Not speaking, just holding his hand, waiting for him to sleep. And as the tensions melted away his heavy eyelids closed and he slept, and she lay on the bed alongside him, her foot touching his leg.

21

BERLIN 1960
About a month after Blake had settled in the rented house at Shemlam a blonde woman was shown into an office near West Berlin's Town Hall. The man who came from behind his desk to show her to a chair was young and fair-haired, and he nodded dismissal at the man who had escorted her to his office. Some instinct kept him from going back behind his desk and he sat in the red leather chair facing her.

'They told me that you had phoned and asked to speak to a security officer. My name is Berger. I'm an officer of the BfV. What can I do to help you?'

He watched her face as he spoke. He guessed she was in her middle thirties. An attractive woman who must once have been pretty. But now her face was gaunt and pale, her eyes red-rimmed and strained.

'I want to report a man who is a spy for the Russians.'

'Are you sure that you're not mistaken?'

'Quite sure.'

'OK. Tell me about it.'

'What do you want to know?'

'Is the man German?'

'Yes.'

'In Berlin?'

'Yes.'

'What makes you think he's a spy?'

'He told me so.'

Berger smiled. 'You're a very attractive lady, if I might say so. Men sometimes do claim to be involved in espionage to impress their girl-friends.'

'He's not my boy-friend.'

'Could I ask you your name, madam?'

'I'd rather not say.'

'OK. What about the man's name?'

'Horst Heinz Eitner.'

'Tell me what he told you.'

'He said his code-name is "Paulus" and he reports to a Colonel Willi Seegebrecht, head of an East German intelligence organization.'

'Go on.'

'And the Russian he reports to is based at Karlshorst, and his name is Petrov. He's KGB.'

Berger looked at her for several minutes before he spoke.

'Am I right in thinking that Herr Eitner is your husband?'

He saw the flush suffuse her face, and she said in almost a whisper, 'How did you know that?'

'I didn't, Frau Eitner. But to know that kind of specific detail you would need to be either his wife or his mistress. You already said you were not his girl-friend.'

'It's true all the same, what I told you.'

'I'm not doubting that for a moment, Frau Eitner. But I have to ask you why you are telling me this.'

'Why is that necessary?'

'Let me explain. Before we can take any action against Herr Eitner we have to have evidence that would be acceptable to a court. A statement by anybody that he told them such and such is not evidence. It's what the courts call hearsay. When that evidence comes from the accused's wife it creates other problems. There are two possible motives for a wife to give evidence that would convict her husband. If she were doing it because she was a patriot it could carry some weight. If the defence could suggest to the court that it was done out of jealousy or spite then that evidence would not be enough. In either case we should have to carry out our own investigations and provide quite independent evidence.'

'You think I'm lying out of jealousy?'

'By no means. Eighty per cent of information given us, or the civil police, with jealousy as a motive, turns out to be true. There are many other ways a jealous woman, or man, can take revenge. But I do need to know your motive.'

'He wants to leave me for a young girl.'

'Has he said so?'

163

'No. But he sees her every day. Most afternoons at her flat.'

'How do you know this?'

'I paid a private detective to find out.'

'Have you got reports in writing?'

'Yes.'

'Where are they?'

'In my hat-box at home.'

Berger reached into his inside pocket and pulled out a leather wallet. He took out a card and reached over and gave it to her.

'You can ring that number any time of the day or night. Ask for me — Major Berger. What's your forename?'

'Brigitte.'

'Right. Just give the name, Brigitte. If I happened to be out of Berlin they will tell you so, and when I shall be back. If I am in Berlin, ring again fifteen minutes later, and they will put you through to me. Don't use your own telephone at home. If Herr Eitner really is doing what he told you the telephone might well be tapped. Does your husband have a job?'

'Just what I've told you.'

'Does he have money enough?'

'Plenty. He's got all the money he needs.'

'Just from these two sources?'

'And from the British.'

'What does he do for the British?'

'He spies for them too.'

'Are you sure?'

And for the first time she saw that he was really interested.

'He does it with a Dutchman who works for British intelligence.'

'What's the Dutchman's name?'

'Max van Vries.'

'Your . . . Herr Eitner told you this?'

'Max comes to our house. He's a really nice fellow. I liked him.'

'Regularly?'

'Oh yes. Two or three times a week.'

164

'*Do you know when he's due to come again?*'

'*Oh, he doesn't come anymore. He went back to England last year. To London.*'

'*Have you got a family, Frau Eitner?*'

'*A little girl.*'

Berger sat in silence for several minutes. Then he reached out his hand. 'Give me back the card, please.' He took it and placed it on his desk.

'*Frau Eitner. Unless you were actually afraid for some reason, don't ring me. I want you to go back home and forget that you've ever been here. Forget our conversation. Put all this out of your mind. Understand? It never happened. Just continue whatever relationship you have with Herr Eitner as normally as you can.*'

'*What will happen?*'

Berger stood up and smiled. 'So far as you are concerned, nothing. But I am grateful for your help. I shall do my best to see that you are not involved in any way.'

'*What will happen to him?*'

He took her arm gently, opened the door and led her down the corridor. 'I'm taking you down to the side door. Walk down the side passage and you'll come out by the shops. It's more discreet this way.'

She took the hint and accepted that he didn't intend answering her question. She wished that he had asked the girl's name and address. And that reminded her.

'*Do you want my address?*'

'*No, that's all right. Leave it all to us.' He took her hand, holding it for a moment. She really was quite attractive. 'Thank you again. If you need help some time in the future, please contact me.' He bowed slightly and she turned and left.*

He walked slowly back to his office and dialled a number on the internal phone. When the red light came on he said, 'I think we've got a real lead to Viktor at last.'

Berger and the lawyer from the Office of the Public Prosecutor went through the reports page by page, and Berger answered the lawyer's queries from a pile of official notebooks. It was the third full day given to examining the case of Horst Eitner.

'And that's the lot, Karl. What do you think?'

'You've certainly got enough to pull him in and interrogate him.'

'No more than that?'

'It depends on what his answers are. The court won't like the jealousy motive on the part of the wife.'

'Do we need to use her?'

'Definitely. She's the only evidence that this Dutchman Max van Vries was ever in the flat. We'll have to declare the jealousy angle. If we don't the defence will.'

'What do I need to establish when I interrogate him?'

'The money in the three banks. He'll try all the usual things. Gambling winnings. Gifts. Maybe black market. Make him give detail after detail. He won't be able to, he'll claim he can't remember. Tell him we shall class it as obstruction of evidence.

'Then you've got the meetings in East Berlin with known KGB and SSD agents. The court will agree to evidence in camera *on that sort of stuff so that you don't have to give away too much. Try and get the British to give evidence that they used him and paid him. They'll have dates and amounts of payments that you can relate to bank deposits.' He pursed his lips. 'And that's about all you've got.'*

'Will it stick, d'you think?'

Karl Bonner shrugged. 'It's hard to say. Fifty-fifty as it stands. Anything more could turn it our way.'

'I'm going to pull him in tomorrow at the girl's place. When are you back from leave?'

'Two weeks. I'll leave a number, but don't use it unless you have to. I need all the sunshine I can get.'

'Where are you going?'

'Costa del Sol. A small place called Nerja.' He smiled. 'Why are you picking him up at the girl's place?'

Berger smiled back. 'That poor bloody wife deserves some sort of pay-off, doesn't she?'

Bonner nodded. 'I guess so.' He picked up his brief-case and walked to the door. 'Try and get the British to make that fellow van Vries available to give evidence. He at least establishes that Eitner dabbled as an agent.'

'They're never very co-operative when it means exposing one of their people in court. We should be the same.'

'Try anyway.'

'OK.'

Berger looked at his watch and turned to Klaus Messel. 'He's been there an hour. I think we'll go in.'

'OK, Chief.'

When the BMW pulled up outside the girl's building Berger said, 'Cover the fire-escape at the back. I don't think he'll be any trouble. I'll signal from the window when I'm leaving.'

Berger gave Messel ten minutes to get into place and then walked up the stairs to the third floor. He rang the bell and waited. It was several minutes before the door opened. The girl was wearing a man's towelling bath-robe.

'Fräulein Lange?'

She nodded. 'What do you want?'

'I'd like to talk to Herr Eitner.'

'Who are you?'

'My name's Berger. Otto Berger.'

And when she hesitated he spread open his identity card. When she looked back at his face she looked scared.

'I don't understand.'

He said very quietly, 'It's nothing to do with you. Just let me in.'

Slowly and hesitantly she opened the door and he walked inside.

The small living-room was empty, and he pushed open a half-open door. It was the bathroom. The other door was slightly ajar. As he walked in Eitner was reaching for a packet of cigarettes on the bedside cupboard.

'Who the hell are you?'

'Herr Eitner?'

Eitner pushed back the sheets and got out of the bed. He was wearing only his socks.

'Get out, you cheeky bastard, whoever you are.' And he

167

lurched forward, his fists clenched. Berger leaned back against the door to close it. 'I'm a Federal Investigator, Herr Eitner, I should calm down if I were you.'

Eitner stood with one fist raised aggressively. 'You're what?'

Berger showed him his identity card and Eitner's arm fell to his side.

'What the hell's going on?'

'Get dressed, Herr Eitner. I want you to come with me and answer some questions.'

'What authority do you have?'

'A warrant from the Public Prosecutor's Office.'

Eitner took a deep breath, opened his mouth to speak, then changed his mind. Berger stood watching as Eitner slowly dressed. He wasn't going to make trouble.

Eitner had heard about the BfV villa in Grunewald, and the bars on the windows confirmed his worst fears. Berger had left him alone for a couple of days before starting the interrogation. It lasted ten days, almost full-time. It gave him enough to charge Eitner with half a dozen offences but none of them added up to high treason. Eitner was transferred to a normal prison. Berger had made clear that the court would be asked to give consecutive sentences that would add up to over twenty years. He was given no indication of when his trial would take place.

At the end of the first month Eitner had smuggled out a letter to his friend George Blake at his Lebanon address, asking for help. When, after two months, he had received no reply he asked for an interview with Berger. It was a bitter and angry Horst Eitner who was ready to talk. He was taken back to the villa in Grunewald for the interview. It started one mid-evening in February 1961, and Berger was cool and distant as he went down the list of questions.

'Does that mean that you want to retract your statement about being kidnapped by the East Germans and forced to work for them?'

'Yes. But I want to do a deal.'

'What sort of deal?'

168

'I can give you details of a British intelligence officer who is a double-agent for the Russians.'

'Go on.'

'I want charges dropped against me if I give you this information.'

'You've been seeing too many American films, Herr Eitner. We don't work that way. You are a German citizen and you will be tried under German law.'

Eitner shrugged. 'You must have some discretion about what charges you put forward.'

'Look, Eitner, you've wasted days of my time telling me a pack of lies about being kidnapped, and all that crap about Seegebrecht and being forced to work for him. Tell me anything you've got to tell me, and I'll decide what action we take against you yourself.'

'OK.'

'But just remember. The first lie I catch you with you go straight back to jail, and I'll stick down every charge I can find against you. Is that understood?'

'Yes.'

'OK. Carry on. D'you want a cigarette?'

Eitner nodded, and Berger passed him a lighter and a full pack of Benson and Hedges King Size. After he had inhaled, Eitner started.

'I lied about not knowing Max van Vries. I did know him. I worked for him. He wasn't Dutch, he was British, and his real name was Blake. George Blake. He worked for SIS at the Olympic Stadium.'

'What was your relationship with him?'

'He paid me sixty pounds sterling a week and I ran two small networks for him. I was getting the same from the Russians. They just wanted documents. Blake was definitely authentic, I checked on him. A few months before he went back to London he told me how he knew I was working for the Russians. I thought he was going to chop me or put me inside but he didn't. It was then I knew he must be working for the Russians too.'

'Did you ask him about that?'

'I didn't need to. I checked with my SSD contacts in East

169

Berlin. They wouldn't confirm it, but they didn't deny it either. I gather that it caused a few heads to roll. And then Blake took me to meet a Russian named Petrov. He was Blake's controller. I thought he was going to use me, but I heard later that he'd been posted back to Moscow. Almost the same time that Blake went back to London.'

'Is Blake still in London?'

'No, he's just gone to Beirut, to the spy-school there.'

'Have you had any contact with Blake since he went back to London?'

'Just a personal letter to say they'd had another child.'

'Have you still got that letter?'

'I'm not sure, I'd have to check.'

'You realize I can check all this out with the British?'

'Sure I do.'

'And if it's not true you'll be in for life?'

'Do all the checking you like. It's all true.'

'I'll fix you a comfortable room here. You'll be here until I've checked this out. Is there anything you particularly want?'

'Yes.'

'What is it?'

'Who put you on to me.'

'We'd been watching you for quite a time.'

'That's not an answer.'

Berger smiled. 'You know as well as I do that it's all the answer you'll get, my friend.'

'She was in it too.'

'Who was?'

'Brigitte. My wife.'

'Oh. What did she do? You told me originally that she knew nothing about any of it.'

'She was paid for looking after a Soviet agent who was to be planted on the British.'

'We'll talk about that another time.'

Otto Berger had dropped his bombshell on his opposite number at SIS at the Olympic Stadium. Although he obviously wasn't believed he was taken straight away to tell his story to the local Director of SIS who listened impassively and without comment until he had finished.

'Have you informed Bonn, Herr Berger?'

'Yes, sir. They instructed me to see Mr Wainwright.'

'Who else knows? Does Herr Toller know?'

'The only people who know are Herr Mann in Bonn, Herr Toller and myself.'

'What about secretaries?'

'There were no secretaries involved. We have put nothing in writing as yet.'

'This is deeply disturbing, as you can well understand, and I should appreciate your organization maintaining the present control over security. In return we will see that you are kept well informed about our investigations.'

'Thank you, sir.'

'I'll telephone Herr Rudi Mann myself.'

Wainwright accompanied Berger to the car park and as they stood by his car the Englishman said, 'I can't believe it, you know, Otto. Blake was a senior man. He's got a fantastic track record. Not a blot on his copy-book. Didn't drink, didn't womanize, and worked all the hours God sends. It would be incredible if he turned out to be a twicer.'

'It happens, Joe. Burgess and Maclean for instance.'

'I know, but those bastards were drunks and queers. Blake wasn't like them at all. He was a quiet nonentity.'

'Let's wait and see. Maybe our guy is still lying.'

'My God, I hope so.'

But it wasn't going to be SIS's lucky week. An hour before Wainwright and Berger had stood talking in the car park, a BMW car with four passengers and a driver had been passed through the Soviet checkpoint at Brandenburger Tor. There had been no difficulty. The car carried the special diplomatic badge of the Polish embassy in East Berlin. When it was well into West Berlin a black Mercedes tagged in behind it and followed it down to Dahlem in the American zone. In a side-street off Podbielski Allee the two cars pulled up, and the passengers from the BMW got into the big Merc and a US marine sergeant took over the BMW.

The Mercedes drove on to a house standing in its own grounds just beyond the Dahlem cemetery. There were US marines guarding the massive iron gates, and more patrolling the grounds. Two Americans were waiting on the steps of the house.

There were lights on all over the house and the first tentative flakes of snow were beginning to cover the wide lawns and the gravelled drive.

The passengers in the Mercedes were a Pole and his family. A Pole named Michael Goleniewski. To be more precise, Lieutenant-Colonel Goleniewski who two hours earlier had still been the head of Poland's secret service, Z-2, in East Berlin.

Seven months previously he had made his first contact with CIA agents in Berlin and asked for political asylum. Wary that it might be a plant, they asked him to supply various items of intelligence to prove his good faith. The intelligence had been duly provided and he was given the go-ahead to arrange for his family to join him in East Berlin from Warsaw with his birthday as the excuse.

The two Americans who welcomed him had flown over the previous day from Langley, Virginia, and despite their impatience to talk with the defector they had spent that evening going over the arrangements that had been made for the family's future.

They tried to make it more like a conversation than an interrogation, but by midday they knew that they already had enough to justify the operation. They had the names of four Soviet agents working inside CIA units in Hanover, Hamburg and Frankfurt. All in key positions. But they had been shocked by the last item he gave them when they were about to go in to lunch.

'I don't know whether Scarbeck comes into your area or the FBI.'

'Who's Scarbeck?'

'Irwin Chambers Scarbeck.'

'You mean the US diplomat?'

'Yes.'

172

'*You mean* he's *involved with Moscow?*'
'*I thought maybe you knew, or that he was a plant.*'
'*Why did you think he might be a plant?*'
'*We all did. We had meeting after meeting and we never were sure.*'
'*Tell me more.*'
Goleniewski smiled. '*You really don't know about him?*'
'*No. Not a thing.*'
'*He's been passing information and documents for a long time.*'
'*Why? How did they nobble him?*'
'*The usual way. Girls. They've got pictures of him fornicating. Several different girls. They used the usual drill. Threatened copies to his family, the newspapers, Congressional committees, the Department of State.*' *He shrugged, smiling.* '*The old, old story. But he was so stupid, so indiscreet that we thought it must be the CIA playing games. And when he was faced with the photographs he just caved in. No arguing. No bargaining. Just agreement. It was all too easy. That's why we had doubts.*'
'*Jesus. The bastard. What did he hand over?*'
'*Anything they asked for.*'
'*Did they pay him?*'
'*A little. Just enough for him to be committed that way too.*'
By eleven o'clock that morning the Polish ambassador had lodged an almost violent protest at the kidnapping of a Polish diplomat. And after he had been given a not too diplomatic brush-off the Soviet Commander had called for an immediate four-power meeting. There had been no grounds for refusal and four grim-faced men, all of General's rank, had gathered at the Russian Kommandatura.

There was fist-pounding and threats from the Russian. Surprise and indifference from the Frenchman. Mild rebuffs from the Scot, and virtual silence from the American. The threats were reiterated and stepped up, and that confirmed the CIA opinion that they'd got themselves a bargain. It also made them decide that the Pole's life was now in danger and that he should be flown immediately to Washington.

173

They were actually sitting around in Goleniewski's bed-
room, his light luggage already packed as they waited for the
car to take them to Gatow, when the Pole dropped the
second bomb. He had turned casually to Autenowski.
  'I suppose the British already know about Blake?'
  'You mean George Blake?'
  'Yes. Used to be in Berlin. Now back in London.'
  'Actually he's in Beirut. What's he been up to?'
  'He'd been a double-agent for the KGB for years,'
Goleniewski laughed. 'Then they instructed him to double
with the Russians and gave him the perfect cover.'
  'Maybe he really was putting one over on Moscow.'
  'No chance of that. He's been with them since he was a
kid. He was totally committed. No money. No booze. No
girls. A twenty-four-carat Soviet.'
  Joe Autenowski stood up. 'Hang on, Michael. I'll be back
in a few minutes.'
  In fact it was almost an hour before Autenowski came
back. It had been decided to fly the Pole and his family to
London instead of Washington. Autenowski and Wainwright would be going with them.

LONDON 1961
In an isolated cottage near the old-world village of Broad-
way in Worcestershire, Wainwright and a senior colleague
had pieced together George Blake's treachery, although the
Pole could only give the details for 1957-9. He gave general
details of Blake's operation with Moscow for the other years,
but only for those three years could he give evidence of direct
first-hand knowledge of the kind that would be accepted by a
court.
  The head of SIS submitted a full report to the Foreign
Secretary and finally the Prime Minister was consulted and
he ordered that Blake should be brought back from Beirut
for interrogation.
  To arrest Blake in a foreign country could cause unnecessary diplomatic problems and it was decided merely to
send him a telegram asking him to come straight back to
London for important discussions. There were risks in-

volved but it was decided that that was the best way.

The risks were greater than SIS had imagined. Within an hour of the telegram being sent, Moscow had received warnings from two sources that if Blake went back to London he would be arrested. Despite the fact that both warnings were from utterly reliable sources, Moscow, in its wisdom, decided that they were false alarms. In the case of Kim Philby, himself in Beirut, they considered that his nerve had now gone, and in the other case they accepted the advice as prudent but no more.

George Blake responded to the Foreign Office telegram immediately. He would return on Easter Monday, after he had made arrangements for the care of his wife who was expecting their third child in a few weeks' time. They were getting hourly reports on Blake's movements. On Easter Sunday the Blakes had a few friends from MECAS to the house for drinks, and their host had indicated that he would be back in Beirut the following weekend.

On Easter Monday, 3 April 1961, George Blake walked down the steps of the Comet flight from Beirut that had just landed at London Airport. He had been instructed to report at the Foreign Office the next day, and apologies had been offered that nobody would be available to meet him at the airport. It was, after all, a public holiday, and Blake knew well enough the British reluctance to work at weekends and holidays. The characteristic had been helpful to him on many occasions. In fact he had been under close surveillance at Shemlam, on the flight, and for the rest of the day.

On Tuesday morning George Blake arrived at the Foreign Office promptly. He was surprised that he was stopped at reception, and flattered when he was told the head of SIS would see him straight away.

Sir Dick White was standing by the tall Georgian windows when Blake was shown in, and there were two men whom Blake didn't recognize standing by the large desk that dominated the room. The head of SIS turned to look at Blake as the heavy door closed softly behind him. For several minutes he looked at Blake without speaking. His voice was

175

harsh when he finally spoke. His anger was barely hidden.

'Mr Blake. We believe, and have evidence, that you have committed offences under the Official Secrets Act. You will be taken to a police station and charged.' He nodded towards the two men. 'These gentlemen are officers of Special Branch and you will go with them.'

Blake looked back at his chief without any indication of fear or concern.

'I should like to make a full report, sir, that will explain everything.'

Sir Dick White waved his hand dismissively and turned back towards the window to hide his disgust.

The older of the two Special Branch officers stepped forward.

'Mr Blake, please don't say anything right now. I am taking you to a police station where you will be cautioned and charged. If you wish you can then make a statement.'

The other Special Branch officer was the man who had watched him at South Bromley station.

Blake hesitated for a moment, turned and bowed briefly towards the figure at the window, and left with the two men. He was driven to Bow Street police station and formally charged.

Late that afternoon, and long after the courts usually sat, Blake was brought from the cells, and before the Chief Metropolitan Magistrate he was charged with offences under Section 1(c) of the Official Secrets Act of 1911. Only the magistrate, his clerk, Blake and the police officers were present. Neither the court reporters nor the public knew of the special sitting.

With a mixture of creativity and deviousness a brief note was issued to the press which said, 'George Blake, 38, a government official, of no fixed address, has been sent for trial on charges under the Official Secrets Act.'

It could be construed as anything from high treason to a refuse collector who slept rough who had discovered some unimportant official document in a dustbin.

In Beirut the British ambassador sent a message to Gillian Blake that her husband had been delayed in London.

The following Saturday was his son's birthday, and the small party for his children was overshadowed by the fact that it took place without their father. There had been nothing from London. No telephone call, no message, not even a birthday card or a greetings telegram.

Two days later a woman official from the Foreign Office called at the house and broke the news as gently as she could that George Blake had been arrested on serious charges. A flight had been booked for all the family for the next day. Gillian Blake was expecting her third child in six weeks' time. On the advice of the Foreign Office, to avoid the press, Mrs Blake and her children went to stay with friends in Sussex, and the nightmare began.

At the Foreign Office they were sweating over the exact wording of the D-notices to the media that would stop them from printing any details of the arrest and background, without giving them any faint hint of how serious the matter really was. But an establishment that could describe a long-serving senior intelligence officer as 'a government official of no fixed address' didn't have too much difficulty in concocting the words. The problem was how to make them utterly boring without actually lying.

22

Barlow sat on the edge of the bath looking at his notebook as Lawler washed and shaved.

'She goes to the studios most days except Wednesdays and weekends. Usually leaving the house about noon. The man leaves at eight-thirty every day. Sometimes works on Saturdays until about three in the afternoon.'

'Anything about their relationship?'

'Seems OK from what I can gather, but he's definitely a boy for the girls. Mainly young kids hoping to make it in films. He dresses stylishly but informally. Safari jacket and jeans sort of stuff. Made to measure. According to the books he's about fifty. Good-looking in a bored sort of way, grey hair, crew-cut and a deep tan which I suspect comes from a lamp.'

'Do they go out much?'

'The usual studio-type entertaining.'

'How do they behave to one another in public?'

'Friendly, kidding, not over-possessive on either side.'

'How does she dress?'

'Very chic. Very French. If you didn't know you'd assume she was a Parisienne.'

'Close friends?'

'Not on his side. She has a woman friend, another Pole. About the same age. A translator, German–Polish. They sometimes shop together and have coffee at each other's houses.'

'What do you think?'

'About what?'

'Her reaction to my news.'

'I don't fancy your chances.'

'Why not?'

'The guy's doing well. They're living high on what goes

for the hog's back in East Germany. They've lived together for several years and it looks a stable enough relationship. Why should she trade that for your guy?'

'He was her husband, and he wants to marry her again, not just live with her.'

'Oh, come off it, Jimmy. Husbands are ten a penny these days. Especially second-hand ones.'

'Does she know about the young girls?'

Barlow laughed. 'You've got a nasty mind, pal. But I doubt if she does. I'd say he's discreet, and reckons that what she doesn't actually know she ain't gonna grieve over. But I'd guess she doesn't know any details. Probably doesn't ask, so never gets the brush off. They're both in films. She knows what goes on on casting couches.'

'Can you get me details and photographs of a couple of the young girls?'

'I should think so. We may have some on file, but if we haven't it'll take a couple of days at least.'

'Thanks.'

He presented his US passport, paid for the East German visa, and exchanged dollars for East German marks at Checkpoint Charlie. He took a taxi from the stand by the church in Krausen Strasse and asked for the Griechische Park in Köpenick. The driver warned him that it was a long way, and he gave him a five dollar note to encourage him.

From time to time his hand went inside his jacket to touch Petrov's letter and the photographs. There was a lot hanging on that letter. They had gone over it again and again, until it was a mixture of pleading and persuasion, bribery and love. But he knew that the letter alone would never be enough. He had to find words that would at least make her listen.

He looked out of the cab window. The driver had taken him the direct way, straight down the main road, and they were crossing the river at the Karlshorst Bridge. Five minutes later the driver pulled up near St Anton's church. He paid the fare plus two dollars, and the man looked pleased, wished him a good day and turned the cab back

179

towards the bridge.

Lawler looked at his watch. It was barely nine o'clock, and he walked slowly towards the house in Parseval Strasse. The beautiful old houses in Köpenick had, by some miracle, escaped all the ravages of war. They had never been bombed or shelled, and the whole area was like Germany a hundred years earlier. Köpenick had been a town long before the Brandenburgs had made Berlin. Even the Red Army had left it outwardly untouched. Rumour said that it was because even before they took Berlin they had marked down nearby Karlshorst for their head-quarters.

Number 25 was a narrow house set between two double-fronted houses that could have just as fittingly been along-side an Amsterdam canal. It was of old-fashioned purplish brown brick with stone facings to the windows and round the brightly painted blue door. It looked as if it had once been the home of a prosperous merchant, and even now it looked like the house of the well-to-do. There were net curtains at the beautifully proportioned windows, and geraniums and lobelia in the white window boxes. He walked slowly round the block and the sun was already hot on his back. As he turned once again into the cobbled street his hand went inside his jacket to check that the letter was still there.

He crossed the street, walked up the three stone steps and rang the bell. It was several minutes before the door opened and there was no doubt that it was her. She looked at him amiably enough and said, 'Who did you want?'

'I wanted to speak to you.'

She frowned. 'Who are you?'

'It's a personal matter. I'd like to speak to you in private.'

'Are you from the police?'

'No.'

'You've got an accent.'

'So have you.' For a moment he cursed his flippancy, and then she laughed, and opened the door wide.

'You'd better come in, but I can't be long, I've got things to do.'

She closed the door behind him, then led him into a cool sitting-room, which looked out on to a small garden at the back. She pointed to a chair and then sat down herself.

'Now,' she said, 'what can I do for you?'

She looked very little different from Petrov's photograph. Her face was fine. There were lines at the corner of her eyes, but they were smile lines.

'I've tried very hard to think how to say what I have to say. How to begin. I haven't succeeded, I'm afraid.'

She shrugged lightly. 'So just begin.'

'I've brought a letter for you from Anatoli Mikhailovich Petrov. And I've brought you his love.'

She stared at him open-mouthed, her hand to her heart like a woman in a Russian film. But he knew that it wasn't acting. It was as if he'd struck her.

She shook her head slowly and said, almost in a whisper, 'I don't believe it. I don't believe it.'

He handed her the letter, and she stared at the writing on the envelope. It was addressed to Maria Grazyna Petrovna. Slowly she opened it, took out the two pages, and read them. When she came to the end she turned back to the beginning and read them again. It seemed a long time before she looked up at his face.

'How is he?'

'He'll be fine if you come back.'

'How could I?' she said softly. 'After all these years. It's impossible.'

'Would you meet him? Talk to him?'

'Why does he send you? Why didn't he come himself?'

'After they forced him to divorce you, and they sent you back to Poland he was in a turmoil. Finally he was so angry that he defected. He came over to the West.'

'Mother of God. The poor man.' She looked back at him. 'Has he not married? No woman of his own?'

'No. He wants you to marry him again.'

'He doesn't know about my new life?'

'Just the bare facts.'

'He knows I have another man, yes?'

'Yes.'

She briefly closed her eyes, shaking her head.

'This is like a bomb.' She looked towards the garden and the sunshine. 'One minute all is peaceful. Sunshine and flowers, and another good day. Now suddenly . . . all this.'

For long moments they were both silent and then he said softly, 'Are you happy now?'

And suddenly she was weeping, tears streaming down her cheeks. Then she bent her head until it touched her knees, and she sobbed, her shoulders shaking, as if she would never stop. He reached out and touched her hand as it cradled her head and like a child she turned her hand to his and held it. Eventually she was still and silent. Slowly she lifted her head and looked at him.

'I couldn't go back to him now.'

'Don't you care for him anymore?'

'I don't know. I just don't know. The time with him in Moscow is just a dream. A bad dream.' She shivered. 'My God, what a fool I was, for both of us. What the hell did I really care about what the Politburo does to the Russians?'

'Would you meet him and talk to him?'

'Where?'

'It means crossing through a checkpoint but I could bring him through to you, or arrange for you to see him in West Berlin. Whichever you wanted.'

She looked at her watch and then back at his face. 'Have you got time to tell me about him?'

'Of course. Tell me what you want to know.'

'What happened after they sent me back to Poland?'

'You know that they told him you would be sent to a labour-camp in the Gulag if he didn't divorce you?'

'No. I guessed they had pressured him, but I thought it would be about his career.'

'They threatened him about you too. After you had gone they still pressured him. Said he might be sent to a back-number station. The normal kind of thing. He got in touch with us, and over the next six months we made arrangements for him to come over.'

'Are you American or British?'

182

'British.'

'And now he works for you?'

'No. Not really. He is co-operating, but he doesn't work for us. He will have a pension and a house, and be independent.'

'Why does he want me again?'

'He didn't ever stop wanting you. It was forced on him as much as it was forced on you.'

'And no woman?'

'He had a girl-friend. If you saw her you'd know why.'

'Tell me.'

'She looks exactly like you.'

'What happened to her?'

'From the moment we said that we would try to persuade you to come to him she didn't exist for him.'

'And what about her?'

'She liked him a lot, but she didn't love him, just as he didn't love her.'

'And you? I suppose you are secret police.'

'I'm an intelligence officer.'

'And if I don't want to go back to Tolya? Do you kidnap me?'

'Of course not. There would be no point in any of it if you didn't want to go back to him.'

'Why do I matter to him so much?'

'He told me once that the only good and happy part of his life was his time with you.'

'You know about Bubi?'

'Just that you live with him.'

'I have a good life with him.'

'Do you love him?'

'No. But I care about him. I should miss him. And he's been very good to me.'

'Did you love Tolya?'

'Of course. But I was just a girl then.'

'Why did you love him?'

'Who can really say why they love someone? He was a very alive man. Enthusiastic. We just got on well together from the start. I was impressed, of course, that he was a major in KGB, and had so many privileges. But he wasn't pompous like other men. He just laughed about it. And of course I liked that he so obviously loved me.'

'What would make you want to stay here?'

'Obligations. Responsibilities. Habit. The things that are my life now.'

'Will you see him, talk to him?'

She looked away from him again, towards the garden. It seemed a long time before she looked back at him.

'Would it be dangerous for him if they caught him in East Berlin?'

'Yes. And for you too. They would kill him if they knew who he was. We've changed his appearance of course.'

'In what way?'

'He's had surgery to his face.'

'And why do you and your people go to so much trouble for a defecting Russian?'

Lawler looked back at her face, suddenly aware of how like Siobhan's eyes were the big hazel eyes that looked back at him. For a moment he closed his eyes before he spoke.

'Tolya has been telling us about the KGB networks in Britain. It takes a long time to do this. Months. We came to a halt at 1968 because he believed he was in danger from us once he had brought us completely up to date. Our trying to help you come back was a kind of proof to him that we were concerned about his future. It isn't really logical, but it is to him.'

'You're very honest, aren't you?'

'It's important to both of you that I'm honest.'

'So tell me why you closed your eyes before you said all that?'

He smiled. 'It wasn't to give me time to make up a lie if that's what you think.'

'That sounds like Major Petrov KGB at his most cynical. I didn't think that at all.'

'It was a personal thing.'

'So tell me.'

Lawler sighed. 'I closed my eyes because your eyes are exactly like the eyes of the girl who used to be Tolya's girl-friend.'

'And?'

'And what?'

'So why do her eyes matter?'

He said softly, 'Because I love her.'

She smiled. 'Does *she* love you?'

'Yes. We're going to be married when this is all over.'

'Does that depend on me coming back?'

'No. But it would be especially nice if Tolya were happy too.'

'You seem to like him.'

'I do.'

'You're a bit like him, you know.' She paused. 'Why do you look so surprised?'

'Other people have said I was like him. Then they list our mutual bad points. In what way do you think we're alike?'

She smiled. 'It's like talking with him to talk to you. Both of you an odd mixture of innocence and ruthlessness. I feel as if I've known you for a long time.'

'I'm glad.'

She laughed softly. 'That's because my eyes are like her eyes.' She sighed and looked again at her watch. 'I have to make a telephone call. I won't be long.'

'Would you prefer me to come back some other time?'

'No. I can cancel what I was going to do.'

When she left the room he knew he was taking a risk. She could be phoning the police or SSD. But he didn't dwell on it. Out of the score of reactions he had rehearsed in his mind he had done better than he expected. She was still interested in Petrov. That was obvious. It could have been an outright refusal. Anger, derision, fear for her own safety if they found out that she had been contacted. But except for the one outburst it had been like she said, as if they had known one another for years. He had expected to have to be an advocate. To make a case. To lay out what she had to gain. It would have been a mistake. Nothing like that would impress or persuade her.

He looked around the spacious room. It was elegantly furnished and the decorations were modern, the paintings

185

on the wall were modern too. There were indoor plants everywhere, and small signs of her life in an open book turned face down on the settee. And patience cards already laid out on a card table. He wondered if perhaps she was lonely.

It was almost fifteen minutes before she came back and she was carrying a tray with glasses and a jug of orange juice which she placed on a stool between them.

She smiled. 'Help yourself.'

'Will you have some?'

'Yes. Why not?'

He poured them both a glass and as she went to sip he held up his glass.

'*Na zdrowie.*'

She smiled again. '*Na zdrowie.* Do you speak Polish as well as German?'

'I'm afraid not. Just Russian.'

'What's your name?'

For a moment he hesitated. 'James Lawler. But that's not the name on my passport.'

'So what do we do now, James Lawler?'

'Would you like to see him and talk with him?'

'That wouldn't be fair to Tolya.'

'Why not?'

'I would be sitting here in my pleasant house and my secure life and he would come here to persuade me. I know how he would be. He would beg if it were necessary. Plead. He would be risking his life to come. He has no security. Maybe he's not your prisoner, but it is something very near to that. A man shouldn't have to go through that.'

'Maybe he would want to remind you of good times that you had.'

She smiled. 'James Lawler, I'm a woman, I haven't forgotten the good times we had.' She laughed softly. 'Maybe I can remember more of them than he can.'

'What would you like to do?'

'Perhaps it would be . . .' She paused, and then as if she had thought of something else she said, 'So what about Bubi?'

186

'I only know who he is, and a bit about his background.'

'So. Tell me something. Just one thing, that puts him in a bad light. Just one thing to convince me that says he cares less for me than Tolya does.'

The big hazel eyes were on his face, half amused as she waited for his answer.

In the outer pocket of his jacket were the three postcard-sized photographs of Bubi and the two young girls. All three of them were naked and what they were doing was definite and unmistakable. No woman who loved a man would be totally unaffected by them. But this woman was worth more than that sort of bait.

Still smiling, she said, 'Nothing to say, Mr Lawler?'

'The only thing I can think of at this moment might hurt or offend you.'

She raised her eyebrows. 'So offend me. It's in a good cause, surely?'

'Petrov — Tolya — always refers to you as his wife, never his ex-wife.'

She nodded slowly. 'I take the point, Mr Lawler. I take the point.'

'I'm sorry I had to say it.'

'My fault, my friend. Not yours.'

'Tell me what you were going to say.'

'Yes. I was going to ask you if you would trust me.'

'Of course I will.'

'I can't go through checkpoints as you can, but I should like to go into West Berlin and see Tolya alone. Not in wherever you are keeping him, however nice it might be. But somewhere where we are both away from our guards.'.

'You wouldn't mind that people were watching from a distance just for protection?'

'Oh yes. I should mind that very much. I mean really alone. Taking the risk that we may never be seen again. Taking the risk that I might be betraying him. Taking the risk that he may choose to go back through the checkpoint with me.'

Lawler looked back at her, all his confidence gone. And her face was impassive as she waited for his answer.

'I don't think my superiors would allow that.'

'Why not?'

'I think you know why not.'

'So who don't you trust? Me, or Tolya?'

'Why do you need to put us to some sort of test?'

'Because I wonder just how different you are from the KGB.'

'How will this prove it?'

'*They* certainly wouldn't trust us. Either of us. They don't trust anybody. Maybe you don't either.'

'But what else does it prove?'

'It could prove something for Tolya, and it could prove something for me.'

'Tell me.'

'If you let Tolya go off to meet me on his own it would prove that you definitely don't intend to harm him. If you intended to do anything like that you wouldn't allow him to go unaccompanied anywhere. He might escape.'

'And for you?'

'If I went back to Tolya and we lived together in England I would always suspect that we weren't really free. That we were always under surveillance because we were not really trusted. I shouldn't want that. I've got that now. It was even worse when Tolya and I were in Moscow. If you really are offering us both freedom, I would like it to start here – in Berlin.'

'Security officials don't think in those terms. You know that.'

'So what *is* the difference then, between your people and the KGB?'

'I think you know that too.'

'So what do we do?'

He picked up the glass jug of orange juice and looked at her but she shook her head. He poured himself a glass and reached over for it. He took a few sips before he looked back at her face.

'If I make the arrangements you ask for, will you answer me one question absolutely truthfully?'

'Yes.'

'What are the odds that you will want to be with Tolya?'

She looked down at her feet as if she were examining her shoes. It seemed a long time before she looked back at his face.

'Let me say the exact truth. If I had received Tolya's letter through the post, I would have been very moved by it. I *think* I would have wanted to go to him.' She paused. 'But I don't think I would have gone. I should have needed something more. Some sign. But now we have talked I think that has been almost enough.'

'So what are the odds?' he said quietly.

'I have two tests I want to apply. I have applied one while we were talking, and I was satisfied with the result. If you agree to what I ask, for me to talk with Tolya, then you will have passed my second test. And if that happens, I can say that I would want to be with Tolya once I am sure he really wishes it for the right reasons.'

'What was the first test?'

She smiled. 'I'll tell you some other time. Not now.'

'When could we do this, *if* I can arrange it?'

'That would be up to you.'

'Tomorrow?'

'After midday, yes.'

'Are you scared about going through the checkpoint?'

'Yes.'

'Have you got a passport?'

'You forget. I was thrown out of Moscow. I'm an undesirable. My passport is always with the secret police. In Poland with Z-2, here with SSD.'

'Have you got a photograph I could take?'

'Of course.'

'Can you get it for me now?'

She came back with several and he took two of them, handing the others back.

'Do you know the Operncafé in Unter den Linden?'

'Yes.'

'What time could you meet me there tomorrow?'

'One o'clock?'

'Fine. I'll be there before then. I'll try and get a table at

189

the back of the room. Can you write down your telephone number for me?'

She reached for her handbag, took out a small leather case, and gave him her visiting card. He looked at it and slid it into his breast pocket, then looked back at her face.

'If it had to be the day after tomorrow, could you manage that?'

'Yes. How would I know?'

'A girl would call you on the phone. She would just say, "Krakow" and hang up. That would mean same place, same time on Friday. OK?'

'Yes. Does all this mean that you agree with what I asked for?'

'It means that I shall not ask my superiors. I shall arrange it myself, and take the responsibility myself.'

'And what would happen if you never saw Tolya again?'

'I've no idea. And I'm not going to think about it.' He stood up. 'Thank you very much for listening to me, and for being so kind.'

She put out her hand and he took it. 'I'll see you tomorrow then,' she said, 'or the next day. What, by the way, if you're not in the café at one o'clock?'

'You look around, make sure that I'm really not there, and leave straight away. You come back here, and you'll be contacted again. I'll be there.'

'I'm sure you will. What are you going to tell Tolya?'

'That you will see him and talk it over.'

'Give him my love.'

'Are you sure you want me to do that?'

'Yes. Quite sure.'

She walked with him to the door and she seemed relaxed as she let him out.

He walked to the park before he looked at his watch. He seemed to have been with her for days but it was barely eleven. He had to walk almost to the bridge before he found a taxi stand.

23

The sign over the swing doors was plain and simple. Hand-drawn, black lettering edged with gold, on a narrow oak strip. It said 'Court No.1', and not even its several coats of varnish could disguise its grim message. Court No.1 at the Old Bailey had been the scene of all the most serious criminal trials in recent British history. Even the most hardened criminals were aware of its atmosphere of State power. Outsiders would describe it as impressive, even awesome. To those in the dock, guilty and innocent alike, it was merely grim.

On the morning of 3 May 1961 the court was due to sit at ten o'clock, and when the court usher shouted his traditional cry for the court to rise there was only a handful of people in the public gallery as the Lord Chief Justice of England bowed briefly to the court and sat down. But the three benches reserved for the press were full to overflowing. Lord Parker of Waddington was as aware of the air of drama as the rest of the assembly, but his face was impassive as the Attorney-General, who was prosecuting, exchanged last minute words with the Director of Public Prosecutions who sat on the bench in front of the Treasury junior counsels.

The Lord Chief Justice glanced briefly at the prisoner in the dock. George Blake's face was impassive as he looked back at the judge. Clean-shaven, and soberly dressed, his sun-tanned face looked innocent and youthful.

The Clerk of the Court slowly and carefully read out the indictment, giving precise dates and periods relating to the five charges under the Official Secrets Act.

When the prisoner was asked how he pleaded, his reply of 'Guilty, sir' was barely audible.

The Attorney-General, Sir Reginald Manningham-Buller, a tall, burly man, rose slowly to present the pros-

191

ecution's case. He looked briefly around the court before he started, and his deep voice seemed to emphasize the seriousness of the charges.

'The charges to which the accused pleaded guilty are of a very serious character. I shall tell the court a little about them in open court, and about his history. Until these matters came to light it was right to say that Blake enjoyed the reputation of a good character. In October 1943 the defendant, who was a British subject, volunteered for service in the Royal Navy, and served until 1948, when he was demobilized. From that date until his arrest he had been employed in the Government service both in this country and overseas.'

Pointing to the great pile of papers in front of him, the Attorney-General continued: 'As your Lordship knows from the depositions, he has made a complete and detailed confession. That is in Exhibit One, and no doubt you have read it. Its contents, except for the short passages to which I propose to refer, must remain secret, and if there is any question of referring to the confession, apart from those parts I shall mention, I shall have to ask you to close the Court and sit in camera.

'In that statement Blake says that more than ten years ago his philosophical and political views underwent a change and in the autumn of 1951 he held the strong conviction that the Communist system was the better one and deserved to triumph. To quote his own words, he resolved to join the Communist side in establishing what he believed to be a balanced and more just society.

'Having reached this conclusion he did not take the course of resigning from the Government service. What he did was to approach the Russians and volunteer to work for them.

'His offer was accepted, and I use his own words, he agreed to make available to the Soviet Intelligence service such information as came his way in the course of his duties in order to promote the cause of Communism.

'It appears from his statement that for the past nine and a half years, while employed in the Government service, and drawing his salary from the State, he had been working as an

agent for the Russians, as a spy for them and communicating
a mass of information to them. In short, for the past nine and
a half years he had been engaged in betraying his country.

'I cannot publicly reveal the nature of the information he
has communicated,' the Attorney-General went on, 'but in
his statement he says this, and again I quote his own words:
"I must freely admit that there was not an official document
of any importance to which I had access which was not
passed to my Soviet contacts."

'And he had access to information of very great
importance,' Sir Reginald added gravely. 'Although he held
responsible positions, his employment fortunately did not
give him access to any information relating to secret weapons
or nuclear or atomic energy, but it was the case that he had
done most serious damage to the interests of this country.
Recently your Lordship tried in this Court another serious
case where the charge was conspiracy to commit breaches of
the Official Secrets Act. That was a grave case, but it is right
that I should say that the facts of this case bear no
resemblance or connection to the facts of that case, but that
this is an even graver case is, in my submission, clearly
shown by the confession made by the accused. It is not
necessary for me to say anything more at this stage on behalf
of the prosecution.'

As he finished his presentation the Attorney-General
adjusted his wig and sat down. The Lord Chief Justice was
still writing his notes. When he eventually looked up he
asked the Attorney-General if he now wished the court to be
closed and, standing to address him, Sir Reginald submitted
that it would be of assistance to counsel for the defence in
putting forward his plea in mitigation if the court was
cleared. The Lord Chief Justice expressed his dislike for
hearings in camera *but agreed to do so if both sides so*
wished. Mr Jeremy Hutchinson, QC, counsel for the
defence, stood up.

'I have indicated, my Lord, some of those matters which I
wish to urge in mitigation and which are most vital to this
man. I am told that much of what I wish to say should not be
said in public and, therefore, my choice must be whether the

full facts should be put before you, or whether I should leave out much that should be said, but at least some mitigation should be known to the world in general. That is the choice I have had to make this morning because I had no idea that these proceedings were going to be held in public. In those circumstances my client wishes, in spite of the disadvantages in many ways, to him, that I should have complete freedom to address your Lordship on all matters.'

The Lord Chief Justice ordered the court to be cleared. Members of the public were asked to leave the public gallery, and the media reporters reluctantly left the press benches. Meanwhile extra ushers were fitting wooden shutters to all the windows of the court and the glass panels in the two entrance doors. Police officers patrolled the corridors outside No.1 Court as the hearing continued.

Defence counsel took just under an hour to present his case for mitigation on behalf of George Blake, after which the shutters were removed and the locked doors opened.

When the court had settled into silence the Clerk of the Court rose and looking directly at Blake he said slowly, 'You stand convicted of felony. Is there anything you wish to say why sentence should not be passed upon you according to law?'

Standing upright in the dock Blake shook his head. His lips moved, but the sound of his 'No' was scarcely audible. He looked hesitantly up towards the gallery as if looking for someone, and then he turned to face the Lord Chief Justice as he began to address him.

Lord Parker said: 'Your full written confession reveals that for some years you have been working continuously as an agent and spy for a foreign power. Moreover, the information communicated, though not of a scientific nature, was clearly of the utmost importance to that power and has rendered much of this country's efforts completely useless.

'Indeed, you yourself have said in your confession that there was not an official document of any importance to which you had access which was not passed to your Soviet contact.

'When one realizes that you are a British subject, albeit not

194

by birth, and that throughout this period you were employed by this country – your country – in responsible positions of trust, it is clear that your case is akin to treason. Indeed, it is one of the worst that can be envisaged other than in time of war.

'It would clearly be contrary to the public interest for me to refer, in sentencing you, to the full contents of your confession. I can, however, say, without hesitation, that no one who has read it could possibly fail to take that view.

'I have listened to all that has been so ably said on your behalf and I fully recognize that it is unfortunate for you that many matters urged in mitigation cannot be divulged, but I can say this, that I am perfectly prepared to accept that it was not for money that you did this, but because of your conversion to a genuine belief in the Communist system. Everyone is entitled to their own views, but the gravamen of the case against you is that you never resigned, that you retained your employment in positions of trust in order to betray your country.

'You are not yet thirty-nine years of age. You must know and appreciate the gravity of the offences to which you have pleaded guilty. Your conduct in many other countries would undoubtedly carry the death penalty. In our law, however, I have no option but to sentence you to imprisonment, and for your traitorous conduct extending over so many years there must be a very heavy sentence.

'For a single offence of this kind the highest penalty laid down is fourteen years' imprisonment, and the Court cannot, therefore, even if so minded, give you a sentence of life imprisonment. There are, however, five counts to which you have pleaded guilty, each dealing with separate periods in your life during which you were betraying your country.

'The Court will impose upon you a sentence of fourteen years' imprisonment on each of the five counts. Those in respect of counts one, two and three will be consecutive, and those in respect of counts four and five will be concurrent, making a total of forty-two years' imprisonment.'

Two minutes after sentence was passed the telephone kiosks were crammed with struggling reporters, and the *banner headlines that night proclaimed,* 'THE LONGEST PRISON SENTENCE EVER IMPOSED IN BRITISH HISTORY'. *But with the newspapers still gagged by D-notices, only the vaguest details could be printed about the trial and its background. German, American and other foreign newspapers had no such restrictions, and printed every detail they could discover.*

Pressure mounted from both sides of the House of Commons for a statement by the Government on how such a gross security lapse could have occurred. MPs began making their own enquiries and a long list of questions were tabled with the Speaker's clerks. Finally the Prime Minister agreed to make a statement.

Mr Macmillan started by saying: 'I am informed that Blake has ten days within which to apply for leave to appeal against sentence; and if he does apply, some time must elapse before the matter is discussed. But I naturally wish to give the House as much information as I can, consistently with the national interest and without prejudicing any appeal. Blake, who is a British subject by birth, served with credit through the war with the RNVR. In 1948 he was temporarily employed as Vice-Consul in Seoul, where he was interned by the Chinese and held for nearly three years in captivity. Although he no doubt underwent a certain amount of ill-treatment in common with others who were interned, he was subject to none of the brainwashing which military prisoners suffered. After his release, and after having been subjected to a very thorough security vetting, Blake was employed for a period with the British Military Government in Berlin and subsequently attached for a time to the Foreign Office in London. In September 1960 he was sent to learn Arabic in the Lebanon. Blake was never an established member of the Foreign Service. There is no reason to doubt that until 1951 he gave loyal service to this country. It was during his internment in Korea that he decided to join the Communist side. It would appear that he voluntarily became a convert to what most members of this House would regard as an evil faith. However regrettable we may regard such a conversion, it does not, of course, constitute criminal con-*

196

duct. But to this he added treachery to the State. He agreed, in his own words, to make available to the Soviet Intelligence such information as came his way in the course of his duties. It was for doing this that he was tried and sentenced.

'Blake's action was not the result of brainwashing or intimidation while a prisoner. Nor did he fall to any of the other kinds of pressure which are sometimes employed in these circumstances. He received no money for his services. He was never at any time a member of the Communist Party or any of its affiliated organizations. What he did was done, in the words of the Lord Chief Justice, as the result of conversion to a genuine belief in the Communist system. In these circumstances suspicion would not easily be aroused in relation to a man who had served his country well for some eight years, who gave every appearance of leading a normal and respectable life, but who had decided to betray his country for ideological reasons. Indeed, having agreed to work for the Russians, he was careful not to arouse suspicion and to conceal his conversion to Communism. Eventually, however, his activities were uncovered and the result was his trial at the Old Bailey. He had access to information of importance and he passed it on. As the Attorney-General said in open court, he has done serious damage to the interests of this country. As to that it would not be right, nor would it be in the public interest, for me to say more than was said in open court yesterday.'

Pausing for a moment, the Prime Minister continued with emphasis: 'But I can assure the House that Blake's disclosures will not have done irreparable damage. In particular, he had no access to secret information on defence, nuclear or atomic matters.

'Such cases as this are, I hope, extremely rare. But by reason of their very nature they are very difficult to detect or prevent by security procedures. No such procedures can guarantee to catch a man who changes his allegiance and skilfully conceals his conversion. I do not, therefore, think that any inquiry such as that now being conducted in relation to another case with which Blake's case has no connection and affords no parallel, would serve any useful purpose. But

197

I can assure the House that I am reviewing all the circumstances with very great care to see whether there are any possible further measures which could be taken to protect this country from treachery of this kind.'

The Prime Minister concluded: 'While I recognize to the full the responsibility that rests on HM Government, I should be very willing to discuss with the Leader of the Opposition and any Privy Councillor that he might wish to have associated with him, the circumstances of this case and the matters that arise from it.'

The Leader of the Opposition, Mr Hugh Gaitskell, welcomed the statement because ' . . . there was widespread disquiet that this kind of thing could have been allowed to happen and a man could for nine and a half years supply information to the Soviet Union and, in the words of the Lord Chief Justice, "render much of this country's efforts completely useless". In these circumstances I consider it right to accept the Prime Minister's invitation for talks, but the Opposition felt that, to reassure public opinion, private conversations between the leaders of the Government and Opposition did not quite match up to the case. Some kind of inquiry was necessary to assure the public the right things were being done to prevent this sort of thing happening again.'

Mr Richard Marsh, Labour MP for Greenwich, said, 'Although Blake might not have been an established servant at the Foreign Office he was, in fact, employed by Foreign Office Intelligence.'

To this the Prime Minister replied: 'It would not be right for me to add anything said in the court in camera.'

Mr John Hynd, Labour MP for Attercliffe, who at the time of Blake's service in Hamburg had been the Minister in charge of German affairs in the Labour Government, had already seen the details published in the German newspapers the day after Blake's trial, which stated that Blake had been a senior agent of the British secret service for four years in Berlin. British newspapers were prevented from revealing this damaging information by the Government's 'D' notices, and neither the public nor Members of Parliament knew of the real facts or even that the Government was 'gagging' the press.

Then Mr Patrick Gordon Walker, MP for Smethwick, made a statement in the House alleging that the Government '. . . had introduced political censorship of the Press over the Blake case.' He said: 'While accounts of Blake's activities had been published in European and American papers, British newspapers are unable to tell their readers what people are reading in newspapers in other countries. Once such information is out in the world, its suppression in Britain is no longer security censorship but political censorship.'

Eventually the Government offered a committee to enquire into the workings of the Security services, and the doubts of the Government's party MPs were assuaged by hints that the evasions, delays and censorship had saved the lives of many British agents operating abroad. The summer holidays, the traditional wave of strikes, industrial disputes, and a sinking Financial Times Index, soon took over the headlines.

24

Lawler was back at the house in Grunewald by two o'clock, and he spent half an hour talking to Petrov; putting over hope not certainty. And even the hope was made dependent on Petrov carrying out Lawler's instructions to the letter.

He talked to Siobhan very briefly, and she let him borrow her passport. In the basement rooms with the steel doors he explained to the technicians' team exactly what he wanted. The walls of one room were lined with metal shelves divided off into small sections which held passports of every country in Europe and several in South America. In metal boxes were rubber stamps for visas, exits and entries, special facilities, and the other niceties that immigration authorities employ. Travel passes, transit documents, identity cards, oil, petrol and food vouchers, residence permits and security clearances were all available, with details of current practice, signatures and current stamps. The basic material was almost always genuine. The working details were up-dated every twenty-four hours and if an operation warranted it, the information could be no more than two hours old.

It was five in the morning before he slept, and by then he had worked out the final details of his plan. There was a call from Silvester in London which he avoided, promising to phone back later. Barlow found him the girl he wanted, and he briefed her carefully and told her where she would be accommodated and how she would be brought back some time during the weekend.

At ten-thirty he breakfasted with Petrov and went over the details yet again. Petrov's part was simple, and involved no obvious dangers, but the Russian was already tense and apprehensive about the meeting with his wife. At eleven the guards changed at the gates, and as Lawler stopped the car the relief sergeant bent down, saw Lawler and said, 'OK, sir. When will you be back?'

'This evening, about nine or nine-thirty.'

The sergeant glanced at Petrov and then waved the car through the open gates. Twenty minutes later he drove into the multi-storage car park near the entrance to the Zoo. Petrov was shivering despite the hot sunshine, and he was like a man in a dream as Lawler bought tickets for the Zoo. It was hard to believe that Petrov had once run the KGB networks in Berlin, but was so disturbed about the meeting with Maria. It really was as if the Russian felt that his life was in danger if it didn't work out. It had become an obsession.

Five minutes later they were at the ice-cream kiosk.

'This is where you meet her, Tolya. Sit on one of the benches over there, and she'll come to the kiosk.'

'And I am to be here at one-thirty, yes?'

'Yes. If she isn't here by four-thirty phone this number. It's the number of the house in Grunewald. Ask for Mr Barlow, and tell him you want to be picked up.'

Petrov looked at the number on the paper and then back at Lawler's face.

'You could come even if she doesn't come.'

'Look, Tolya. She's coming. There's no doubt about that. But something *could* go wrong. She'll be coming through the checkpoint with me. If one of us is picked up, then we'll both get picked up. If it goes wrong Barlow will look after you.'

'She doesn't deserve risks like that, Jimmy.'

'I know, but we have to take risks.'

'If you are taken I'll get you both out.'

'Don't be crazy, Tolya. Leave all that to me and the others. There's nothing you could do.'

'I could offer myself in exchange.'

Lawler looked open-mouthed at the Russian. And suddenly he was cold himself, despite the heat. It was something he hadn't thought of. And now it had been said it didn't bear thinking about. He looked at the Russian's pale, strained face. 'If you tried playing games like that, Tolya, you wouldn't last more than a couple of days. Both sides would have a vested interest in killing you. And just remember; I'd be far more valuable to the KGB than you would be. They'd only want you to discourage others, they would want me because of what I know. And you know who they'd choose.'

'You're taking big risks for me. Not just this, but not telling London about today.'

'The only risk I'm taking is that you do something bloody stupid.'

'And the checkpoint?'

'You know as well as I do that we're passing people in and out a dozen times a week. It's only honest people who have problems at checkpoints.'

Petrov nodded, his shoulders hunched, stamping his feet as if there was snow on the ground. Then he looked up at Lawler's face. 'Whatever happens today I co-operate with you. I start talking now if you want.'

'Thanks. But I can't stop now, Tolya. I need to be over in good time. But thanks for the offer. Don't worry. And one more thing. Where did I say we should meet?'

'In the new *Gedächtnis* Church any time after two-thirty.'

'OK. I'll be there, waiting for you.' Lawler grinned and squeezed the Russian's arm. 'Be good, Tolya.'

Petrov nodded without speaking, like a child being sent on an errand.

Lawler watched as the Vopo checked slowly through his passport, his money declaration, his Ost-mark receipt, and his visa receipt. The policeman wrote down the passport details, its number and his name. Reluctantly the man handed his passport back and nodded him through. The girl had gone through before him.

He walked slowly up Friedrich Strasse, gazing in the shop windows, his light raincoat over his arm. He looked up as the girl asked him the way to Unter den Linden, and as he turned to point the way she slid the passport into the pocket of his raincoat. He said softly, 'Go to the bookshop and buy two Falk street-maps of Berlin. They'll look after you.'

She smiled, thanked him, and walked on as Lawler turned back to look again at the watches in the shop window. He stopped further on to look at a display of furs from the Soviet Union. He looked at his watch and then walked up to the crossing and turned right into the broad avenue of Unter den Linden. It was twelve-thirty when he went into the café. It was half-empty, and all the tables at the far end were empty. The waitress took his order for coffee and brought him a copy of the *Berliner Zeitung*.

As he sipped his coffee he watched the street as shoppers and tourists walked slowly by, and in the distance he could hear, faintly, the band at the Brandenburger Tor. It was barely audible but it sounded vaguely like the waltz from *Eugene Onegin*.

At ten to one he saw her, crossing from the other side of the broad avenue, walking under the trees, and at the centre kerb she stood looking each way before she crossed the rest of the street. She was wearing a black silk dress and a rope of pearls. She saw him as soon as she came through the door. She smiled and walked towards his table. He stood up and pulled out a chair. She was still smiling as she looked across the table, sliding her gloves from her hands.

'Have we got time for a coffee together?'

'Of course. And the pastries are very good here.'

She smiled back at him. 'Just a coffee.'

After the waitress had brought them both coffees and cream he said softly, 'Put your hands under the table. I'm going to give you a passport. Is your handbag on your lap or on the floor?'

'On my lap.'

'Open it first. And put the passport straight inside it.'

'I'm ready when you are.'

He felt her take the passport and was pleased that she had the sense to go on looking at him as she fiddled with her handbag.

'We'll leave here in a few minutes and walk down to hear

the band. While we're there I'd like you to look at the details in your passport. Just the name, and the date of birth, and the place of birth. I'll check them over with you before we go through the checkpoint.'

'Do we go through the German one, or the one for foreigners?'

'The one for foreigners. Checkpoint Charlie.'

'Where do I meet my friend?'

'We'll talk about all that outside. Do you feel OK?'

'No.' She shook her head. 'I feel very nervous. It's foolish, but I do.'

'When I left your friend he was shaking like a leaf.'

She laughed. 'That's not very romantic.'

'It is actually. He's afraid that his fairy castle could come crashing down.'

She sighed. 'Shall we go?'

He paid his bill at the cash desk, and in the street she slid her arm under his as they walked to the end of the avenue. The benches were occupied so they sat together on the low stone wall, and the band was playing 'Moscow Nights' as she looked through the passport. Then she closed it, and slipped it back into her handbag.

'You didn't use my photograph?'

'No. That passport's totally genuine.'

'Is that your girl?'

'Yes.'

'We *are* very much alike but she's much younger than I am.'

'We've changed the birth date. The photograph is enough like you. They won't query it.'

'You sound so sure of everything.'

He touched her hand where it lay on the wall. 'Don't worry. It's all been done before. Hundreds of times.'

She sighed. 'I shall still be glad when it's over.'

'OK. Let's go.'

As they walked off slowly, her arm linked with his, he said, 'Feel in my jacket pocket. There's an American Express card and a Diners Club card in the same name. Slip them into your handbag and let the Vopo see them when he checks your passport.'

'OK.'

'Your name, *fräulein?*'

'Siobhan Nolan.'

He laughed softly. 'No. You say it like Sha-von. Try it.'

'Shavon.'

'Can you manage simple English?'

'Yes, I think so. Most film people can. But I've probably got an American accent.'

'There's the queue, we'll go in behind the two Japanese. You came through here about twelve o'clock. They'll have your name and passport details on a list. And the time. It all corresponds. You came through just in front of me. I'll go first this time and make clear that we're together.'

She frowned. 'How on earth can those details be on their list?'

'That's a trade secret. They're there all right.'

Ten minutes later he handed over his passport. He declared his currency and his passport was stamped. He stood aside and Maria put down her passport. The man motioned to him to leave and Lawler smiled amiably as he said that he was waiting for his fiancée. The man turned sulkily back to the girl's passport and the currency documents. He seemed to take hours with his hand poised before he finally applied the stamp, closed the passport and pushed it back to her as he nodded to the elderly American behind her.

'OK?' Lawler said, as he took her arm, and she nodded. He could feel her trembling. There was a line of taxis waiting on the stand and he asked for the Zoo as he opened the door for her.

When they stood on the corner opposite the entrance to the Zoo he took her hand. 'He's waiting for you. When you go in you take the right-hand path past a kiosk selling postcards, then, over by the first pool there is a café. In front of the café is a kiosk selling ice-cream. That's where he's waiting for you. Whatever you both decide I shall stick by. There'll be no persuasion and no pressure. A lot is hanging on all of this, but this is the two of you. On your own. Deciding what's best for you both. I want you to

205

remember that. All you need think about is your future and his. That's all that matters this afternoon. I'm going now to the *Gedächtnis Kirche*, the new building. I'll be in there, waiting for you both.' He bent and gently kissed her cheek. He saw tears glistening in her eyes and she said softly, 'It will seem strange seeing him, talking to him, after all these years.'

'How long is it?'

'Ten, nearly eleven years. Will you do something for me?'

'Of course. What is it?'

'Tell me something nice that you know about Tolya that I don't already know. Just some little thing. Nothing big.'

'Why do you want that?'

'I want to walk towards him smiling, knowing something about him that isn't something from the past.'

He hesitated, then he said, 'Before I came for you today I told him what to do if you and I were caught. He insisted that he would give himself up to the Russians in exchange for you being released. Very stupid, but very nice. Good luck, Maria. I'll be waiting for you.'

He turned and walked to the car park and checked out his car. The Kurfürstendamm was crowded, and there was single-line traffic where the road was up for pipe-laying. The lights changed three times before he got over the crossroads. By the church a bus had broken down, and a policeman was letting only a trickle of cars edge their way past. They would have barely had time to find each other let alone talk, but he was impatient to get to the church. As if his being there could affect the issue. At the junction he took the right fork, missed a turn-out and cursed as the lights went red. He turned impatiently at the next outlet and went round the block at Willenberg Platz and on to the parking block at the far end of Bayreuther Strasse. He stuffed the parking slip into his pocket and hurried back down to the street. There was a taxi at the far end of the street putting down a passenger and he waved frantically. The driver flashed his lights and cruised down towards him. It dropped him outside the bombed remains of the old

Gedächtnis Kirche that a shrewd administration had left as a permanent reminder of World War II. Only tourists noticed it any longer, and Berliners did their best not to remember. It was part of what they wanted to forget.

The architect of the new church, next to the ruin, had been asked for something different. More modern, even theatrical, to match the liveliness of the besieged city. Modern it certainly was, and despite its pagan exterior it had an elevation that commanded awe if not respect. It was an awesome building and its clusters of coloured windows gave out some kind of message. The message was undoubtedly defiant.

He walked slowly up the wide steps, through the massive open doors and into the church. He had never been in it before, and he was immediately aware of its calmness and stillness. The soft light filtering through the stained-glass windows gave it the light you get in spring in northern Italy. A Canaletto light that was soft and pure. Somewhere an organ was playing a thin, wandering voluntary that further emphasized the church's tranquillity.

He sat in one of the modern chairs at the back of the church and tried not to look at his watch. Inside, the church seemed smaller than its exterior indicated. There were about twenty or so people in the church. Some with their heads bowed, some just sitting, inhaling its peace. There were two massive candles set in heavy brass pedestals but there were no flowers anywhere – unless a wreath in the shape of a cross at the foot of the altar could count as flowers. He looked at his watch. It was two-twenty-five. He wondered if it would be a bad sign if they came early. It was almost like waiting for a jury to come out. Wondering if the longer they took the more chance there was. They would hardly make their minds up quickly after ten years apart. Maybe she wouldn't like his new face. Or perhaps the emotional beating he had had in the last two years would have so changed him that he was too different from the self-confident KGB major she had once fallen in love with.

He heard a clock outside strike the half-hour, and he knew he needed to think of other things or the time would never pass. He closed his eyes and tried to remember the start of the Schubert Trio. His mind reached for the cello line but after a few bars it slid away into the opening theme of the Elgar concerto. And then it came back. From nowhere. Sixteen lush bars before he lost it again. He must concentrate harder. It just wouldn't come, and he was wandering into some other theme. The Tchaikovsky variations. He must think of something else. Siobhan. She was naked, her beautiful breasts lifting and falling as she breathed, her long legs slightly apart, smiling as she . . . He cursed silently, and thereby added a second act of sacrilege to the one he had just committed. He opened his eyes and looked at his watch. It was four minutes past three. And for no reason he could understand he thought of young Sarah. It was always the same thought: who would be loving her, comforting her, cuddling her? He was in a church. He could pray for her.

He bowed his head and clasped his hands. It was a long time since he had prayed, and all he could remember was the prayer routine of his childhood. Half-whispered, half in his mind, he slowly recited the Lord's Prayer. But when he got to 'Give us this day our daily bread' he couldn't remember what came next. He went back to the beginning and started again. But it was hopeless, and he shook his head as he went to the last few words. Then, in his ritual, you prayed for people. Parents. Uncles and aunts and friends. He prayed for his mother and father, for Siobhan, for Petrov and Maria. And finally for Sarah. A long, wandering prayer that made his eyes prick with tears. And if you were a Christian you prayed for the others. And that meant he prayed for Joanna. But he couldn't find words that were not accusations, and as he struggled as if the words might be a legal commitment he rationalized and gave up. If God were really all-knowing he would know that the prayer was spurious. A hundred times he had visualized the messenger who announced her death and the news that Sarah was his to care for.

Beads of perspiration lined his eyebrows, merged and slid down to sting his eyes. His head still bowed, he reached in his pocket for a tissue, and wiped his eyes and his forehead. Slowly he raised his head and the church was dark. And from a long way away a woman's voice said in German, 'What is it, Jimmy? What's the matter?'

They were both there. Standing in front of him, looking surprised and concerned at his face. He took a deep breath, then another, and then he said, 'Tell me. Just tell me.'

Maria sat down beside him and took his hand. 'Tell me what's the matter.'

'Nothing. I think I fell asleep,' he said wearily.

'It's going to be fine, Jimmy. Where do we go for tonight?'

25

LONDON 1966
'Plea-bargaining' is almost unheard of in British courts, except where, in some very minor crime, the accused's co-operation with the police deserves rewarding. The practice is never available to lawyers in normal criminal trials. However, in George Blake's case there were pre-trial discussions between counsel on both sides. The main point was the defence plea of mitigation, which would involve the revelation in open court of what were still State secrets. It was agreed by both sides that if the evidence were given in open court it would definitely damage national security. Yet without those matters being put forward the mitigation pleas would be hopelessly weak. Agreement was reached that the evidence should be given, but in closed court. There was possibly an assumption by the defence side that the defendant's co-operation and his plea of 'Guilty' would warrant consideration when sentence was passed. From previous spy cases it looked as if between ten and fourteen years would be the sentence pronounced.

When the sentence of forty-two years was passed Blake showed no sign of emotion in court but when taken to the cells he collapsed from shock and was taken to the prison hospital at Wormwood Scrubs. An appeal was lodged but, despite all submissions from the defence, was dismissed by the Court of Criminal Appeal. Their dismissal was on the grounds that Blake was not being convicted for his ideological convictions but for using his position to betray his country's secrets. Blake himself was too ill to be present at the appeal.

There was a strange twist of fate in Blake being incarcerated in Wormwood Scrubs, for the prison itself had been cleared of prisoners early in the war to become the tem-

porary headquarters of MI5. And it was near where he himself had been interrogated when he first landed in England after escaping from Holland.

There is a special smell about long-term, high-security prisons that is almost impossible to describe. It isn't the stench of sweat or urine, more the smell of some unfamiliar incense. Acrid, warm, rotting, like the odour from the old lion-house at the zoo. Visitors try hard to hold their breath but eventually inhale, and the smell becomes sickly sweet. Romantics would describe it as the smell of fear. The more practical would ascribe it to bad drains or bad ventilation. Neither would be right. It is just the stench of an ancient prison, and its load of sick humanity.

Blake was put in 'D' block with a cell to himself, and prisoners in 'D' block were under constant surveillance. All their clothes had to be left outside the cell at night, and their cell lights were on continuously with frequent random inspections. They were allowed no association with other prisoners apart from those in 'D' block itself.

There were at least three alleged plots to free Blake which were investigated thoroughly by the security services. They were taken seriously but never found to have more than a vague justification for suspicion. He was a model prisoner, popular with other 'D' block prisoners, spending his time in the prison book-binding shop and eventually continuing his Arabic studies with a correspondence school. Another prisoner in 'D' block was Gordon Lonsdale, who was in reality Colonel Konon Molody of the KGB, and he was traded back by the Russians in exchange for the alleged British spy Greville Wynne.

On Friday, 21 October 1966, a mountain of wet coal-dust slid down and over the small Welsh village of Aberfan. By the following day the whole country mourned the deaths of 166 children, and tried hard not to imagine too vividly the last minutes of the infants' lives as they suffocated in their village school under the relentless, moving mass that careless officialdom had neglected to make safe. South Wales was inured to the sadness of miners dying below the ground, but there was a special kind of sickness to the thought that their children had been killed by the detritus of the coal their fathers mined at such risk to their own lives. It was almost too horrible to bear thinking about, so perhaps people far away from South Wales can be forgiven for pressing on with their lives that ghastly Saturday.

By 5 p.m. the football matches were over, girls sat looking in mirrors to prepare for their evening dates, and forward-thinking young men polished the back seats of their cars.

In 'D' block at Wormwood Scrubs, 5 p.m. saw the start of the 'free association' period. Prisoners could leave their cells, stroll through the corridors, and join others in the ground-floor recreation rooms. They could play table-tennis, chess, or even musical instruments. Like a good many others George Blake sat watching TV. It was Associated Television's usual Saturday offering of all-in wrestling, and the prisoners' amiable but scathing shouts reflected their views on the contrived gymnastics that purported to be wrestling. Blake watched for some time and then stood up, strolling to the door where the two prison officers who were in charge of over two hundred prisoners in the block stood casually watching the men. He chatted to them for a couple of minutes about the wrestling and said he was going up to his cell to read. It was just 5.30 p.m.

He walked slowly up the iron stairs to the second landing, and along to the big window above the entrance to the hall. It was protected by a series of vertical iron bars. At the second bar Blake stopped and pulled off the strip of adhesive tape that had been blackened with shoe polish. The bar itself had been loosened from its concrete seating a week before, and came away easily. Blake stood it carefully and quietly against the wall. He looked around cautiously but the landing was still empty, and the noise from below was deafening. He turned and put his foot against the glass. For a moment it bowed under the pressure and then it collapsed and shattered, to fall in the yard below.

Slipping on black leather gloves he slid through the window and hung for a second before dropping to the roof

212

of the covered walk-way that joined 'D' block to the next building. The second drop was to the top of a wooden bin, and finally a few feet to the ground. Thirty seconds later he was running in the shadow of the covered way. The slight drizzle had become a heavy downpour. He could barely see the high prison wall but when he heard the car engine race he ran towards the darkness of the wall and the sound. The nylon ladder came over as he reached the wall, and his foot in its heavy prison boot found purchase on the bottom rung. The rungs were only nylon thread reinforced with steel knitting needles, and the ladder's lightness made it difficult to control. It took longer than they had allowed for before he was at the top of the wall, but the car was there, its engine running. He swung his body over the blanket on top of the wall and the waiting man guided his feet to the roof of the car. Five minutes later they were passing the BBC TV Centre as they headed for Shepherd's Bush.

It was nearly two hours later when it was discovered that Blake was missing, and one of the largest and costliest man-hunts for years was put into operation.

The first handicap for the police was the two-hour start. Blake could already be out of the country before the hunt began. It wasn't likely but it was certainly possible. A small private plane from a farm air strip and he could already be in Holland or France.

The second handicap was that the only photograph held by Scotland Yard was well out of date. It showed Blake on his return from Korea, bearded, smiling and thin-faced. He was clean-shaven now, and his face much fuller. A recent photograph taken in the prison was discovered, and the Criminal Records Office photographers worked all night to produce the hundreds of copies that were needed.

Already a general call with a full description had been sent to all police forces, Special Branch, ports, airports and flying clubs. All Warsaw Pact embassies and offices were put under immediate surveillance, and Communist countries' vessels and aircraft were being checked and watched.

The editor of the News of the World stopped the presses to

accommodate a photograph and description, and several other newspapers included a photograph in their last editions. Certain members of the Communist Party were put under surveillance, and at least one was questioned. There were three separate clues of a practical nature. At the foot of the wall under the ladder was a pot of pink chrysanthemums still wrapped in the florist's paper. There were the knitting needles in the nylon ladder. But the florist's was a firm with a hundred shops, and several were within a mile or two of Wormwood Scrubs. And the pot of flowers left at the foot of the wall to mark the spot where the ladder should go over, and the car should be parked, indicated that the escape had been well planned. The firm who manufactured the knitting needles confirmed the suspicion that they were available in thousands of outlets. The third clue was to be more useful — a set of tyre tracks near the wall, and marks on the prison wall where the car had been backed up against the stone surface. It would take time before these clues were useful but they were photographed and filed for the record.

There were three men from Special Branch, an assistant commissioner, the governer of the prison and two prison officers. They sat around the table in the prison office canteen with files laid out down the centre, and a large-scale plan of the prison and the surrounding roads spread out at each end.

The assistant commissioner said, 'Go over the visitors again. Right from the first day.'

The governor looked at the list. It was quite short.

'Three visits from his solicitor. Four visits by his mother and twelve visits by his wife. That's all.'

'None of those would be involved. What about associates in "D" block?'

'He was quite popular but he wasn't the kind to have friends in a place like this.'

'You've talked to the prisoners about his contacts?'

'Yes. Every one of them.'

'And no significant names come up?'

'None at all, just casual, random contacts.'

214

'What was the date of his divorce?'

'Petition filed on June 18th. I gather the relationship had come to an end about April. He filed the petition, but I'd say it was for his family's sake, not because he particularly wanted it.'

One of the prison officers put up his hand and the governor nodded to him.

'What is it?'

'What about New Horizon and the Daily Sketch?'

The governor turned to the assistant commissioner. 'You remember that, I expect?'

'Some article by Blake, wasn't it?'

'Yes.'

'Remind me.'

The governor pointed to the prison officer. 'Harvey is in charge of the magazine. Go over it, Harvey, but be brief.'

Harvey looked towards the AC. 'We have an internal prison magazine produced by prisoners themselves. It's called New Horizon. It's not allowed to go outside the prison, and the governor examines it before it's distributed. The articles are never attributed. Just pen names. In the June issue last year there was an article called "Knaves and Fools" that was put in under the by-line "By the Humanist Group". The magazine is just run off on a prison duplicator. A reporter on the Daily Sketch got hold of a copy somehow, and they published an article about the magazine and the "Knaves and Fools" article was attributed to George Blake. Their duplicated copy was checked by the Home Office and on that particular copy the article was actually attributed to Blake. But there was no other copy that was the same. The Mountbatten enquiry team had it analysed for codes and the rest of it but found nothing. I just thought it might be relevant.'

'What was the article about?'

'Routine stuff about most prisoners being stupid rather than criminal.'

'Why did Blake write it? Was he asked to?'

'He didn't write it. The editor wrote it.'

'Who's the editor?'

'*He's been released since then. His name was Bourke.*'

'*Sean Bourke?*' It was one of the Special Branch officers who asked the question.

'*Yes.*'

'*Sean Adolphus Bourke?*'

'*Yes, I believe that was his full name.*'

The Special Branch man turned to the AC. '*Sean Bourke is ex-IRA. The man who was arrested by Detective-Sergeant Sheldon. He was released from the Scrubs about July this year, and has been making threats by letter and telephone to Sheldon and his family, saying he's going to "get" him or his wife and children. We've been looking for him.*'

'*Call a meeting at the Yard for six this evening. Get the files and anyone who's been dealing with the Bourke case.*'

'*Right, sir.*'

At the meeting, two of the facts that came out were that Blake had been allowed to have a portable radio set in his cell, and that Sean Bourke was an expert radio technician. It was just possible that he could have had radio contact with people outside the prison.

Two senior Special Branch officers were sent to Ireland on the night flight.

The small house in Highlever Road was in North Kensington, which sounds rather more exclusive than it really is. Highlever Road itself is only a few minutes' walk from Wormwood Scrubs prison. The owner, a respectable sixty-year-old lady of German extraction, was highly satisfied with the new tenant of her two-roomed flatlet. He paid monthly in advance and was no trouble at all. No noise, apart from his typewriter, and no girls. He was a tall, well-built, good-looking man in his early thirties with a fine dark beard and a moustache. Even when he was away the rent would come through the post, paid by postal orders, and always on the correct day. Mr Sigworth was an ideal tenant.

He had taken the flat in October, and she had been surprised when she saw him a week later clean-shaven. He had smiled at her comment and said that his mother didn't like *the beard or the moustache. He looked younger clean-shaven, she thought, but not so masculine, not so striking.*

George Blake grinned at the Irishman as he slid into the back seat of the car and lay down as it sped away. By the time they were at Chelsea Bridge he had struggled out of his prison clothes into a tweed jacket and a pair of cavalry drill trousers with well-polished brown brogues and a check Viyella shirt.

The driver stopped the car for Blake to join him in the front at Lavender Hill. They talked very little until they were well clear of London and its sprawling suburbs. In East Croydon they stopped to buy a couple of beef sandwiches, and ate them as they travelled towards Sanderstead and the Downs. It was an easy run through Limpsfield and Eden-bridge to where the signpost pointed right. It was a quiet country lane, and the signpost said 'Cowden ½m'.

The house lay back from the road, up a tarmacadamed drive that ended at a double garage. There were lights on in the house, and a man stood smiling, just inside the open door.

Once inside Blake was grinning, and the two men hugged each other, overcome with emotion. It was Blake who broke away first, standing back to look at the other man's face.

'It was fantastic, Tolya. It went like clockwork.'

'Are you OK? You look fatter, my friend.'

'Lack of exercise and fresh air.' Blake laughed. 'Take me outside for God's sake. Let me walk around.'

'There's been nothing on the radio or TV as yet.'

'Give them a chance. They probably didn't discover I'd flown until 7.30 or so. I want to breathe some real air.'

Petrov smiled and took his arm. 'OK. It's got a hectare of garden, and big paddocks, and a small wood.'

'Show me.'

There was a fallen oak almost at the edge of the wood and Petrov and Blake sat on it in the warm, autumn sunshine.

'How far back did you go for them?'

'Back to Seoul and Pyongyang.'

'Nothing before that?'

217

'No. I told them that that was where I changed sides.'

'Did they believe you?'

'Oh yes.'

'How much about Berlin?'

Blake sighed. 'Most of it. There was no point in keeping it back. They would have ground it out of me anyway.'

'Names?'

'Yes.'

'And procedures?'

'Yes.' Blake looked at Petrov. 'Were Moscow angry about it?'

Petrov shrugged, looking at his shoes. 'Worried of course. We lost a lot of people. Hard to start all over again.'

'Why didn't they try to trade me? They traded Lonsdale, and he only had a few years' sentence.'

'He was a Soviet citizen, Georgi. It's not policy to trade non-Soviets.'

'Not even after nearly thirty-five years' service?'

Petrov pursed his lips. 'They're bureaucrats. You know what they're like. Always the same. The rules are the rules.'

'I'll make up for it when I'm in Moscow. I can train people and evaluate the stuff you get.'

'Of course. Of course.'

'How long before I go?'

'They want you to lie low until it all dies down. They're going to put out a few stories to confuse the issue so that they'll believe you're already in Moscow or East Berlin.'

'How long will that take?'

'A couple of months.'

'Isn't that dangerous? They'll still go on checking everything here no matter what stories are planted by Moscow.'

Petrov smiled. 'We shall know well in advance if there's any danger.'

'How?'

'Friends in the right places.'

Blake looked surprised. 'You mean inside the security services?'

'Of course.'

'Who?'

'*You know I can't tell you that, Georgi. Just rest assured we know what we're doing.*'

'*Can you get me some newspapers and books?*'

'*Anything you want. Just make out a list.*'

In Tunbridge Wells Petrov phoned a London number from a public call-box and when he heard the voice at the other end say, "Primrose," he said, 'The day after tomorrow,' and hung up.

Blake stood watching the two ponies and the donkey in the field, the donkey cropping the grass, oblivious to the pounding hooves of the two young animals cavorting around it. He looked up at the blue sky to where a skylark still sang, rising and falling on a fountain of sweet sound. He wondered for a moment if there were skylarks in Moscow. It was roughly the same latitude as Glasgow and they surely had skylarks in the fields around Glasgow.

It was then he heard voices and he turned. Petrov and another man, a taller man, were walking towards him. The man waved to him, smiling, and he couldn't believe it.

26

It was Petrov who waved down a taxi while Maria sat in the church with Lawler, and by the time they had collected the car from the car park Lawler was beginning to realize what had happened. He turned into a side-street and pulled up the car, turning to look at Maria who was in the passenger seat.

'Tell me all about it.'

She laughed. 'There's nothing to tell except that we talked, and I'll be staying with Tolya.'

Lawler turned in his seat to look at Petrov who was smiling but subdued.

'I'm so pleased for you, Tolya.'

Petrov nodded. 'I talk with your people OK. As soon as you want.'

'I'll arrange for us to fly out tomorrow.'

'There will be KGB agents watching at the airport. You can be sure of that. They will guess where she has gone.'

Lawler nodded. 'We shan't be going back from Tegel. We shall fly from Gatow on an RAF plane.' Lawler looked back at Maria. 'Is there anything you need in Berlin?'

'Maybe clothes. I couldn't bring anything with me.'

'We can fix you up with all the things you want in London tomorrow. It will be easier, and safer. Let's go back to the house.'

Petrov grinned. 'They will be pleased with you, Jimmy, when you phone London?'

'They'll be pleased with you, my friend. They'll probably send me to Ireland or Abu Dhabi for disobeying orders.'

He switched on the engine and headed back for the main road, and half an hour later he was introducing Barlow to Maria. Barlow doubled the guards around the house and

Lawler phoned London. Silvester sounded pleased but pre-occupied. He made no comment about Lawler having deliberately ignored his instructions. Silvester wondered if perhaps they couldn't fly back that night but he didn't press the point when Lawler didn't respond.

RAF Gatow were co-operative. They had a plane flying back to an airfield near Banbury the next morning at eight o'clock, but they couldn't provide onward transport to London. Barlow arranged it all for him so that he could sleep for an hour before dinner. He didn't sleep, because the tight internal security inside the house was no longer necessary, and making love to Siobhan Nolan was far more appealing than sleep.

They all dined together, and Barlow laid on champagne for their quiet celebration. As Siobhan Nolan looked round the table she was aware of the fact that she was the only one there who was celebrating a simple, normal pleasure. Poor Petrov had his Maria, but he'd also got SIS. Jimmy Lawler had completed his operation successfully, but he too had SIS. She had her one, simple pleasure. James Lawler had asked her to marry him, and she had said yes. But they weren't telling anybody until they were back in London.

In the next room they watched the TV news. Aldrin and Armstrong had landed on the moon. Maria leaned across to Lawler and said softly, 'Can I speak to you alone for a few moments?'

'Yes. Of course. Let's go in Barlow's office.'

He turned to Siobhan. 'I'll be back in a moment, sweetie.'

'OK.'

He switched on the light in Barlow's office, closed the door, and perched himself on the edge of the desk. She opened her handbag and took out an envelope, handing it to him. He looked at the writing, and it just said 'Bubi'. When he looked back at her face she said, 'Will you see that he gets that as soon as possible?'

He looked at his watch. 'It won't be tonight but I can get it there early tomorrow morning.'

She nodded. 'I haven't sealed it. It's only personal, but

221

you can read it if you want. I shan't be offended. I've not mentioned Tolya or said where I've gone.'

'It's not necessary for me to read it, Maria.' He licked the edges of the flap and pressed them together.

'There's something else I want to say.'

He looked up at her face. 'Go ahead.'

'When you came to see me yesterday I asked you if you could tell me something unfavourable about Bubi. Do you remember?'

'Yes.'

'And I told you that I had two tests to help me decide whether to see Tolya. It wasn't that I doubted Tolya, but if I joined him we should both be dependent on you and your people. We should be at your mercy. That's why I wanted to meet Tolya alone. If you would let us do that, then it was a good sign. Do you agree?'

'Yes. I understand.'

'The other test was when I asked you about Bubi. When I left you to make a phone call yesterday I was calling the KGB.' She smiled as she saw the horror on his face. 'It's all right. Don't worry. I've got a close girl-friend who works there. In their translation set-up. She told me some days ago that Bubi was being watched by people who were not KGB. She thought it might be the West Germans. I phoned her yesterday to ask if she had found out who was watching him. She said she hadn't heard anything. But she told me that they'd picked up a man, a photographer, who was used by them for blackmail jobs, and among his stuff they'd found compromising photographs of Bubi. He said he'd been paid two hundred marks for prints of them by some fellow. They had found the man and interrogated him. He had sold the photographs to a man who was known to work for British intelligence. The KGB couldn't understand why the British should be interested in Bubi. But I could.'

'So what was the test?'

'Like I said. I asked you to tell me something unfavourable about Bubi. I was sure you had those photographs. But when you had the chance to use them you

222

didn't. I liked you for that. The KGB would have used them. Why didn't you?'

He shrugged. 'I don't deserve the good marks, my dear. I *was* going to use them. They were in my pocket.'

'But you didn't. Why not?'

'Because by the time the opportunity came round I'd talked to you. I liked you. I didn't feel you deserved that sort of crap. Neither did Tolya.'

She kissed him gently, on the mouth, and even her mouth was like Siobhan's.

The summer sun slanted through the stained-glass windows, casting red and yellow diamonds of light on the soft white pile of the carpet. Silvester sat facing Petrov in a high-backed chair and Lawler was perched on the edge of the table, one leg swinging as they waited.

Silvester said softly, 'Go on, Petrov.'

'I was Blake's controller in Berlin. We got on well. We did good work together. When he went back to London I went back to Moscow. He didn't like his controller at the embassy in London so I was put back with him to sort things out. Dyer was one of our people in SIS. We only used him operationally if it was very important. Otherwise he just passed documents. But it was Dyer who recruited Blake for SIS in Hamburg. KGB knew he was available and they made him operational. He doesn't know about Dyer, but Dyer watches him for us.

'Dyer warned Moscow that if Blake came back from Beirut he would be arrested. They thought he was panicking. So Blake confesses and goes to prison. Dyer tells us that Blake has told them everything. Names, safe-houses, dead-letter drops, codes. Everything. Blake thinks if he talks that they give him only short sentence. At first Moscow don't believe that he talked so much, then in ten days we lost many networks. You know all about that. Serov gives me orders to arrange for Blake to escape and I make arrangements. I came over to London embassy for that time. Is Dyer who organizes the escape. He is brought down to the house in the country and when I signal Moscow he is free, I get a personal message from Serov that Blake is to be killed and I am to do this with Dyer.' Petrov shrugged. 'And that's what we did.'

'What made you stop co-operating with us?'

'One day in interrogation room Mr Reid doesn't lock the door. There is a knock and Dyer looks in for a moment then closes the door. I was sure he recognize me and inform Moscow and Dyer fixes for me to be killed.'

'And now you'll co-operate?'

Petrov grinned and pointed to Lawler. 'For this man I do anything.'

Silvester ignored the praise. 'Tell us about what happened when Blake met Dyer at the house in the country.'

'We talked in the garden for a few minutes. Blake was obviously surprised, shocked even, that the Englishman had been working for Moscow all those years. He kept asking him questions as if he couldn't believe it. Then we went inside for a coffee. I put the pill in Blake's cup. He complained about the taste but he drank half of it, and that was enough. When he was out I gave him the injection, and that was it. He died in a matter of seconds.'

'What did you do with the body?'

'We buried it that afternoon. The hole had been dug a few weeks before by a contractor's man. We told him we were checking the soil structure. We filled it in ourselves afterwards and planted a willow tree on top. It took us nearly four hours.'

'Where was the house?'

'A village in Kent. Edenfield or a name like that.'

'Edenbridge?'

'That's it.'

'Could you identify the house?'

'Yes. It was right on its own.'

'And this matter, and your wife, were your only problems?'

'Yes.'

'Well, let me tell you what's going to happen. First of all the Englishman who was with you at the house in Edenbridge. He was under suspicion already. Not about Blake, but more recent things. He's been under surveillance for some time. He will be sent overseas tonight. To Rome. If he wants to head for Moscow nobody will stop him. Meanwhile, you and I and James, and a few others, will look into this burial at Edenbridge. When that's been dealt with I'll want you, Tolya, to make a signed statement. It won't ever be used, but I need it so that others will agree with what I intend doing. Then it will be destroyed. The Englishman will be dealt with so that he will never be a problem to you again.

'Now we come to you and Maria. We've asked our embassy in Warsaw to get hold of the necessary documents. Birth certificate and so on. There will be no problem there, but it might take a couple of weeks. I'd suggest you plan your wedding for late August or early September. All right?'

Petrov nodded but didn't speak.

'We've found a very nice cottage for you in Sussex, and when you've both seen it and approved it, we'll buy it in your name, you can furnish it at our expense and move in as soon as you like. We shall provide you with a completely new identity and all the supporting documentation. For both of you.

'We shall pay a lump sum into a bank account in your new name, and you will receive a pension of six thousand a year through a well known insurance company. Nothing will connect you with SIS.

'Meanwhile we've rented a house for you in Northumberland. A decent-sized place, a five-minute walk from the sea, and if you're agreeable I should like the rest of your de-briefing to be carried out with Mr Lawler.'

'That's OK with me, Mr Silvester. How long is the pension paid for?'

'For as long as either you or Maria are alive.'

'We can move around? Holidays and outings?'

'Of course. You'll live a perfectly normal life. You'll both have British passports. You can travel wherever you please.'

'And we are not watched?'

'Not unless you ask to be.'

Petrov turned in his chair to look at Lawler.

'Is this all OK, Jimmy? You agree with it for me?'

'Yes. There'll be no problems, I assure you.'

Petrov looked back at Silvester. 'I trust this man.'

Silvester stood up, hiding his irritation, and Lawler smiled to himself. Silvester didn't like his underlings sitting in judgement on his proposals. He interposed before Silvester could work out how to reply without giving offence but without going along with Petrov's Good Housekeeping Seal of Approval.

'I think I'll hang on for half an hour or so, Tolya. You go back to Maria and Siobhan at the Hilton, and we'll have dinner together.'

Petrov shook Silvester's hand and gave him a tentative Slav hug that was most reluctantly accepted, and nodding to Lawler went out to the waiting car and driver.

When they were alone Silvester opened the drinks cabinet and poured himself a whisky.

'A drink, James?' he said, with no effort that could be construed as persuasion.

'No thanks, Adam.'

Silvester sighed deeply. 'Don't know how you survived all that Slav drama and schmaltz.'

'Well, you did say right at the start that you thought we were much alike.'

'Did I say that?' Silvester looked astonished.

'You did.'

'My apologies, James.'

'I think you were partly right.'

Silvester looked at him. 'Ah well, we'll have to do something about that. Are you happy about doing the rest of his de-briefing?'

'Yes. I think it'll work well. The time in Berlin helped a lot.'

Silvester looked at his empty glass. 'Maybe. Anyway, I'd prefer to draw a veil over that little lot.'

'What put you on to our mutual friend?'

Silvester sniffed robustly, hooked his foot round the leg

226

of a chair and pulled it towards him. When he was sitting down he looked up at Lawler.

'There's some lessons to be learnt there, James. I was careless and stupid. That man Ridger was thrown out of Special Branch for blackmail. He had been working on checking the backgrounds of suspected illegal immigrants. He was taking money, hundreds at a time, to give favourable reports. And then there was a girl. Chilean or Peruvian, I've forgotten which. He had sex with her instead of cash. She wasn't all that unwilling but she happened to be the mistress of one of the attachés at her embassy who laid an official complaint with Immigration. There was an investigation and Ridger got the chop. Very quietly, of course, for everybody's sake. A warning was circulated about him to various departments including us. Our friend saw it, passed the name to the Soviet Embassy and they hired him to keep tabs on you. Ridger was given a photograph of you, but he wasn't told about Petrov. Just told to report on all your contacts. When I interrogated Ridger myself it was obvious that he'd been ripping them off. His reports were quite useless. But in the end they were desperate and they showed him a photograph of Petrov, but he didn't recognize him. Said he wasn't the man who was with you. The fact that the embassy connected you with Petrov meant that there was a leak somewhere in SIS. I put a special team on it. In the end it came down to only two names left in the hat. One was you, and the other was Dyer.

'Then I realized that despite all this, Ridger was still very cocky. Very sure of himself. So I put Sanders on him from Legal. He made clear that we were going to prosecute him under the Official Secrets Act and he stood to get fourteen years and maybe the blackmail charges would be put up too. And then he spilled the beans. The Russians had hinted that he had protection inside SIS before he took on the job. He didn't believe it, so they gave him a very brief meeting with a man who obviously knew his way around SIS. I showed him half a dozen photographs and he picked out Dyer without hesitation. That was the day before I told you to take Petrov and the girl with you to Berlin. As I told you, I knew something was going on but I didn't know what.

'I made them work round the clock, and put a documents team on it. They came up with the original copy of Dyer's recommendation in Hamburg that Blake should be transferred from the Royal Navy to us. We found that Dyer had made a dozen or more trips to Berlin when Blake was operating there. It's all circumstantial. Not a shred of evidence that would stand up in court. Not unless we put Petrov in the box and even *in camera* I wouldn't be prepared to do that. There are other ways we can deal with Dyer.'

'Like what?'

'Never you mind. Just you concentrate on Petrov and the de-briefing.'

'How long will you need Petrov for the Edenbridge business?'

'I don't know. We've got to locate the place first, and then work out a cover story that will satisfy the people who live there now. Geological survey, buried treasure, God knows what. I'd allow for a couple of weeks anyway.'

27

Silvester sat on the bench seat on the patio to pull on his wellingtons, and Lawler stood waiting with the Assistant Commissioner (Crime). The three of them walked in silence through the garden, across the paddock as far as the edge of the copse. Petrov and the two police constables stood together by the big, yellow-painted, mechanical digger. Twin great mounds of soil rose up at each end of the pit.

As Lawler looked down into the earth he could see the beginnings of the layer of lime. A few, small, compacted white clusters that were startlingly white against the smooth clods of heavy red clay.

Then Silvester nodded, and the two constables with their shiny spades made their way down the rough steps that had been cut into the sides of the pit.

Slowly and carefully they dug down, a few inches at a time, taking depth measurements in the dug earth, and scooping samples into plastic bags. Twenty minutes later one of the constables knelt down, and after a few moments he stood up and nodded to the Assistant Commissioner. He went back to the police car and radioed for a police forensic scientist to be sent from Tunbridge Wells with a police photographer.

It was an hour before they came, and after a brief examination of the section of the skull uncovered from the soil he supervised the rest of the digging and photography. The present owners of the house were told that the remains were of a pilot brought down during the Battle of Britain.

The lime had not destroyed the body. In fact, even vital organs had been preserved, apart from the skeleton itself. Two dentists who had cared for Blake's teeth gave positive identifications from plaster casts of the jaw bones.

Sir George Andrews sat behind his leather-topped desk, his right hand on a thin file and a large buff envelope. The three men facing him sat waiting for his answer. The Commissioner of the Metropolitan Police was in uniform. The Attorney-General was in a dinner jacket with medals, and Silvester looked sombre in a plain, dark blue suit. Eventually Sir George looked directly at the Attorney-General.

'You're quite sure that you couldn't prosecute?'

'Quite sure. If we could have the Russian to give evidence there might be a chance. But even then I couldn't guarantee it.'

'Commissioner?'

'Without that witness we haven't a shred of evidence. A public inquest would certainly end up as either "Death from unknown causes" or "Murder by a person or persons unknown". And like Sir Alec, I'm not even sure that if we had that witness we could get a conviction.'

Sir George turned to look at Silvester.

'How much harm would it do?'

'We have an agreement with—'

'No. No. No. I'm not interested in that aspect. Forget Petrov. I mean harm to national security.'

'It would be devastating, sir. We'd be forced to reveal things that are absolutely secret. It would put us back years.'

'Would it involve loss of life?'

'Almost certainly.'

'What about our relationship with the Americans?'

'They'd probably be delighted about what had happened way back, but we could expect no co-operation from them in the future. At least four of their German networks would go down.'

Sir George shook his head slowly, reached for the silver cigarette case, and offered it to the others. They all refused, and sat in silence as he lit his own cigarette. He looked back at Silvester.

'If not murder charges, what about high treason

230

charges?'

Silvester said, 'The same applies. I've been over that with the Attorney-General. Unless he pleaded guilty, and the court sat *in camera*, and we used Petrov, we should do just as much damage that way. Maybe more.'

Sir George shifted in his chair.

'I'm not in any way trying to spread the responsibility for this . . . er, decision. It's mine alone. I recognize that absolutely. But it would help me . . . assist me, if any of you were to disagree with my inclination to deal with this our own way.'

The Commissioner didn't hesitate. 'I go along with you. I don't think you have any choice.'

The Attorney-General, an essentially cautious man, as his office required, said quietly, 'I concur.'

Sir George didn't wait for a reply from Silvester. He went on, 'And we do all agree that the matter ends in this room? With the four of us?'

The Attorney-General stood up, his black leather briefcase in his hand. 'I couldn't go further than I have done, George. You wouldn't expect it. Whether you tell the Prime Minister or not is in your capable hands. You have the discretion. Every enquiry and every commission, and God knows there's been enough of them, have left the passing of information to the PM in your hands. So far as I am concerned we have discussed a hypothetical case, and my lips are sealed, as they say. I leave it to you.'

Sir George nodded. 'I understand, Arthur. Thank you for your help. I much appreciate it.'

When the senior law officer left it was the Commissioner who spoke. 'You couldn't expect any more from him, George.'

'I agree and I meant what I said. The . . . never mind. It's done with now.'

'What are you going to do with him?'

'What would *you* do, Colin?'

The Commissioner smiled grimly. 'I guess it would be short and sharp in somewhere like Tehran or Abu Dhabi.'

'Right idea, wrong places.'

'D'you think he knows we're on to him?'

Sir George looked at Silvester.

'What d'you think, Adam?'

'He's been running scared ever since they found out that Petrov and Lawler had left the flat, but he's got no idea we're on to him. I'm sure of that.'

The Commissioner stood up. He would read it in the newspapers in due course. Along with everybody else. And that was enough.

'Can I give you a lift anywhere, George?'

'No thanks. I've got a few things to go over with Silvester here.' He held out his hand. 'Thanks for the help.'

The Commissioner nodded to Silvester and let himself out. Sir George turned back to Silvester.

'You've made the arrangements, Adam?'

'Yes, sir.'

'When?'

'In the next two days.'

'Right. You just get on with it.' He shook his head angrily. 'The bastard.' He handed the file and the envelope to Silvester. 'Take these bloody things and burn them.'

It rated a couple of paragraphs in the evening papers and a paragraph in four of the dailies, and none of them went beyond the first brief details put on the wire by PA-Reuter.

BRITISH DIPLOMAT CYPRUS. BRITISH FOREIGN OFFICE OFFICIAL KILLED NEAR FAMAGUSTA YESTERDAY. RICHARD NEVILLE DYER WAS VICTIM OF MISTAKEN IDENTITY IN TERRORIST SHOOTING APPROX FIVE FIGURES FIVE KILOMETRES SOUTH OF BRITISH ARMY BASE AT FAMAGUSTA. THIS AREA DISPUTED BETWEEN TURKISH AND GREEK AUTHORITIES HAS BEEN SCENE FREQUENT ATTACKS ON VEHICLES BY TERRORISTS FROM BOTH SIDES. LOCAL POLICE OPINION DYER MISTAKEN FOR LOCAL POLITICIAN. ENDS.

A vigorous protest had been lodged by the Foreign Office

232

with both the Turkish and Greek administrations in Cyprus who each rejected the protest and blamed the other.

Anatoli Mikhailovich Petrov married Maria Grazyna Felinska at Chelsea Registrar's Office on 15 September 1970, although those were not the names on their birth certificates, their National Health cards or the marriage certificate. She kept her Maria and he became Michael and his surname was Keller. German enough to explain his accent and unobtrusive enough to come easily to an English tongue.

They settled down easily in the Sussex village. As victims of Nazi oppression, their German background was a help rather than a hindrance. There was some speculation at the vicarage and the manor house as to whether or not they were Jews. Most refugees were and they obviously made good money from the two well-managed newspaper and tobacconists' shops that they owned in Bexhill and Hastings. If there had been any lingering doubts about the newcomers they would have been dispelled when they bought the chestnut gelding and the palomino mare from the manor house stables. From that time on they became locals. Although they were both amiable and active they kept themselves to themselves and that was considered as fitting behaviour. Maybe in three or four years' time they would be accepted as belonging; until then, a nod and a smile and a greeting were all that was called for.

Freedom, like great wealth, takes time to get used to but the two Alsatians were the only outward signs of their doubts. They rode, whatever the weather, over the rolling Sussex downs, visited their two shops twice a week and went to the theatres on the coast no matter what was on. The visits to the shops were social rather than commercial for both shops were run by retired policemen and their wives. SIS had seen to that. During the summer months they paid visits to the Lawlers' in Buriton who returned the visits from time to time.

They had talked in the early months about having children but they knew in their heart of hearts that it was only talk. They didn't lack courage but if you knew as much about the world as they did you knew that with children you would be vulnerable. Better to be as they were. Survivors rather than inhabitants. Neither of them suffered nostalgia for Moscow or Warsaw. The names represented regimes rather than people. And Petrov would have been surprised if a visitor, walking down to the stream that ran through their garden, had connected the silver birches he had planted as nostalgia for the silver birches that relieved Moscow's gloom every spring and summer.

To say that they were happy would be an exaggeration but they were content, and to them the difference between the two states would have been seen as a mere problem of semantics. Once a year they travelled to Ireland to see the other Lawlers.

Siobhan and James Lawler hadn't married until March 1971. It had taken some months for Lawler to make up his mind about whether he would continue his career in SIS. Eventually he knew that to continue would harm his marriage in many ways. Not just the sudden departures, or the dangers, but the cynicism that was essential for survival in that arcane world. So he opted for early retirement and a reduced pension. Silvester had done his good deed stealthily, recognizing where the younger man's thoughts were leading him. The pension of a 37-year-old depended on his rank and, almost two months before he decided to leave, Lawler had been promoted two grades. At the time he saw it as part of his superior's attempts to induce him to stay but Silvester wasn't a man who looked for other people's approval of either his good or bad deeds.

They could have lived modestly on the pension alone but by moving to the Republic they lived more comfortably, and it gave much pleasure to Siobhan, who was typically Irish in that she constantly derided her fellow countrymen and pined for the country itself.

Three months after they had bought the house in Cork Siobhan was offered the post of Women's Page editor on a local paper, a job she thoroughly enjoyed. Lawler himself is part owner and active director of the most successful bookshop in the city.

After being married to Siobhan for some time he made a happy discovery. They were walking one evening along the upper reaches of the river and stopped to look at the cascade of water around a rock formation. They had watched it for several minutes and Siobhan had pointed to the lichen on one of the flat outcrops of rock that was beginning to change colour from grey-green to orange, when Lawler turned impulsively to the girl and said, 'I'm so lucky to have you.'

'Why?' But she smiled.

'I'm so happy it's almost unbearable.'

She laughed. 'How can being happy be unbearable?'

'It's the thought of what I might be doing this moment if I hadn't met you. I've done a pleasant day's work and now I'm here with you, in peaceful countryside, looking at water and rocks and wondering why a lichen should be changing colour. We'll be going back to our house and then to the concert. If I hadn't met you I'd still be in SIS playing games against the KGB and going back to some lonely room in a Berlin hotel.'

The big hazel eyes looked back at him, and she said softly, 'It wasn't SIS made you lonely, it was the people in your private life. They ran down your batteries because they were weak and selfish. You picked lame ducks. They wore away your armour and left you too vulnerable. And as those kinds of people always do, they made it seem as if it were you who was inadequate, not them. You're a per- fectly normal man, my love, and I'm a normal woman. Just as you count your blessings, I count mine. I'm lucky to have you. We're both lucky.'

Lawler stood, awkward and embarrassed, and she laughed and took his hand. 'We'd better get back to the car. Remember, we promised to pick up the Foleys.'

As they walked back to the road, hand in hand, he smiled to himself and she said, 'Why the smug smile, my boy?'

'I was thinking of the day you came to my office at Century House and you stood staring at the thing on the wall.'

235

'There's nothing to smile at there, my lad. You English are cheeky bastards. Always have been, always will be if we don't watch you.'

Despite what she had said Siobhan Nolan had made Lawler's early retirement a condition of marriage, and when she's in the right mood Siobhan Lawler sometimes admits that she might have been influenced by the faded front page of a newspaper that hung in its frame on Lawler's office wall at Century House, whence it had come from his old office at Queen Anne's Gate. It was the front page of the *Skibbereen Eagle,* and its banner headline read: 'The *Skibbereen Eagle* has its eye on Moscow'. Skibbereen, with a population of about 3,500, was in County Cork.

There are times, when he's tired, or home before Siobhan, that his mind goes to a small girl. The healing of that wound was not in Siobhan's benefit, and those who could have healed the wound were not healers of wounds.

F   Allbeury, Ted
ALL
           Shadow of shadows

DATE			

C. 1